W9-CRW-842

St. Rose Goes Hawaiian

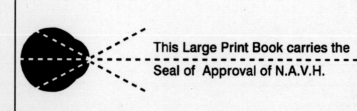

This Large Print Book carries the
Seal of Approval of N.A.V.H.

A ST. ROSE QUILTING BEE MYSTERY

St. Rose Goes Hawaiian

Annette Mahon

WHEELER PUBLISHING
A part of Gale, Cengage Learning

GALE
CENGAGE Learning

Detroit • New York • San Francisco • New Haven, Conn • Waterville, Maine • London

GALE
CENGAGE Learning·

Copyright © 2012 by Annette Mahon.
The Additional Copyright Information on page 5 constitutes an extension of the copyright page.
Wheeler Publishing, a part of Gale, Cengage Learning.

ALL RIGHTS RESERVED
This novel is a work of fiction. Names, characters, places and incidents are either the product of the author's imagination, or, if real, used fictitiously.
The publisher bears no responsibility for the quality of information provided through author or third-party Web sites and does not have any control over, nor assume any responsibility for, information contained in these sites. Providing these sites should not be construed as an endorsement or approval by the publisher of these organizations or of the positions they may take on various issues.
Wheeler Publishing Large Print Cozy Mystery.
The text of this Large Print edition is unabridged.
Other aspects of the book may vary from the original edition.
Set in 16 pt. Plantin.

LIBRARY OF CONGRESS CATALOGING-IN-PUBLICATION DATA

Mahon, Annette.
  St. Rose goes Hawaiian / by Annette Mahon.
    pages ; cm. -- (A St. Rose quilting bee mystery) (Wheeler Publishing large print cozy mystery)
    ISBN 978-1-4104-5212-2 (softcover) -- ISBN 1-4104-5212-3 (softcover)
  1. Quilting--Fiction. 2. Large type books. I. Title. II. Title: Saint Rose goes Hawaiian.
PS3563.A3595S7 2012b
813'.54--dc23   2012028289

Published in 2012 by arrangement with Tekno Books and Ed Gorman (USA) Inc.

Printed in the United States of America
  1 2 3 4 5   16 15 14 13 12
FD271

ADDITIONAL COPYRIGHT INFORMATION

The recipes contained at the back of this book are supplied by the author. The Publisher is not responsible for your specific health or allergy needs that may require medical supervision. The Publisher is not responsible for any adverse reactions to the recipes contained in this book.

In loving memory of
Josephine Agnes Edwards.

Chapter 1

She could hardly stand it. Finally, after all this time. After all her planning. It was going to happen. See if he didn't regret what he'd done to her.

Years of pain and planning had gone into her revenge. Searching the Internet, hiring detectives. She'd reinvented herself, just as he had done. But she hadn't forgotten.

Sometimes she thought that her mind was ill, she was so obsessed with getting back at him. But he had betrayed her, destroyed her life. Completely destroyed it. Lost for her the only good thing she'd ever had. People thought she was lucky. Independent, successful. But they didn't know. She'd come here to start over, to try to forget about the past. And she had had success in her new career. But you never forget. That was what she had discovered. You never forget. The only thing that would help her get on with her life was destroying his. Then perhaps she'd be able to put his betrayal behind her.

And now this. It was ideal. She was so excited by the perfectness of the opportunity, she hoped she could keep the glee from showing on her face. But she'd had years of practice at controlling her innermost thoughts and feelings. She'd manage. And, in the end, she'd have her revenge.

CHAPTER 2

Scottsdale, Arizona. How it all began . . .

It was a bright and beautiful morning in early June, and the quilting group of the St. Rose Catholic Church Senior Guild was busy as usual. Although the weatherman promised temperatures approaching one hundred later in the day, the morning was a comfortable seventy-five and the door to their room was propped open. The frame held a pieced quilt in the classic nine-patch pattern, a top contributed by member Edie Dulinski and made from fabric donated by Candy Breckner's family, a Bee member who had passed on. Edie had used a variety of blue prints and they looked especially lovely as the quilting proceeded. A shaded blue quilting thread enhanced the design and showed up beautifully in solid cream squares. The quilting was going quickly — straight lines in the pieced squares and a feathered circle in the plain alternate block.

It was one of their most popular patterns and they did at least one every year.

"We should be able to roll this again before we leave today, don't you think?" Louise Lombard asked.

The Quilting Bee worked on an old-fashioned type of frame, basically four boards covered with muslin to which the quilt was pinned, the whole held in place by specially constructed legs. In earlier times, women used to prop these boards on wooden kitchen chair backs. As they completed one section of the quilt, they rolled two sides of the frame so that they could reach further into the piece to continue their stitching.

Louise looked toward Maggie Browne, who nodded her agreement. A rancher in north Scottsdale for most of her life, Maggie's strong personality and take-charge attitude made her the group's unofficial leader.

Before any more could be said about their progress, however, Dolores Newcomb blew into the room. A tote bag bright with a Hawaiian floral design swung from her arm, slamming against the side of the door as she entered. If not for the soft materials, there would have been a loud thud. Dolores was a longtime friend of the Bee women, though she did not quilt. She did do a lot of sewing for Guild projects, both on the sewing machine and by hand, and they continued to urge her to try quilting.

"Aloha!" she sang out. "I just got back from Hawai'i."

She was greeted with smiles and exclamations, as well as hopes that she'd had a nice trip.

"Hawai'i! Where were you?"

Iris Fleming's sharp words were an odd note in the rush of good-natured questions and comments. Their newest member seemed to notice this, as she quickly added, "I've been there a few times myself of course. Which island did you visit?"

"We were on Maui," Dolores said, still gushing with excitement. "And it was terrific."

"Maui," Iris said. "That's nice." She returned to her stitching without further comment.

Undaunted, Dolores continued her chatter. "In fact, we just got back last night, really late, and I overslept." She shook her head. "I'd wanted to get here early, before you all settled down to quilt. I couldn't wait to show you what I did while I was there."

"Jet lag," Edie pronounced.

Distracted, Dolores turned toward Edie.

A small woman with an often-ferocious frown, Edie was a plain speaker who frequently rubbed people the wrong way. But she had a good heart, and she was a terrific quilter. Since Dolores had known Edie for years, Maggie was sure Dolores was not offended by Edie's rough tone.

"What?" Dolores said, looking over toward Edie.

"You said you overslept," Edie explained. "It's probably jet lag."

"Oh, I guess." Dolores seemed to have lost her train of thought and stood silently for a moment.

"What was it you couldn't wait to show us?" Maggie smiled at Dolores. The regular Bee members were used to ignoring Edie's comments or just gliding over them as they talked while they stitched, Edie's favorite topics being the proliferation of property crimes and the threat posed by the increase of local gang activity.

"Oh, the most wonderful thing." Her confused expression vanished, replaced by excitement. She plunged her hand into her tote bag while she spoke in a voice gone reedy with pleasure. "The hotel we stayed at had Hawaiian quilting lessons," she said, grinning widely as she pulled a piece of yellow fabric from her bag.

"Vince and I always said we were going to Hawai'i for a second honeymoon," Louise said. "Took us thirty-five years, but we did it. We had a wonderful time, but I didn't get to do things like that since Vince was along and he wanted us to do things together. It's been almost ten years ago now."

"I think it's sweet that he wanted to spend his time with you," Anna said.

"Well, it was supposed to be a second honeymoon," Louise said. "And we did have a nice time."

"You should have sent him off to the golf course the morning it was offered," Maggie said, to some general laughter.

"I tried," Louise replied. "But he wanted me to ride along with him. He said the course was really beautiful and I'd enjoy it. And he was right."

As they spoke, Dolores unfolded the large fabric square. "Here's what I made," she said, revealing an appliqué in a dark-green fabric that displayed a pattern of leaves that repeated four times in the manner of a paper snowflake. There was a circular shape between the leaves that Maggie thought might be the bud of a flower or a fruit of some kind. "This is the breadfruit pattern. You're supposed to start with it, so that you'll have good luck in your quilting."

"Ooh, I love hearing that kind of thing," Clare said. "It's like when you first hear about the humility block, you know, and you think, wow, this is really special. Or the stories about quilts showing the way in the Underground Railroad."

"The humility block?" Iris said. "What's that?"

Theresa and Dolores also looked puzzled.

"In pioneer times, women would often leave an obvious mistake in one of their quilt blocks," Edie explained. "That was their 'humility block' and proved that the maker was not perfect, because only God could create perfection."

"Interesting," Iris mumbled.

Meanwhile, the women set aside their needles so they could examine Dolores's Hawaiian block. Those sitting across from her got up and walked around the frame for a closer look.

"I've always meant to try Hawaiian quilting," Victoria said. "The full-sized quilts are so beautiful, but they are so large. They must take a long time to work."

"Oh, yes." Dolores nodded eagerly. "My instructor said some women spend years doing one. I bought a couple of patterns for full-sized quilts," she added, pulling more items from her tote. "And a couple for wall hangings, since I thought those would be a more manageable size. The instructor also said that it's hard to work on the full-sized quilts because it's very difficult to hold all the fabric in one hand while you appliqué."

There were several nods as the more experienced appliquérs agreed.

"Especially for those of us with arthritis." Anna rubbed her swollen knuckles. Maggie was surprised at the comment because Anna rarely complained.

"It's love at first sight," Victoria whispered to Maggie, nodding toward Theresa.

Indeed, Theresa was sifting slowly through Dolores's new patterns, exclaiming over each one. Her eyes were wide in appreciation, drinking in every detail of this new art form. A newer member of the Bee, Theresa had joined recently when she retired from her job as cashier at one of the larger car dealerships.

"I think I've found my passion," Theresa finally said, her voice reverent with awe. "These are so beautiful, and so unique. This is definitely what I would like to do. I've never seen anything like them. Will it be hard for me to learn?"

"Not at all," Edie told her, much to the others' surprise. Edie could be harsh and plainspoken, but she was basically a good person. And she was an extremely talented quilter. "I could help you learn to appliqué. Once you catch on to the basic technique it won't be hard to adapt it to that particular style."

"And you're a good quilter, so you should pick it up in no time," Victoria added.

Dolores agreed that the Hawaiian technique wasn't difficult. "It's the cutting and laying out that's the real trick," she added. "I thought folding the fabric was rather complicated. It has to be done just right, or you end up with either two or four separate pieces instead of just one."

There were further questions from the quilters for Dolores, and compliments over her pillow top and the beautiful patterns she had purchased. Her sample block passed from hand to hand while each quilter studied the technique.

"Tell us how you're going to quilt this," Edie urged.

"Will it be a pillow or a wall hanging?" Anna asked.

Everyone listened, though they drifted back to their own chairs and took up their stitching as the dialogue continued. This was their usual morning routine, enjoying both stitching and conversation. Talking about one another's quilting or sewing projects was a favorite topic.

Suddenly, Clare paused, sitting straight up and looking around the room. "We should all go on a quilting tour to Hawai'i," she said. "You know, set up something where we could see some quilts and have lessons. Wouldn't it be fun?"

"I know someone who did a tour like that in Japan," Edie said. "She called it the trip of a lifetime."

While the others agreed that it would be fun to have a quilt tour in Hawai'i, Iris picked up the suggestion in all earnestness.

"We could do it," Iris said in her confident, all-business voice. "I'll look into it. I'll bet I can arrange something affordable for us."

Shocked, the other women looked at Iris. They were great talkers, the women of the St. Rose Quilting Bee. In their conversations over the quilting frame, they traveled all over the world. But they rarely took real-time trips, except to visit relatives. Perhaps Iris didn't know they were all such home-bodies. She had only joined the group a few months ago, had only lived in Scottsdale for a year.

"Really go to Hawai'i?" Anna asked.

"Why not? Wouldn't it be fun?"

They all agreed that it would.

"It probably won't be Maui, though," Iris

warned. "The prices are sure to be high there because it's such a popular vacation spot."

"I've always wanted to do one of those quilt tours," Edie admitted. "But wouldn't it be expensive?"

Leave it to Edie to get right to the point. Maggie knew that much of the group's hesitation was due to the anticipated expense. While they would all enjoy such a tour, cost was a major issue. Almost everyone at the Senior Guild was retired and living on a fixed income. Except, perhaps, Iris, who still sold expensive real estate in Paradise Valley and Scottsdale. Even with the slow economy, expensive homes did sell. And it didn't take many sales of million-dollar-plus homes to produce a good income. So "affordable" was a relative term.

"Look, I'll check things out and let you know," Iris said. "Then we'll talk about it. I used to have a travel agency, you know," she continued, "so I'm sure I'll be able to find a really good deal for us. I still have some contacts in the business, and I know where to look online for the best deals."

Maggie and Victoria exchanged a meaningful look. They certainly did know that Iris used to own her own travel agency. She now worked part-time selling real estate, which gave her mornings to devote to the Quilting Bee, though she often talked about her years as a travel agent and all the wonderful places she'd visited. In fact, she spoke of it so frequently, some of the other Bee members had taken to pantomiming yawns behind her line of sight.

Maggie and Victoria considered Iris a type A personality, and it surprised them that she wanted to join them at the Senior Guild. She seemed the kind of person who would remain a workaholic through her seventies. Of course, they appreciated the fact that she had joined the Quilting Bee, and she did produce some fine quilting. But Victoria often said — to Maggie, in private — that she got tired just *sitting* beside Iris, who talked virtually nonstop from the moment she arrived in the Quilting Bee's room. And her restless energy drove her up and about at least once every half hour. She made countless trips to the refreshment room, took bathroom breaks, and visited with other groups working in various parts of the church complex. Louise once said she suspected adult ADHD was involved.

"I'd like to do it," Iris assured them. "Travel to Hawai'i is always popular, but I'll bet I can get a really good deal if we go after the holidays. There's a lull in travel between the new year and spring-break season. Things are slower then and it would give us lots of time to plan. And to budget for it," she added.

"I know you'll get the best price, Iris," Dolores said, "and I really want to learn more about Hawaiian quilting. If it's after the holidays, I'd love to join you." She turned a proud eye on her pillow top. "In fact, there's a woman in the sewing room, Bernadette, who is from Hawai'i, and I'm sure she'll want to go too. You should talk to her before you start, because she still has lots of relatives there and I think one of them is a quilter. Bernie's the one who told me to watch out for the quilting demonstration at the hotel." She pushed the pillow top into her tote bag and stood. "Why don't I go get her? I bet she'll love hearing about this proposed tour."

It didn't take long for her to return with Bernadette and another woman. Bernadette, or Bernie, spent her mornings at the church stitching up small items like doll clothes and tote bags. The second woman, Lydia, liked to embroider, so she embellished the dolls, baby clothing and other items the women in the sewing room stitched up.

Bernie beamed. "Dolores told me about

the quilt tour. I'm so excited. I'd love to go. I was born in Honolulu, but most of my family is on the Big Island, including a cousin my age who quilts." This was met by excited chatter from the Bee members. "We used to be pen pals but switched to e-mail." She grinned, proud of her advance into the technological age, then continued with a nod of emphasis. "In fact my cousin designs quilt patterns and sells them on the Internet. You should see the wonderful things she creates with embroidery embellishments. I can put you in touch with her and she might be able to help," she added, speaking directly to Iris now. "And of course, I'll do whatever I can."

Iris seemed delighted with Bernie's suggestion. "The Big Island is wonderful," she enthused. "I was going to suggest it myself. Mountains, volcanoes, beaches. Wonderful flowers. And there's that fabulous collection of Hawaiian quilts at the Mauna Kea Hotel. It would be perfect."

Bernie pulled an extra chair up next to Iris, who quickly abandoned her stitching. She fished a notebook out of her large designer purse and turned toward Bernadette.

"I'm so excited," Bernadette repeated. "If you can work out a tour on the Big Island, I could join you and see my cousin and her family. It's been years since we've been able to get together. And learning about quilting will be a nice bonus. I've seen the gorgeous work she does and I'd love to learn."

"Tell me how to get in touch with her," Iris said, pen at the ready.

Bernie took the pen and scribbled something in Iris's notebook.

Meanwhile it was Lydia's turn to chime in. "This is great. I'm excited too, and I'd love to help out. My neighbor and best friend moved there — to the Big Island — two years ago. Her husband is an astronomer, and they have these huge telescopes on the mountain there," she explained. "We keep in touch by phone and e-mail, but it's not like actually seeing one another. If we had a tour, she could join us, couldn't she?" In her excitement over the trip and seeing an old friend again, she went right on speaking without waiting for a reply. "Oh, that would be so wonderful. We haven't seen each other since she moved."

"Does she quilt?" Edie asked.

"I don't know." Lydia's brows drew together as she thought it over. "Judy sews a lot, but I don't know if she's tried quilting. I never thought to ask. But I'll be calling her as soon as I get home today. It's three

24

hours earlier there, you know."

"I had no idea we had such a Hawaiian connection here at St. Rose," Louise said. "There are so many people here from the Midwest, but I've only met a few parishioners from west of Arizona. Or the Pacific northwest," she added, remembering a woman in the knitting room who hailed from Oregon.

"I didn't know you were from Hawai'i, Bernie," Clare said, surprising them all. Clare was the Quilting Bee's go-to person when it came to learning personal information about parishioners. She always seemed to know where people were from and how many children and grandchildren they had. Clare had such a sympathetic manner, people just naturally confided in her.

"How is it we've never thought about doing any Hawaiian quilting before?" Victoria asked. "I've seen the blocks in books and magazines, and always admired the style."

"I think it's just that we've always had certain things we prefer," Maggie said. "And we always do the rose blocks for the church quilts, so I think we've just always veered toward rose patterns and more traditional piecing and appliqué patterns."

"There's a more practical reason, too," Edie added. "The Hawaiian quilts are very large and they are a tremendous amount of work. As Dolores said, it can take years to do the appliqué and then quilt one of those large quilts. We have to work faster than that in order to have a good amount of quilts for the auction."

The St. Rose Quilting Bee auction was a staple of the Senior Guild's All Hallows Eve Bazaar. Held on the weekend closest to October thirty-first, the Guild sold craft objects made by their members. The biggest fund-raiser by far was the auction of the quilts made by the Quilting Bee throughout the year. The quality of their quilts had become known across the country, so bidders came from far afield and the prices had risen accordingly.

Maggie nodded. "It's true. I've always admired the Hawaiian quilts, but they are intimidating. Now a pillow top like Dolores showed us, that would be fun. And hearing about the style from a local quilter would be the best way to learn."

While the others continued to discuss Hawaiian quilts, Iris conducted a brief meeting with Bernie and Lydia, busily jotting notes into her notebook.

"This is going to be great," Iris said as she finished up. "With your local connections I think it will be easy to set up something wonderful. I can't wait to get started."

Chapter 3

Iris began work on their tour immediately. Interest was strong, but everyone was awaiting word on the cost before committing to the trip.

By September, Iris had a discounted price at a small bed-and-breakfast on the Big Island run by a local quilter, and a tentative schedule of quilting classes and quilt-related events. She credited Bernie's cousin with finding "the perfect venue" for their tour.

"Bernie's cousin knows a quilter who runs the Blue Lily Bed and Breakfast Inn in Hilo. Hilo is kind of a quaint old plantation town that you'll enjoy visiting. The inn is near the ocean, and they have a bus that can take us to the other places we'll want to visit. Best of all, she has a large classroom right on the site. You'll love it. All the beds at the inn have handmade Hawaiian quilts on them. The quilter's name is Lurline Ilima, and she's very excited about hosting our group."

Iris even brought in her laptop to show them online pictures of the bed-and-breakfast. Edie grumbled that it all cut into their quilting time, but even she enjoyed hearing Iris's plans. And especially the prices Iris had obtained for them.

"We won't just be sitting in a classroom sewing, either," Iris told them. "Lurline and Rita — that's Bernie's cousin — have set up a full schedule for us with visits to the local places of interest. And they assure me it will all tie in with the quilt designing. We'll get to see quilts and the things and places that influenced their creators."

"I didn't know you were interested in quilt design, Iris," Edie said.

Iris waved away the comment. "I knew the group would be interested. For myself, I'll make one of those pillow tops like Dolores did and be perfectly happy. But I'll enjoy seeing the Big Island again. It's a really lovely place and not nearly as crowded as Maui."

"I can't wait," Louise said. "It sounds wonderful. Vince has been listening to me talk about it and would love to join me, but I told him it's a girls'-night-out kind of trip. He's quite impressed with the prices you got for us, Iris."

"Would you really want him along?" asked

Edie. "Having him there would cut into your sewing time."

"You're probably right, but I have to admit I'm of two minds about it. Even with classes and touring the various places, there are bound to be some romantic moments." Louise kept her eyes on the line of quilting stitches she was putting into the quilt top, but her cheeks turned pink.

Maggie had to smile. She understood what Louise was feeling. If Harry was still alive, she would have liked to have him along on such a trip. Spending time with "the girls" was all well and good, but there was nothing like a spouse for sharing romantic moments and to hold close on cold nights. And they had already been warned that January evenings on the Big Island would be cold.

"I'm sure it would be nice to have Gerald come," Clare said, "but it works better for me to have him stay. Then I won't have to worry about Samson. He's getting old, and it would really upset him to go to a kennel."

Clare doted on her aging miniature schnauzer, so they well understood how she felt about leaving him with strangers. With her children and grandchildren all still in the Midwest, the dog was like her child. And while Gerald often grumbled about the dog, they knew that he loved him as much as Clare did.

"Well, I've just been there with my husband, so I'm all for a women-only excursion." Dolores, the inspiration for the trip, was eager to join them, even though she had recently returned from a trip to Hawai'i. "There were some stores I would have liked to explore, but Peter isn't much of a shopper. I'm sure there will be similar places on the Big Island."

"Well, you'll have to decide quickly if you want to go as a couple," Iris said. "The Blue Lily is a small inn and we already have quite a few quilters who want to go."

"We should probably limit it to those taking the classes," Maggie suggested. "It will make it easier for everyone that way."

Iris was happy to agree and gathered up her things. Within minutes she was bustling from the room, on her way to check in with groups in other rooms in order to see if she could finalize her tour list.

The others breathed out in relief.

"I'm afraid I don't find the quilting as relaxing these days," Anna said. "Iris wears me out. She has so much energy, she makes me twitchy."

"Twitchy?" Maggie repeated with a chuckle.

"I think she's been much better since she began planning our tour," Louise said.

"True," Maggie agreed. "Of course, she's only been coming a few days a week since she's been spending so much time setting up this tour."

A few guilty smiles were exchanged across the quilt frame.

"There's something odd about Iris," Edie said.

"You're always so suspicious," Clare scolded. "She's working so hard on this, and she's doing it all for us."

"Odd how?" Maggie asked.

"Nothing specific. Just a feeling," Edie admitted. "But you know how she's always going on about that travel agency she used to own? One day I tried to Google Iris Fleming and travel agency, and nothing came up. Or at least, nothing I could see that tied in with her having her own agency."

"But she lost it years ago. Because of her ex-husband running off with their money." Anna always believed whatever she was told and hated to think there might be something suspicious about their friend.

"Perhaps you're getting a strange vibe because she's getting a lot of help from Bernie's relative, and maybe trying not to give as much credit as is due," Louise suggested. "Iris does like to bask in the spot-light."

"Maybe that's it," Edie said. Still, she looked far from certain about that explanation, Maggie thought.

"She is putting a lot of time and energy into this," Louise said. "We're lucky to have her. None of us would have pursued this otherwise, and think how much fun it will be."

"I'm getting so excited." Clare was almost bouncing in her seat. She said over and over again each day how much she was looking forward to their quilt tour.

"It should be quite the experience," Edie allowed. High praise indeed from the group's pessimist.

CHAPTER 4

Quilt tour, day one. Tuesday, the afternoon of their arrival.

It was a perfect Hawaiian day in January when the St. Rose Quilting Bee tour group deplaned at General Lyman Field in Hilo. The sky was a clear azure blue; only a few cottony white clouds marred its pristine surface. The sun blazed, bright and hot. Mauna Loa and Mauna Kea towered over the city, bright white snow shining at the top of the latter, higher mountain.

Clare was thrilled with their warm welcome. A handsome local couple clad in colorful, matching Hawaiian clothing met them, with big smiles of welcome and armfuls of flower leis — the fragrant garlands presented to each tour member with a kiss of aloha.

They easily recognized Lurline from her Web-site photo. She was tall and Rubenesque with quantities of dark, gray-streaked hair coiled neatly into a bun at the nape of her neck. Beside her stood an equally tall, extremely handsome older man, with a marked resemblance to actor Cary Grant in his heyday. Maggie heard Clare suck in her breath, and she knew she'd just caught sight of him. Clare *loved* Cary Grant.

Beside the couple from the Blue Lily were two local women, also holding armfuls of leis to present to the new arrivals. A small, wiry woman with a gray streak in her mahogany-colored hair — greeted with a shriek and a hug by Bernie — turned out to be her cousin Rita. The paler, blonde woman beside her was former Scottsdale resident Judy Hayden, Lydia's best friend. They were less exuberant in their reunion, but Maggie could see how happy they were to be together again, however temporarily.

There were introductions and handshakes, but the small airport turned out to be quite efficient at producing luggage, and their bags were quickly collected on a cart by the handsome older man — who was Lurline's husband and their tour-bus driver, "Sam" Samson.

With a flair much like the famed actor, Sam led them to the B and B's bus. The women took a moment to admire the old school bus, repainted a pale golden yellow and decorated with colorful Hawaiian quilt snowflake-like designs. *Blue Lily Bed and Breakfast* was inscribed across the side in pretty calligraphy, in paint that exactly matched the shade of the agapanthus lilies blooming along the bottom edge of the vehicle, illustrating the derivation of the inn's name.

"It will just take a few minutes to get to the Blue Lily," Lurline assured them as she seated herself at the front of the bus. Then, as Sam started the engine, she picked up a microphone. She provided a running commentary on the places they passed as they drove to the Blue Lily, but, as promised, it was a very short drive. They were shown to their rooms and given a half hour to freshen up; then everyone gathered in the large classroom.

"This must be an addition to the main house," Maggie commented, as she and Victoria found seats at one of the long tables. "It looks much newer than the main part of the house."

Lurline overheard and smiled. "You're correct. The house has been in my family for many years. We had to renovate extensively for the bed-and-breakfast, of course. But this classroom was added on a few years ago."

She glanced around the room, counting heads, Maggie suspected.

"Shall we begin? I wanted to start right away because we have a lot to cover. My experience has been that people arriving are anxious to begin their vacation and don't mind an immediate class. It's the anticipation of a good time and the experience of actually being in the islands, perhaps for the first time. It seems to delay the jet lag caused by the three-hour time difference."

This was greeted with applause.

"We might be senior citizens, but we can't wait to get going," Louise said.

Her comment was met with agreement and laughs.

"Why don't we begin with introductions? I'll start with the people here at the Blue Lily. I am Lurline Ilima. I learned to quilt right here in this house, from my mother and grandmother. I started designing about ten years ago, and discovered that I love that best of all. I've made many quilts for businesses, and all of the quilts on the beds here in the inn."

There was a break in the introductions as the tour group took time to exclaim over the beautiful quilts each had encountered in their rooms and to compliment Lurline on her work.

"But my favorite thing of all is sharing my knowledge of Hawaiian quilts with people who don't know about them. It is rewarding and fulfilling."

This statement was so moving, Anna had to wipe away a tear. Lurline's cheeks turned pink when she noticed Anna's reaction.

"Now, let me introduce my family members, who all help out here at the inn."

A tall young woman stepped forward — a younger, slimmer version of Lurline. She had deep, soulful eyes the color of semisweet chocolate, and long brown hair hanging past her shoulders and streaked with red highlights.

"This is my number-one daughter, Makana."

"Your *only* daughter," Makana countered with an eye roll, drawing laughter from the group.

Lurline smiled, probably used to what Maggie suspected was a regular part of their presentation.

"She, too, is a quilter and will be helping with the classes and the field trips." Lurline smiled at her daughter. "She just graduated from the University of Hawai'i in Honolulu with a degree in design," she added proudly.

After a moment of congratulatory applause, Lurline continued.

"I didn't ask him to come inside, but you all met Sam, our driver and my husband. He drives our little bus and he had another group to pick up just now, so he had to leave. He mainly drives the people who stay here at the inn, but he does take other jobs now and then. Don't worry. We plan his outside work carefully so that it won't interfere with your tour."

As she finished speaking, the door opened and a grinning, middle-aged man appeared. He was shorter than Maggie, and rather round, with a full head of dark, wavy hair and the warmest smile Maggie had ever seen. She later told Victoria that he reminded her of her Golden Retriever back at the ranch in Scottsdale, with his big brown eyes and friendly, eager-to-please manner. Victoria, in her turn, thought he looked like a teddy bear.

"This is Manu, the best cook in the islands. You'll get a chance to sample his work this evening. We'll be having an early dinner, as I'm sure you'll be noticing the time change and will want to get to bed before it gets too late."

"Aloha!" Manu greeted everyone with a wave. "Like Lurline said, I'm making early dinner. You'll like it. I'm the best cook in Keaukaha."

And with those brief words and another friendly wave, he turned and returned to his kitchen.

Lurline then called up Bernie's cousin, Rita Lindsey. "Rita is a local quilter who lives in Waimea, an inland community in ranch country. We'll be going to Waimea on one of our excursions because there's a nice little quilt shop there. I'm sure you all know that Rita is Bernadette's cousin. She helped Iris and I put your tour together. Rita is also a talented quilter and designer who sells her patterns and kits on the Internet." Lurline paused, then added with a good-natured chuckle, "In other words, she's my competition."

This was greeted with polite laughter.

"Iris put me in touch with Rita early on and we planned your tour together. She'll be helping a lot with the classes, and if any of you need help with the stitching."

Rita added her "Aloha," but had little more to tell them. "I think Lurline said it all." She offered the group a friendly smile as she returned to her seat beside Bernie. "Though I do want to add that I'm very excited about having this time with Bernie, who I haven't seen for years." She covered her cousin's hand with her own and they exchanged affectionate grins. "I'm so happy that she's finally going to learn how to quilt."

"Now, let's meet all of you," Lurline said, looking around the room for someone to start off the introductions.

One by one the Quilting Bee members introduced themselves. Maggie, Victoria, Louise, Anna, Clare and Edie began, then Theresa and Iris.

"I've really enjoyed putting this trip together," Iris said. "I used to have my own travel agency," she explained to Lurline and the other two local women, "but I sell real estate now. This was so much fun, perhaps I should go back to travel planning."

The St. Rose women exchanged looks at this last. Louise raised her eyebrows at Maggie, and Maggie pursed her lips. It seemed the wrong time to be making such personal statements. Feeling sorry for herself, Maggie thought.

"Anyway," Iris continued, "our trip was inspired by a fellow parishioner named Dolores. She and her husband vacationed on Maui last summer and she brought in a pillow top she made. She loved the short quilting lesson she had at the hotel on Maui, and she really wanted to come and learn more."

Several of the women murmured agreement. "She was really looking forward to coming," Clare said.

"Unfortunately, her husband had to have surgery," Iris said. "This was apparently the only time they could arrange to do it, so she had to cancel."

Lurline made the appropriate sympathetic noises, and they moved on to Lydia.

"I do a lot of embroidery at the Senior Guild," Lydia said, "mostly embellishing items the other women sew. Lots of baby clothes, and doll clothes, tea towels, things like that. I saw some of Rita's designs online that have embroidery on the Hawaiian quilts, so I'm very excited." She smiled over at Rita, who looked flattered at her praise.

"Also, I wanted to come to meet up with my dear friend," Lydia gestured toward the woman sitting next to her. "This is Judy Hayden, who now lives on the Big Island. I don't know if any of you remember Judy from the parish. She lived next door to us when we moved to Scottsdale, but she moved here two years ago. We had become very close friends over the years and it was hard on me when she moved. We've kept in touch by e-mail and phone calls of course, but it's so exciting to have her here with me for the week of classes." Her smile widened as she glanced at Judy seated beside her.

Judy returned the smile, covering her friend's hand with her own. "I can't tell you how glad I am to be here, and especially to be with Lydia again. I sew a lot, and I do some painting. I've wanted to learn to quilt, but just haven't found the time. You know how it is." There were several murmured agreements. "But once I heard about the tour group, I knew I had to come. I can't wait to get started. And of course, I'm rooming with my old friend, and we're anticipating some girly pajama-party-type sessions."

Laughter greeted this last comment.

Bernie was the final member of the group. "I'm very excited about learning to appliqué and quilt. I was born in Honolulu and moved to the mainland to go to college, got married, and never moved back." She shrugged.

"It's a common story in Hawai'i," Lurline murmured. Maggie saw her look quickly over at Makana, love shining in her eyes. And probably relief that her daughter had come home after graduation, Maggie thought.

"At St. Rose," Bernie continued, "I sew small items for the bazaar — doll clothes, aprons and tote bags. Sometimes I piece quilt blocks for the front of the tote bags.

43

But I've never tried appliqué and I can't wait to try it. I've always loved Rita's quilts and patterns, and I don't know why I haven't tried making something from them before now."

There were some murmurs of agreement as the others commiserated. They all knew how that went. You wanted to try something new but somehow the time just never arrived. It was always easiest to keep with what you knew best.

"There we go," Lurline said, her eyes glowing with enthusiasm. "Now we all know one another. Let's get started, shall we?"

There was a resounding "yes" from those sitting at the tables.

"I'm going to start you all off with a pillow kit to work." She gestured toward Makana, who held a number of colorful packages in her hands, ready to begin distribution. "This will help you all learn about the Hawaiian quilting techniques. By the time you finish this pillow top, you'll know enough about technique to appliqué any Hawaiian quilt pattern. The colors vary, so you may select your favorite. But they are all of the *ulu,* or breadfruit, pattern. This is traditionally the first design you should work, so that you will have a long and fruitful quilting career."

She smiled as her gaze roved around the room, stopping briefly at each woman in turn.

"This is going to be a wonderful group," Lurline said as she began their first lesson. "There's a lot of stitching experience here. I foresee amazing things happening this week."

Unfortunately, her prediction would prove all too true.

CHAPTER 5

Quilt tour, day two. Wednesday, early morning.

Although they started their quilt sessions immediately on arrival, and everyone was anxious to get stitching, the three-hour time difference and the long trip called for an early night. However, everyone was up early the next morning. It was partly due to the time difference between Hawai'i and Arizona, but they were also eager to begin the first full day of their schedule.

Lurline was waiting in the dining room to greet everyone at six-thirty, welcoming them to enjoy a hearty breakfast. "We have a lot to do today, so be sure to get your nourishment now."

"I'm glad I brought a cardigan," Victoria told Maggie as they entered the dining room. She pulled the edges of her sweater together, fastening several of the buttons. "Even though Bernie warned us, I didn't expect it to be quite so cold."

"I suspect it's the chill from the dampness that's getting to us," Maggie said. "We're used to a dryer atmosphere."

"It can get quite cold here in the wintertime," Lurline said. "Especially when there's snow on the mountain, as there is now. It will warm right up to the mid-seventies or low eighties once the sun comes up. And once the rain stops," she added. "But you'll need that sweater for the trip to the volcano," Lurline continued. "That's on the side of the mountain, at a much higher altitude, and it can be very cold and windy."

"I hadn't expected it would be so cold at night," Anna said. "Inside, I mean. It was very chilly. I guess we're all spoiled with our central heat and air."

"I closed the window, and we made good use of those beautiful quilts on the beds," said Clare, Anna's roommate.

Maggie had noticed the patter of raindrops hitting the corrugated tin roof. It seemed quite loud compared to the sound of rain on the insulated roofs on the mainland, but not unpleasant. In fact, when she'd awakened during the night, she'd found the steady rhythm of the rainfall on the roof soothed her right back to sleep. For the first night in a strange bed, she'd slept very comfortably.

Now, on the lower floor and further from the roof, she could hear the softer sound of raindrops hitting the foliage outside the open windows. It was a soothing sound, like listening to the music of the water in the fountain at St. Rose. One of the reasons they liked to keep the door to the quilting room open was so that they could hear that lovely susurration as the water tumbled from one level to another in the courtyard fountain.

There were tall open windows at the end of the dining room, and a refreshing scent of damp foliage and rich soil floated in, along with a faint perfume from the tropical flowers growing in profusion outside. Maggie sniffed appreciatively. The only thing better than the refreshing scent of blooming flowers was the smell of bacon, eggs, and potatoes coming from the sideboard.

Although officially a bed-and-breakfast, the Blue Lily Inn had agreed to provide or arrange for all meals during the quilt group's stay. True to Manu's boast when they'd first met, the meal they enjoyed the night before had been excellent. So everyone was happy to see Manu again as he presided over the buffet hot trays and checked to see that each woman got what she wanted.

Breakfast was as excellent as their dinner the previous night, and the women were urged to enjoy the meal while Lurline made a final check on Sam and the bus.

"The local people have such interesting names," Anna said, watching Lurline exit the room.

"Lurline told me she was named after a ship that used to travel between the islands and the mainland," Clare said.

Iris nodded. "It was *the* ship for travel to Hawai'i for many years. The original ship was named after the daughter of the Matson line owner. And here's an interesting bit of trivia for you: during World War II, they used it as a troopship."

"It must have been nice traveling to Hawai'i on a ship. So leisurely. You'd probably meet lots of really interesting people." Clare sighed. Maggie imagined she was already weaving wonderfully romantic stories about the ship and its passengers.

"As long as you don't get seasick," Lydia said. "Which I do."

Several people commiserated with her over this revelation.

"What a shame," Anna said, adding to several other similar comments. "I went on a cruise once, and it was lovely."

"Makana's name means 'gift,' " Maggie

said, bringing the conversation back to the original topic of interesting local names.

Clare nodded then took a quick glance around before lowering her voice. "Did you realize that Manu is Makana's father?"

"I did hear her call him Dad last night," Victoria replied.

All around the table, heads dipped forward and voices lowered.

"And Sam, who picked us up in the bus," Theresa said. "Lurline said he's her husband."

"He is," Rita said. "Their last names aren't the same because Lurline had already established herself as a quilter by the time they got married, so she kept her name. A lot of professional women do that. Manu was her first husband," she added.

"So do she and Manu share a name? And Makana?" Anna asked.

Rita nodded. "Lurline probably didn't get her quilt business going until after she married Manu," she said. "Because she, Manu and Makana all have the same last name: Ilima."

"She might have married young," Clare said, always willing to consider the romantic side of a story. Thinking that Lurline and Manu might have been high school sweethearts would be her style, Maggie thought, and Clare's soft heart was probably already aching for the demise of the sweet love she envisioned. Maggie doubted the truth was quite so idealistic.

"What a situation!" Edie clucked her tongue. "It's a disaster just waiting to happen. Especially since Sam seems to be the kind of man who can't resist flirting with anyone with two X chromosomes."

"I wondered if I'd imagined that." Victoria's soft voice was thoughtful.

"Oh, no," Theresa said. "I noticed it too."

"I was embarrassed at the airport when he kissed me right on the lips," Anna confided, almost whispering the words. Apparently, she still felt embarrassed by that offense to her personal space. "The lei was nice, but a kiss on the cheek would have been more appropriate."

"Oh, it's just a bit of harmless flirting he's doing," Iris said in dismissal. "Like what you do if you go to a club. He's trying to make the vacation fun for everyone." But Maggie thought her smile seemed brittle. Was she feeling bad about Sam's behavior because she'd been the one to make the arrangements and choose the inn?

"That's not what I consider fun." Anna's somber voice left no doubt how she felt about strange men taking liberties.

Maggie understood. She had received her lei from Lurline, who had placed a light kiss on her cheek, so she had not been a recipient of a kiss on the lips from Sam. And she couldn't relate to Iris's statement, as she'd never been to a club. And didn't want to go to one, either. But she knew she didn't need false flattery to have a good time — in fact, just the opposite — so she didn't appreciate Sam's attitude either.

"Have you noticed the way Sam acts around Makana?" Theresa asked. "It's disgraceful."

Edie gave a grunt of disapproval. "Some men just can't help acting that way with every woman they meet," she said. "At least Makana is sensible enough to ignore him."

"But his own stepdaughter!" Theresa said, keeping her voice low in case Makana or Manu should hear from the kitchen. "And with her father right there in the kitchen."

"Not to mention her mother, his *wife*," Edie said dryly.

"It might still affect Makana, even if she seems to know how to handle him," Louise said. "Did you see how she ate at dinner last night? Or perhaps I should say how she didn't eat. The poor thing barely touched a bite."

"Poor Lurline," Theresa said. "Maybe

that's why she keeps Manu around. Did you see the way he looks at her? Pure adoration. I wonder why they ever divorced."

"Oh, that was the talk of the quilting community when it happened," Rita said. "Lurline was already an established quilter when her mother died about ten years ago and left her this house. She had a dream of opening a bed-and-breakfast and offering quilting seminars on site, so she and Manu opened the Blue Lily together. They were a happily married couple then. But things went bad, and Lurline filed for divorce. Manu never wanted a divorce, so he wouldn't agree to splitting the B and B."

"That must make it interesting, working together with an ex who didn't want a divorce and your new husband right there all the time," Louise said.

"But he's such a wonderful chef," Clare said. "Who would she have gotten to cook if they had broken the place up? Makana told me he takes care of the yard and garden too."

"He sounds like a treasure," Edie said. "I wonder why they broke up."

"That was the juiciest part of the gossip," Rita said, her voice rising somewhat with the tidbit she had to share. With a guilty look toward the door leading to the kitchen, she quickly dropped her voice again.

"A few years after they opened the Blue Lily, Manu went to some kind of special cooking class on Maui and had a moment of madness. While he was there, he ran into an old girlfriend from his school days — a rival of Lurline's. She lives on Maui and just happened to be at the resort restaurant that night with some girlfriends. Another classmate saw them cuddling in a booth late that night, and took a picture and posted it on the Internet."

"Oh, dear," Anna said with a sigh. "There are so many wonderful things you can do with a computer. But it can also be used to destroy lives." Anna did not participate in social media herself, but she helped with her grandchildren, and her daughter kept her well informed about online dangers. So she knew how quickly that kind of thing could take off.

Rita nodded. "Of course old classmates were falling all over themselves telling Lurline all about it. She filed for divorce right away and the ink wasn't even dry when she met Sam. The day the divorce went through, she flew to Vegas to celebrate and she met Sam there. She was definitely on the rebound. Makana says her dad never wanted a divorce and had hoped they could make up, since they would still be working together."

"Her haste makes sense if it was an old school friend. They were probably rivals back then, and it would really hurt for her to see him getting back together with her, even if it was just a one-night fling," Louise said.

"Everyone around here agreed she and Manu probably would have reconciled if she hadn't had her own moment of madness in Vegas," Rita said.

"I wonder how long she's been married to Sam."

Maggie didn't think Clare expected an answer, having voiced it as a musing thought, but Rita replied anyway.

"About six or seven years . . ."

"Well, maybe it's the old seven-year itch making Sam act so silly around other women," Edie said.

"Oh, no," Rita said. "That Sam, he's got a reputation. All the local waitresses know about him. They don't turn their backs on him. He and Lurline have had some big kine arguments in restaurant parking lots . . . yelling at each other about the way he acts."

Edie shook her head, her lips pursed in a moue of disgust.

"Manu does look at Lurline like a man

who's still in love." Anna, who probably read as many, if not more, romance novels than mystery ones, felt very sad for his unrequited love.

Clare agreed. "It's hard to believe he was so foolish."

"Not really," Louise said. "Men — and even women — often think they can get away with anything when they're away from home. Lots of happily married people have one-night flings while at conventions. They just think they won't get caught. It's the whole idea behind that campaign of 'what happens in Vegas stays in Vegas.' Add to that liquor consumption and a woman determined to seduce him . . . well, the poor man never had a chance."

With a "tsk" and a shake of her head, Edie agreed.

"I think Manu is wonderful," Anna said. "And his cooking . . . !"

"Everyone loves Manu," Rita said.

As though called by their flattering remarks, Manu walked into the room with a fresh platter of pancakes.

Rita sent him a wink, sure he'd heard her earlier comment. "Manu is so nice. And the man can cook, yeah?"

Manu bowed good-naturedly, a wide smile on his round face. "Anything you'd like, ladies, just ask and I'll see if I can make it."

"These macadamia nut pancakes are unbelievable," Clare said, and several others agreed.

"Would you share the recipe, or is it a secret?" Judy asked, tempering her request with a smile.

"No, no, I share. Tomorrow, macadamia nut waffles."

They continued to praise Manu's abilities until he retreated to the kitchen. A few of the women returned to the buffet for seconds while others turned their attention to the day's schedule.

"I can't believe we're actually going to see an erupting volcano," Anna said with a delicate shudder. She pulled her jacket across her chest, as though the wool could protect her like some kind of suit of armor. "It's a bit frightening, isn't it?"

CHAPTER 6

Quilt tour, day two. Wednesday morning.
Hawai'i Volcanoes National Park.

The morning's trip brought the tour group to Hawai'i Volcanoes National Park to view the longest-running eruption in the history of Kīlauea. At the visitor center where they started their tour, they learned that the Pu'u Ō'ō vent had been erupting steadily since 1983 and showed no signs of stopping any time soon. It had already added more than 500 acres of new land to the Big Island as it flowed into the ocean several miles away. More accessible to viewing, however, the Halema'uma'u crater was shifting and steaming. Huge plumes of steam were streaming upward from inside the crater, and seismic rumblings continued beneath the surface.

"Oh, darn," Clare said when she heard how the crater glowed after dark. "I wish we could see that."

"Don't worry," Lurline told them. "After the luau this evening, we'll go to see the lava entering the ocean. That's a much better sight than a mere glow from the crater. You'll be able to see the lava streams coming down the hill and going into the sea."

Lurline explained that the lava from the current eruption was traveling toward the ocean through tubes underground, so the best views were from the ocean, after dark. "It's an incredible sight at night," Lurline continued, "especially from the water. The luau wraps up early, and we'll go directly from the hotel to the harbor. We'll board a boat in Hilo and have a leisurely excursion out to the area where our island is growing. People from the mainland are always amazed by the sight."

"Oh, dear, a boat," Lydia moaned. "I'm glad I brought some Dramamine."

There wasn't time to commiserate with her now, though, as they pulled into the parking lot at what Lurline called the best viewing spot above the crater. Clothing billowed in the wind as they dismounted the bus and headed for the overlook. The women snatched at the edges of their sweaters and jackets, pulling them together as best they could as they made their way to an overlook above the Kīlauea caldera and beside the Jaggar Museum. Lurline told them that the current museum had once been the whole of the Volcano Observatory, but that particular building was now a separate unit and not open to visitors.

"We used to be able to drive in a circle around the crater — on Crater Rim Road," Lurline told them, gesturing with her hands at the surrounding area. From their high vantage point, they could see much of the road, currently closed off because of dangerous fumes. "But the eruptions have always played havoc with the roads in the park and a lot of the roads are closed right now. The Pu'u Ō'ō eruption destroyed a large portion of the Chain of Craters Road, the section that ran down to the ocean and back to Hilo. And the Rim Road is currently closed because of the steam venting from Halema'uma'u. There are high levels of sulfur dioxide present in the gases, and it could be dangerous to move through that area."

A wide spectrum of comments issued from the tour group as they looked out over the desolate landscape of the Hawai'i Volcanoes National Park.

"Isn't it beautiful?" Victoria said.

"Rather frightening too," Louise observed.

"So much devastation," Anna said.

"Doesn't it remind you of Meteor Crater?" Lydia asked.

"It does," Victoria agreed. Meteor Crater, in northern Arizona, was a huge crater in a desolate area, created in prehistoric times when a meteor hit the earth. "Only Meteor Crater was created fifty thousand years ago with one great hit, and this is an ongoing process."

"That can't compare to this." Despite the wind disrupting her usually impeccable hairdo, Clare was excited to be present in such an amazing place. "This is even better than the geysers at Yellowstone," she insisted, staring intently at the floor of the crater they had been told was Halema'uma'u, the home of Pele, Goddess of Hawaiian Volcanoes. The ranger had explained that deep within the pit was another, smaller crater, and the floor of this smaller *"puka,"* or hole, seemed to be undulating as it expelled gases. The latter steamed upward in a huge white cloud — a cloud filled with the sulfur dioxides Lurline had warned them about.

"That must be the lava pool they told us about," Louise said, pointing in the direction of the white plume. One of the park rangers had given them a rundown of what they might expect on this particular day, and Maggie knew Clare hoped to see something of that shifting and undulating — even though they were told it would not be visible to the naked eye.

"Did you see it moving?" Anna asked, more hopeful than not.

"No, but I'm sure I can see a glow," Clare said.

Edie frowned. "They said there was a noticeable glow at night, but it can't be seen in the daylight."

"I'm sure there's a glow," Clare insisted.

A thick plume of steam rose from the vent, luckily blowing away from their vantage point.

Maggie watched their erstwhile guides move off. Sam had hold of Lurline's upper arm, and his head was angled close to hers as he spoke earnestly into her ear. The wind was brisk, blowing their hair and clothing, and making it difficult to hear people a few feet away. Lurline and Sam stopped some twenty feet away, their body language indicating a disagreement of some kind. Maggie would have been interested in hearing what they were saying, but the wind and the distance made it impossible.

"Looks like there's something going on there," Maggie said.

"I'm so glad you didn't say 'trouble in

paradise,' " Victoria responded, smiling at her friend.

Lurline and Makana had joined the group for breakfast, but Sam had not appeared. Once they all gathered outside, they found him standing beside the door to the bus, ready to chauffeur them on the day's tour. He'd greeted all the women with smiles and compliments, but sent a beseeching look toward Lurline. Lurline, they'd all noticed, ignored him, stepping into the bus with her eyes focused straight ahead.

Everyone had noticed that the coldness between Sam and Lurline continued for the duration of the bus ride. Edie even made a remark about tension thick enough to slice. Lurline took her usual seat immediately behind the driver, but it was as though she was trying to lean away from him at the same time. Maggie wondered if Sam was talking, trying to win her back — or making excuses. Was she attempting not to hear him?

Now, standing on the rim of a live volcano, Maggie stared at the couple for a few minutes, shaking her head. Just to the other side of her was a sight that must qualify as one of the wonders of the modern world. How could she let a domestic spat distract her from such an amazing view? Still, she'd always maintained that it was the people who made places exciting, not the static landscape.

Maggie almost laughed at herself. This particular landscape was anything but static.

She sent another look toward their hosts. "No surprise, if you ask me. Lurline strikes me as a smart woman who knows what she wants. I can't understand her putting up with a phony like Sam."

"Rita did say that they often argue in public because of his womanizing, remember?" Louise said.

Anna looked around, a furtiveness in the movement. "He has been flirting a lot with Iris and Judy," she whispered.

"He's been trying to flirt with everybody. Iris and Judy are just letting him do it. The rest of us don't have time for that kind of chauvinism." Edie, as usual, was decisive in her pronouncement.

"Lydia and Rita are allowing him to flirt too. Even Bernie to a lesser extent," Victoria observed. "Did you get the impression that Judy knew him before this quilt tour?" She added the latter in an undertone to Maggie.

Maggie nodded. She'd seen Sam put his arm around Judy as he helped her from the bus. But then she'd seen him do the same with Bernie when they were boarding.

"If he's always like that, Lurline should be used to it," Louise commented.

"I don't know that you ever get used to that kind of thing," Theresa said. "I sure wouldn't want Carl acting like that. I'd set him straight right quick if he did."

"I'm going to move inside and check out the gift shop," Edie said. "I don't care to put up with this wind for more than a few minutes at a time. And I see there's a nice big window, so we can probably look our fill from there too."

As most of the tour members followed Edie inside, Maggie and Victoria remained in place. Maggie couldn't help a feeling of being on top of the world, even if there was a higher point behind them.

"There is a certain charm about Sam," Victoria said, still thinking of the couple standing so close by. "I think he likes to play up the suave sophisticate, pretend he's Cary Grant. Clare was certainly taken with him at dinner last night. You know how she loves Cary Grant. And you have to admit to the resemblance."

Maggie nodded. "Still, it's got to be difficult for Lurline. With her business centering on quilting, the inn is probably always full of women. And she's got such an idiot playboy for a husband."

"It takes all kinds," Victoria said.

With a final glance at the feuding couple, they followed their friends into the building. They spent an enjoyable half hour browsing in the museum and gift shop. Sam entered a few minutes behind them and caused a bit of a sensation as he moved from one group to another, passing out his sometimes risqué compliments and being much too free with touches and pats. At one point Edie even snapped, "Get your hand off me, please."

To Maggie's relief, Sam wandered back outside after that. It was a much lighter atmosphere in the shop once he'd gone, and the women were able to choose souvenirs from among the books, postcards and DVDs.

As they approached the bus in the lookout parking lot, the main part of the group was distracted by the sight of several Hawaiian *nene* geese, the Hawaiian state bird, and a name often found in crossword puzzles — another favorite pastime of the quilting women. Maggie and Victoria, a little ahead of the main group, continued on their way while some of the others paused and pulled out cameras.

"What do you think you're doing?"

In what was probably an attempt to maintain control because her students were nearby, Lurline spoke in muted tones. Yet Maggie and Victoria heard her clearly. If she'd been a cat, Lurline would have been hissing at her husband. The women seemed to have walked in on what appeared to be a full-blown argument between their hosts. Lurline and Sam were huddled together beside the bus, and not in a romantic manner.

"Nothing, sweetheart."

Maggie and Victoria, who had stopped short of the couple, not wanting to embarrass them by making their presence known, exchanged a glance. "Smarmy," Maggie mouthed. Victoria nodded.

"Just having a little fun," they heard Sam continue, "making sure our guests have a good time. You know the tourists enjoy a little flirting. Makes them feel good, gives them something to brag about when they get home."

"Well, you can darned well stop it, or you can have your fun somewhere else, without me. Remember, these are church ladies." The words were bitten off, hard, her voice as sharp as a brand new knife. "And the tourists like having a little fling with a handsome young beach boy, not an over-the-hill *haole*."

Victoria winced at both the words and the acid tone.

"I've been through one divorce. I'm sure it will be a lot easier the second time around."

"Now, Lurline . . ."

"Don't you 'now Lurline' me," she said. Her voice was hot and angry, filled with pain. Maggie suspected tears were not far behind. "I don't know why I put up with you — your freeloading ways, your flirting. It's making me old before my time. Manu and I are the same age and he doesn't have any gray hair. *Look* at mine. All your fault. You're killing me with your philandering ways."

They heard a loud sniff and indecipherable murmuring from Sam.

"And I repeat, this is a church group. So quit trying to get too close. It's a conservative group, and I already heard a complaint about you kissing them at the airport. Right on the lips. What were you thinking?"

Maggie and Victoria exchanged a significant look, embarrassed to witness this conversation that the couple thought private. Had Anna complained to Lurline about the kiss? Or had she overheard them at breakfast?

Edie and Louise were the next to arrive,

68

and stopped behind Maggie and Victoria. They caught Lurline's final words and also stopped, embarrassed to go on around them and expose the fact that a private conversation had been overheard. Even Clare stopped short, though she was leaning forward, avidly listening and probably hoping for more.

But the rest of the group approached en masse at that point, and the noise of so many chattering women alerted Lurline and Sam to their presence.

For a second, Lurline looked like a deer in the headlights. But her professional demeanor quickly reappeared, and she stepped away from Sam, a smile of welcome on her face.

"Ready to move on to the next lookout point?" she asked, her voice bright but brittle. "We'll make a brief stop at the steam vents, which you really have to see. Then we'll go back around to the Chain of Craters Road and to the Kīlauea Iki site and show you Devastation Trail. It's changed a lot from the way it looks in my wall hanging, but you can find photos of the original trail online."

In relating all of their side trips to quilting topics, Lurline had used the drive time from Hilo to show off a pillow pattern of flowing lava called Kīlauea Iki and a wall hanging of an area called Devastation Trail. The women had loved both designs. The former showed what appeared to be a pool of red lava dribbling into an overlay of black fabric and done in a technique called reverse appliqué. The Quilting Bee veterans were familiar with the method, but it required an explanation for those newer to appliqué methods.

The wall hanging was an amazing piece of stitching. It depicted a desert-like area of grays with some leafless trees and a narrow trail of wooden slats. Lurline's use of varying degrees of gray fabric was expert, creating a realistic representation of the famous photo she had used as inspiration. Maggie thought the piece well worthy of the blue ribbon from the county fair that was pinned to its border. As the wall hanging made its way around the bus, Lurline explained that the trail led through the devastation around an eruption at the Kīlauea Iki crater in the 1950s.

"My mother saw that eruption live and especially liked this photograph." She indicated the copy affixed to her wall hanging showing a desolate area of gray cinders and skeletal trees. "She got to walk the trail when it looked just like this. It was after she died that I decided to make this quilt as a tribute to her. The trail is still there, but has changed a lot in the past fifty years. There's a lot of new vegetation, which will be interesting on its own. It will show you how the earth replenishes itself."

"Be sure to listen to the birds," Rita suggested. "I've done a series of blocks with native birds that were inspired by visits out there. The local species are making comebacks in the area and their song is lovely."

While the women bombarded Lurline with comments on the sights so far, and questions about what was to come, Maggie kept her eyes focused on Sam. His smile came quicker than his wife's, as he moved from her side to Judy's, making a comment that caused the local woman to blush. But Judy returned the smile and made a remark in her turn, causing Sam to laugh in response. Maggie wanted to slap Sam upside the head. But she already knew that with some people, nothing that simple worked.

Lurline was still acting very cool toward Sam when they left the park.

"We'll be having bento lunches at Punalu'u Black Sand Beach Park," Lurline announced.

"Black sand!" Anna said. "I've heard of

black sand beaches, but seeing one will be something. It's hard to even picture it."

"Hilo Bay has black sand," Lurline said, "though I don't know if you'll be able to see that from any of the places on our tour. But the whole stretch along the front of the town is a black sand beach."

While this was interesting, Theresa's stomach was already rumbling, and she was more concerned about the food. "What are bento lunches?"

Lurline smiled. "They are the local box lunches, a tradition brought to the islands by the immigrant Japanese, of course. We thought we'd let you try them. You'll be able to say that you went native, yeah?"

There were a few chuckles, but Maggie could tell not everyone liked the idea of a strange meal. Makana jumped in to explain about the local food.

"Don't worry. There will be fish and chicken. Your imagination will make it much stranger than the reality."

Which proved to be true. Upon their arrival at Punalu'u, they wandered on the beach for a while to drink in the atmosphere. The long, wide stretch of black sand was a shock to those used to white sandy beaches, and Edie even called the scene oppressive. But the sight of a large sea turtle sunning himself (or herself) on the beach suddenly made the experience worthwhile. They were able to get up close to the beautiful creature and take photos to show off at home.

Lurline explained that the Hawaiians called the turtles *honu*. Also, that they were an endangered species and people could be fined for touching them or interfering with them in any way.

"My family's *'aumakua* is the *honu*," she said. "An *'aumakua* is a protective ancestral spirit," she explained.

"Do you have any quilt patterns with the sea turtle?" Theresa asked.

"Yes, I do," she replied. "I have a pillow pattern. And Rita has a beautiful wall hanging with *honu* and embroidery embellishments."

Theresa smiled happily as she adjusted her camera and snapped more pictures.

"I foresee some sales," Victoria said with a smile.

By the time they settled themselves at the picnic tables where Sam and Lurline waited with their lunches, even Theresa declared herself hungry enough to face the unknown. A self-proclaimed conservative when it came to food, Theresa had not been happy about the bento lunches.

"I've changed my mind," Edie declared, sitting down and opening her box lunch. "This place isn't oppressive at all. It's just different," she finished. "Like this lunch." Using the chopsticks, she picked up a piece of teriyaki chicken and popped it into her mouth. Theresa watched with interest from an adjacent table, her own lunch open before her. "Umm. It's good," Edie said.

Encouraged, others began to taste the food.

"What is this?" Victoria asked, picking up what looked like a sandwich consisting of rice for "bread" and a thick slice of something pink between, the whole wrapped round with a strip of black seaweed.

"That is a Spam musubi," Makana told her. "It's a great local favorite."

"I'd heard Spam was popular in the islands," Maggie said, picking up her own.

"It is. We often have it sliced thin and fried for breakfast. Maybe Manu will serve some for breakfast one morning. Better than bacon," she added with a grin, but Anna and Edie appeared startled at the suggestion.

As everyone became involved in eating, Maggie leaned forward. "Makana, how did your parents meet? They seem so different. He's not an islander, is he?"

Makana turned in her seat. "He isn't. They met when Mom went on a tour to Las Vegas. It was right after the divorce, and she went with some friends to celebrate. She met Sam in a casino bar the first night. She was very excited, called to tell me how much fun she was having, saying she'd met this nice guy who made her feel great." She sighed. "Next thing I knew she was calling me from a chapel in Vegas, saying she and Sam got married."

"It was that quick?"

"Oh, yes, two days. Can you believe it? Everyone who knew her was shocked."

"So he's from Las Vegas?" Maggie asked.

"No, I don't think so. He's always been a little vague about his background. Over the years he's mentioned several different places where he's lived. California, Texas, Arizona. Vegas too, though I never got the impression that he lived there for long. Maybe he just liked to visit. I'm not even sure Mom knows exactly where he's from. I don't think she cares. He's always said he doesn't have any family, so they don't even go to the mainland to visit. In fact, Mom has suggested going a few times, and he doesn't want to. Says they have everything they need right here, that Hawai'i is paradise and why would anyone want to leave."

"Sam is really . . . friendly," Maggie finally said.

Makana laughed, but it was not because she found the remark funny. There was no joy in her face or her words. "That's one way of putting it." Her tone was bitter, her eyes angry.

With a few deft movements, she threw her chopsticks and napkin into the box her lunch came in. She stood. "I'd better see how everyone is doing."

With that, she hurried off, tossing her box into a barrel labeled "rubbish."

"She just threw out most of her lunch," Louise observed, her voice concerned.

"And she seemed so excited about it," Victoria said.

"I have noticed that she doesn't seem to have much of an appetite." Maggie, too, stared after the young woman. "Do you think she has some kind of eating problem? Those anorexic girls you hear about are usually much thinner than Makana."

Clare, who always managed to discover personal information about people, spoke up.

"She lost almost a hundred pounds in the past year. Didn't you notice that graduation picture of her in the front room of the inn? The one from high school? She was much heavier, though still very pretty. Anyway, she's really proud of losing the weight. You should have seen her face when she told me." Clare's eyes saddened. "Though it didn't help her keep her boyfriend. She said he broke off with her just before graduation — her college graduation, that is. Told her she'd changed. Can you imagine?"

"The poor dear," Anna said.

"She has every reason to feel proud," Victoria said, giving up on her Spam musubi and trying the fish instead. "Mmm, this fish is delicious," she commented.

"I hope she hasn't gone too far in the opposite direction now." Louise, brow furrowed in concern, looked at Makana's new and svelte figure. "Some girls become so obsessed with losing weight, they don't know when to stop. Then they develop eating disorders."

"The Spam musubi isn't bad," Clare said. "But I wouldn't want to eat it all the time."

"No," Victoria agreed. "But I like the fish much better. It's delicious. Very fresh, I'm sure."

Theresa, leaning over from the next table, tapped Maggie's shoulder. "Were you asking about Sam and Manu? What did she say?"

Maggie shook her head. "No. I asked how

Lurline and Sam met. They seem an unlikely couple."

"That's an understatement," Edie muttered.

Theresa nodded agreement. "What did she say?"

Maggie repeated what she'd learned. "Pretty much what Rita told us at breakfast," she concluded.

"It's just like a book, isn't it?" Clare said, her voice filled with delight. "Lurline finding true love in Vegas. A whirlwind romance. And Sam — why, he could be running away from something on the mainland and that's why he came here. Hiding in plain sight, you know, that's what they always say is best."

Edie snorted. "More like a soap opera, you ask me."

"What would he be hiding from?" Maggie asked. She hated to encourage Clare, but the idea was interesting. It would certainly make a good mystery plot.

Clare frowned as she thought. Maggie could see her eyes brighten with each new scenario. "Well . . . ," she finally said. "He could be trying to avoid paying child support. Or he could be running from the law. Or from the mob." She added this last with particular glee. "Maybe he testified against a mobster and had to hide to protect himself. He could have been their accountant."

"He'd probably be in the witness-protection program if that was the case." Edie's dry comment caused the smile to slip from Clare's lips. Sitting beside Theresa at the other table, Judy offered a different possibility.

"Maybe he's hiding from an old girlfriend," Judy said, her voice bitter. "Or an ex-wife."

"Not a bad idea," Clare admitted graciously. She loved plotting out possibilities and didn't mind if she wasn't the one to hit on the best solution.

"And appropriate, too, given Sam's propensity for flirting," Maggie said.

"It would be more exciting if he was a former hit man, but Sam doesn't seem the type."

At this final suggestion from Clare, they all broke into laughter. It was the perfect ending to an interesting meal at an astonishingly beautiful place.

As they reboarded the bus, Maggie and the others noticed a warming in the interaction between Lurline and Sam. Lurline now sported a lovely ginger lei that filled the bus with a heavenly fragrance. Sam, smiling widely — almost a smirk, Maggie thought — must have gotten it from a woman on the beach. Maggie had seen her, a little old lady sitting on a woven mat with plastic grocery bags filled with flowers. She strung them into leis as a toddler played in the sand beside her.

Victoria nudged her as they walked back to their seats. "He's a romantic, that one."

"You mean, he knows how to save his bacon," Maggie replied.

"That too."

"Isn't it nice to see Lurline happy again?" Clare asked, from her seat behind them.

And she was that, Maggie thought, as Sam placed a kiss on his wife's cheek then took his seat behind the wheel.

Lurline picked up the microphone and announced that they would be heading back to Hilo.

"Luau tonight, ladies, so you might want to spend a little time relaxing with your stitching this afternoon. And there are ironing facilities available at the inn if you want to touch up clothes for tonight. You'll want to wear your best Hawaiian outfits," she added.

Groans came from several areas of the bus.

"Oh, dear," Clare moaned, voicing what all the others were thinking. "I don't have a

Hawaiian outfit. I hope slacks are okay."

"No problem," Lurline said with a smile. "Slacks are fine. We'll also be stopping at a very nice store on the way back. Kokonut Kate's. They have a large selection of Hawaiian clothing and some other souvenir goods as well. All their garments are locally made."

There was a low murmur of approval at this last.

As the old bus rattled out of the parking area, Lurline clung to the pole beside the driver's seat.

"The store is named after a local entertainer. Kokonut Kate was a singer and comedian, and quite famous in the forties and fifties, both here and on the mainland. Her specialty was the comic hulas like 'Puka Pants' and 'Princess Pupule,' though nowadays the latter is usually done by male dancers."

Although her mention of the local tunes drew blank stares from her audience, Lurline continued. "When a local entrepreneur decided to start making Aloha shirts and muumuus back in the fifties, he asked Kate if he could use her name and she was happy to agree. It was a successful partnership, though Kate died about ten years ago. My auntie used to work at the factory years ago, back when the store and the factory

81

were housed in the same building. At that time, you could see the women sewing in the factory part of the building while you shopped in the store."

With a bus full of women interested in sewing, this information was met with interest. Except perhaps for Edie. Sitting alone in the seat in front of Maggie and Victoria, Edie leaned back so she could whisper. "Want to bet she gets some kind of commission for bringing in a busload of people?"

"Kickbacks like that seem more Sam's kind of thing," Victoria observed.

"Makes sense," Edie said. "Since he drives the bus, he might be the one who sets up the stops."

Maggie nodded her agreement.

Finished with her spiel, Lurline sat immediately behind Sam. She adjusted her lovely lei, breathing deeply to inhale the sweet fragrance. Then, with loving care, she reached forward and patted Sam on the shoulder. Edie rolled her eyes.

CHAPTER 7

It was a good day for the bottom line at Kokonut Kate's. Everyone in the tour group purchased a new outfit for the evening luau. Several of the women purchased more than one of the comfortable muumuus. A dozen women trying to get into the few dressing rooms to try on clothes made for a wild time in the waiting area outside the small fitting rooms.

"Don't you just love these loose styles?" Clare sighed with pleasure as she modeled one of her choices before Anna. As one who constantly battled the scale, she was delighted with the selection of loose-fitting muumuus. "These will be great to wear during the summer back home. They'll be nice and cool. And don't you love the fabrics?" She brushed her hand over the soft cotton printed with large green monstera leaves.

At the edge of the crowd, their chosen garments folded over their arms, Maggie and

Louise looked out into the store. Sam stood heads together with a young salesgirl, who was pink with pleasure at something he was saying. As they watched, another, older saleswoman approached. She said something to the younger woman, which made her blush bright red. Then the younger woman abruptly turned and walked away, disappearing into an employee-only area. Maggie wouldn't have been surprised to see a few tears, but the retreating woman was facing away from her.

Meanwhile, the new woman began a conversation with Sam. They couldn't hear what was being said, but they could see the smile on her face and the sly look in her eyes. She touched his arm in a personal way, too, and he ducked his head down toward her in an intimate manner.

Maggie turned a significant look toward Victoria, her brows raised.

As they watched, Lydia came out of the dressing room behind them and approached Sam, wearing one of the store's dresses. It was not one of the loose styles Clare had been gushing over. This dress was a beautiful shade of turquoise blue with a pattern of white lilies, and was princess cut to show off a woman's curves. Lydia, a jogging enthusiast with the slim figure of a runner, looked terrific in it. The dress skimmed over her waist and hips, flaring out at the bottom so that it swayed lightly as she walked. Blue was a great color for her.

She must have been asking Sam's opinion since he stepped away from the saleswoman in order to make a production out of looking her over and voicing his opinion. Which was obviously good, as Lydia's face lit with pleasure. The saleswoman, however, was trying hard to hide her resentment. Her smile was ragged at the edges, and her eyes did not show even a glimmer of amusement. But she, too, made a comment that seemed to please Lydia.

Lydia was still beaming when Judy arrived, also seeking Sam's opinion. She wore the same style dress, except hers was lime green with pink lilies. She, too, looked good in the dress, and preened as Sam and the saleswoman complimented her.

"Sam is certainly popular," Maggie said. She glanced around the store. "I wonder where Lurline has gone. I don't think she's going to like that."

"I think she went outside for a cigarette," Louise replied, coming up from behind to join them. "I can't get over how many people over here still smoke."

"It does seem more prevalent here than at

home, doesn't it?" Victoria said. "Though maybe it's just that our little circle of friends is more careful about health issues."

"At least she's good about not smoking around the fabrics and quilting supplies," Louise said.

"Amen," was Maggie's fervent reply.

As they continued to watch the interplay between Sam and the women, they noticed Makana holding up a printed shirt. Deep blue with a green print, Maggie thought it would look very nice on her.

Sam took a step toward Makana and made a comment Maggie couldn't quite hear. But Lurline — who must have just entered the store after her break outside — apparently did.

As Makana's face froze and she turned purposefully away from Sam, Lurline stormed through the clothing racks until she was standing between them.

"What do you think you're doing!"

She didn't quite shout, but her angry voice was clearly heard throughout the store. Lydia and Judy slunk back into the fitting room alcove, and shoppers not in their group turned to stare. While Sam was distracted, Makana inched away from her mother and stepfather. She shoved the hanger holding the blouse haphazardly back toward the rack, and the slippery rayon slid right off the hanger. If Makana noticed, she gave no sign of it. She walked carefully but purposefully toward the exit, never looking back.

"Wow, I wonder what he said to her," Maggie said to Victoria.

"I think it was something rather risqué, about how good she would look in that shirt." Victoria raised her brows as she looked at her friend and added, "With some of the buttons undone."

Maggie stared at Victoria. No wonder Lurline was mad — if she heard something like that addressed to her daughter. From her own husband!

"You heard all that?"

"I heard some of it and deduced the rest from watching his lips move."

His wife's anger didn't seem to bother Sam at all. He remained his cool, charming self. His reply to Lurline's angry question was a calm "Hello there, sweetheart." He might have been merely helping Makana by opening the door for her.

He approached Lurline, trying to put his arm around her, but she was having none of it.

"Judy and Lydia were asking my opinion on their new clothes," Sam said. "And of course I told them they looked lovely."

"Yeah, right." Lurline's voice dripped contempt.

Lurline stood there a moment, staring at Sam, her temper heading toward boiling point. Both Maggie and Victoria thought she would explode at any second. But she surprised them. With a massive effort, she brought her anger under control, turned and stalked off. As she walked, she pulled off her beautiful lei. Near the door, beside a table offering samples of local juices and coffees, there was a small rubbish bin. She threw the lei into it, where it lay half in and half out. Then she disappeared outside.

"Wow," Victoria breathed. "That was quite the statement. And with no words spoken."

"Quite eloquent, in my humble opinion. Good for her." Maggie nodded her approval.

Clare, sympathetic as always, slipped out after Lurline. She returned a few minutes later and approached Maggie and Victoria, who stood behind Louise in the register line.

"She wants me to tell Sam she'll see him back at the inn."

Maggie raised her eyebrows in surprise. "Did she leave, then?"

Clare nodded. "She was already on her phone with Manu when I got outside. She must have him on speed dial," she added. "She said he would come and get her and Makana, and the rest of us should finish shopping and then get the bus back. She said there was no reason for us to hurry our shopping."

Clare bustled off to tell Sam and the others.

"I wonder what Sam will think of that," Victoria said.

"Do you think it will matter to him?" Louise said, turning toward them. Her purchase was complete; she was just waiting for the charge-card slip to sign. "He'll just shrug and say, 'Okay, thanks for telling me.' Then he'll tell her how good she looks this afternoon and ask what is it she uses to get that lovely rosy glow on her cheeks." She sighed. "Give me a break."

Maggie and Victoria laughed. "Did he really say that?" Maggie asked.

"Oh, yes. To me, this morning."

They were still grinning when Louise stepped forward and they moved up to pay for their purchases.

CHAPTER 8

Quilt tour, day two. Wednesday evening. The Luau.

Dressed in their new Hawaiian finery and resembling a flock of brightly colored tropical birds, the tour members gathered on the wide front porch of the Blue Lily, awaiting their gold chariot. Excited at the prospects for the evening, they were laughing and joking, complimenting one another on their new outfits, as they waited for Sam to pull the bus around from the parking area out back. Some wore their flower leis from the airport, sad now with drooping petals and long gaps of empty string.

"I was so tempted to take that ginger lei Lurline tossed out," Clare confided with a sigh. "It was so beautiful. But Lurline and Sam would have recognized it, it was so unique."

"She did throw it away," Edie said.

"Still . . ."

In any case, everyone was delighted when they were presented with fresh orchid leis upon their arrival at the luau.

They passed through the lobby of the resort hotel, and out past the bar to a large lawn sloping down to the ocean. There was no sandy beach, just large slabs of black lava rock edging the shore. But the view across Hilo Bay was spectacular and the sound of the lapping waves soothing. Tables were set out on the lawn beneath rows of coconut palms and other tropical trees.

"This is just lovely," Victoria said, admiring the ferns and flowers sprinkled down the centers of the tables as a casual type of centerpiece.

As the sun began to set behind the mountain, a conch shell sounded and runners sped out to light the torches. The women smiled at the muscular young men dressed in *malo* — wrapped fabric resembling a skirt — as they ran from one torch to the next. Cameras flashed all around them as the diners tried to catch each moment. The flashes became even brighter when the torch lighters reappeared moments later carrying in the roast pig.

Earlier that evening, Maggie had lamented having to attend the scheduled luau. Her fingers were itching to get on with her stitching. On the bus that morning, she'd finished the appliqué on the pillow top kit they'd been given at their first session the day before, and she couldn't wait to begin quilting it. However, as she finished a delicious meal, she found she was glad to be there.

"This is really nice," she said to her table in general. "And the show sounds amazing."

Victoria, sitting beside her, agreed.

"The food wasn't as exotic as I feared," Anna said. "It was all delicious too. That kalua pig that sounded so odd was kind of like pulled pork without the barbeque sauce. I really liked it."

Clare laughed at Anna's description but agreed that she'd liked it very much too.

Clare was having the time of her life. Maggie even noted that, despite her censure earlier in the day, she'd responded to some of Sam's flirtatious remarks with blushes and shy smiles. Maggie thought that, this evening, Clare was seeing him as Cary Grant rather than the faintly sleazy husband of their instructor. It probably didn't hurt that he'd donned a corduroy jacket with patches on the elbows over his Aloha shirt. Clare was probably imaging herself as Grace Kelly in *To Catch a Thief* or Audrey Hepburn in *Charade.*

"Isn't this just wonderful," Clare said, her eyes barely leaving the dancers moving onto the stage. "I should be exhausted, as I didn't sleep that well last night — typical first night away from home, you know. But I'm so excited, I'm not at all tired. I just want this day to go on forever."

Victoria and Maggie smiled at Clare's exuberance.

Louise smiled as well. "This sure is different from my vacation with Vince," she said. "I thought we kept pretty busy, but we weren't nearly as scheduled with activities as we are on this tour. I feel like I've been here for days already."

"I know what you mean," Anna said. "We've barely had time to breathe today."

"Maybe they're trying to keep us out of trouble by scheduling every minute," Maggie suggested with a laugh just as the music once again drowned out speaking voices.

It was true that there was barely any personal time written into their tour schedule. At first Maggie had thought it a shame, as she would have enjoyed some personal time to appreciate the scenery and sew. The long porch at the Blue Lily looked so inviting, she really wanted to spend some time there, just sitting, relaxing with her stitching. But so far everything they'd done had

93

been so interesting, she couldn't regret a moment.

As for the luau, the food was delicious, and the entertainment was turning out to be unlike anything she'd ever seen. Drums, chanting, knife dances and fire dances. The dancers included men and women both, some of the steps defined by sharp movements that looked athletically challenging to an aging rancher like herself. She wondered if they would ever get to the kind of liquid music on guitar with graceful dancers and flowing moves that she had always equated with Hawaiian music.

Lurline had promised the tour women a hula lesson later in their stay — if anyone was interested. Maggie had thought it sounded like fun, but now she wondered. She made a mental note to question Lurline more closely about exactly what was involved before she decided whether or not to participate.

CHAPTER 9

It was time.

Not everyone at the luau was enjoying the entertainment. One person sat, body tense, mind busily running through possibilities. Was this the time and the place? The music was loud enough to cover a minor explosion; everyone was intent on the performers.

She took a deep breath, releasing it very slowly. It was now or never. The killer entertainment that the resorts loved to present was more than enough to draw and hold the eyes of everyone present. Thanks to the large amplifiers, the music was loud. Ear-splittingly loud. Tahitian drums reverberated in the chests of the listeners. No one would be watching the tables. No one would hear anything unusual.

She had spent hours of careful planning that were coming to fruition.

With another deep, cleansing breath, she

positioned herself and her weapon.

There. It was done.

There was no outcry. No one looked around. No one had moved.

Even the victim, that louse, remained seated upright in his chair.

With a tiny smile of satisfaction, something that could easily be construed as a reaction to the performance taking place on stage, the killer secreted her weapon once again.

And the show went on.

CHAPTER 10

Their wonderful evening ended in dismay.

The show concluded with the lovely *auwana*-style songs Maggie had been hoping for — all smooth guitars and ukuleles, with graceful dancers in beautiful flowing dresses.

But as everyone began to rise from the tables, it became apparent that something was wrong. As they all stood and began to gather at one side of the long table, Sam remained slumped in his chair. Maggie assumed he'd nodded off during the program, though how he'd managed it with the loud music and all those drums she'd never know. Of course the end had been mostly guitar music, lovely but still quite loud.

When Sam still didn't move after Lurline called his name, she stepped up to his side and nudged his shoulder.

"Come on, Sam, it's time to go or we'll be late to the boat."

To everyone's surprise, Sam merely slid over to the left, landing with his head on the seat of the chair beside him. Still he did not awaken.

"He's not usually such a sound sleeper." Lurline clasped and unclasped her hands at her waist. She seemed uncertain about nudging him again, reaching out toward him then pulling her hand back before touching him.

"Was he drinking?" Edie asked. Her voice oozed disapproval. While alcohol had not been served at the luau, there was a bar in the hotel that looked out over the grounds where the luau was set up. They had all seen people walking over there to purchase a drink, then bringing it back to the tables to enjoy with their food.

"Just one beer with his food," Lurline said. "He was always careful when he was driving the bus."

Louise rushed forward. "Let me see, Lurline. I'm an RN."

Grateful, Lurline stepped aside to give Louise room.

"Maybe he had a heart attack," Anna suggested. Her fingers trembling slightly, she tugged at the edges of her jacket.

Louise had her fingers at Sam's neck,

checking for a pulse. Her expression was grim.

"Did Sam take any meds that might have reacted with the beer? Not just prescriptions, but over-the-counter stuff? Cold or allergy meds?"

Lurline stared at her, her eyes blank. Then she shook herself back into consciousness and moved her head slowly back and forth. But worry lines appeared across her forehead.

"He never liked to take drugs. He did have some unexplained chest pains back around Halloween. I made him go to the doctor, but he told me it was just indigestion. Too much Halloween candy, he said."

Makana shook her head. "He just didn't want you to worry, Mom. He told me the doctor warned him about his high cholesterol and higher blood pressure. He had some pills he was taking. Didn't you ever notice?"

Lurline appeared shocked at this news. "He said they were vitamins and antacids. He's been having a lot of trouble with his stomach." She shook her head. "Why on earth wouldn't he tell me about this?"

Makana, despite her explanations about Sam's health issues, looked as shocked as her mother. "He was supposed to go to

Honolulu for tests but he kept putting it off."

"Looks like that was a mistake," Edie said, her voice droll.

"Heart attacks can be very sudden," Victoria said, her gentle voice a soothing contrast to Edie's harsher one. "Even young athletes sometimes suffer heart attacks with no probable explanation."

Louise pulled her fingers from Sam's neck and straightened up. She looked at Lurline, her expression solemn. "I'm sorry, Lurline. There's no pulse." Her voice was sad, her eyes filled with compassion. She picked up one of Sam's hands, examined his fingers. "His lips and fingertips are blue," she said. "I'd say he's been dead for a while. It must have happened early in the show."

Lurline stared. There was no other reaction except for her hands pulling the sides of her cardigan together over her chest. Maggie wondered if she was in shock. Behind her she heard Clare's "Oh, my" and Edie's tsk. Judy sniffled, tears already running down her cheeks. Iris had a pocket pack of tissues in her hand and passed them to Judy and Rita, taking one for herself. All three dabbed at their eyes.

"Not a good thing for our trip," Theresa said, voicing a common thought.

But Lurline heard her and hastened to reassure everyone. "No, no. This won't affect your tour. You paid for a quilt tour, and we'll be sure you get it. I'll manage somehow." Her face began to change then and she finally seemed to grasp that Sam was gone. "Oh, dear." Her voice broke on the final word. And the tears came at last. Iris stepped forward with her packet of tissues.

Victoria, who was of a similar height, gathered Lurline to her shoulder and let her cry. She ran her hand over Lurline's back as she muttered a standard "There, there" of comfort.

"We should do something," Clare said.

Maggie, as usual, took charge. "Well, we can't just leave him here for the cleanup crew to deal with. Does anyone have their cell phone to call nine-one-one? I didn't bring a purse so I don't have my phone."

As Edie made the emergency call, Lurline pulled herself together enough to take charge.

"You have to leave for the harbor or you'll miss your volcano tour. It's beautiful to see the lava going into the ocean at night, something you don't want to miss." She used the crumpled tissue to wipe her tears. "I reserved the boat months ago, so I don't know if it would be possible to reschedule.

Obviously, I have to wait for the ambulance, but Makana and Rita can take you."

Rita stepped forward and put her arm around Makana's shoulder. "You stay here with your mother, Makana. I can manage the tour group just fine. I've even driven a school bus before, so don't worry. I'll manage."

To everyone's relief, Manu jogged up just then. His presence instantly calmed both Lurline and Makana.

"What's going on?" he asked, looking around the group, trying to take in what was happening. "Shouldn't you be leaving for the harbor?"

As several people tried to explain, he took Lurline and Makana into his warm arms. He told them he'd been in the hotel bar, and came outside to see what was happening when he saw them standing around instead of leaving. He thanked Rita for offering to handle the volcano boat tour.

Maggie could see that taking care of the tour details was helping Lurline cope. And having Manu there was even more of a help. So, although she initially felt they should stay with their hostess during this difficult period, Maggie decided to go along with those who thought it better to keep the tour on track. While on the bus heading for the harbor, she suggested they say a prayer for Lurline, and in memory of Sam. They all felt a little better after this small gesture.

CHAPTER 11

Quilt tour, day two. Wednesday, late evening. Boat tour of Pu'u 'ō flow.

The shock of Sam's sudden death was somewhat eased by the stark beauty the group encountered on the boat trip. The serene quiet, the sparkling stars overhead and the crisp, clean air was almost enough to compensate for the chill out on the water; everyone was glad to have remembered to bring their sweaters and jackets.

The captain of the boat was a surprise, and a pleasant one. A far cry from the crusty old salt of legend, or the Skipper from the three-hour tour, she was a thin, wiry Vietnamese woman with skin the color and texture of leather. But she had a ready smile, and was as friendly as everyone else they'd met on the trip so far.

"Call me Auntie Mai," she said, flashing a broad smile that showed off a shiny gold tooth to the right of her two front teeth.

She glanced quickly over the members of the group, then checked again. "Where Lurline and Sam?"

Rita quickly explained.

"So some husband finally went get him, yeah?"

"It looked like a heart attack," Louise said. "He just didn't get up from the table when the show was over."

"Ah." Mai chuckled, though without real humor. "One sneaky husband went do it then. Went sneak up and put something in his drink, yeah?" Shaking her head back and forth, still chuckling, she walked to the front cabin to start up the engine.

The peacefulness of the ocean after sunset was unexpected to the group of landlubbers. A half-moon shone bright, lighting the night enough for them to see — once their eyes became accustomed to the dark. The air was cold, but crisp and clear with no rain predicted. The puttering engine was the only sound they heard as they sailed alongside the coast toward the lava flow. The sky was a deep black, scattered with thousands of stars. For Maggie it brought back memories of campouts in the desert, back before everything around Scottsdale became so overdeveloped.

"How lucky there's no rain tonight," Anna said.

Maggie had to agree. The sea mist was more than enough to contend with. She could taste the salt on her lips, a not-unpleasant sensation. She took in a deep, refreshing breath. A bit of cold was a small price to pay for that wonderful air.

And then they arrived in the viewing area. There were other boats milling about, but there was plenty of room for everyone. Mai kept a bit of distance, while other boats sped forward, getting very close to the shore where the lava poured into the water. Maggie was happy to be a conservative spectator. She felt sure the water must be very hot near the entry point, and she wondered if the small boats weren't playing a dangerous game. There were also the fumes to contend with . . .

"Isn't it a beautiful sight?"

Victoria's soft words came at just the right moment. Maggie shook herself. It must be the effect of seeing Sam die that had put her in such a melancholy state. Why else would she be worrying about daredevil boaters and hot water — things that had nothing to do with her and her group.

"Yes," she replied. She fixed her gaze on the amazing sight, determined to make the most of this experience. "I have to remember this, so I can tell the grandchildren all about it."

Out on the shore, thin streams of red hot lava poured down a slope, changing in size and shape as they watched. They had learned that morning that the top layer of flowing lava cooled quickly, forming a thin black crust. But as the hot magma underneath moved, the crust cracked and shifted, revealing the thick red liquid lava underneath. As the red streams approached the ocean, then hit the cold water, the red turned a bright, hot yellow. Huge clouds of billowing white steam puffed up from the spot where the hot lava entered the ocean.

"We no want get too close," Mai told them as she watched for a minute before returning to the cabin. "That not just steam there," she said pointing to the billowing clouds rising into the night sky. "Got bits of lava in there, and gases and stuff. Not good."

"It's okay," Iris assured her. "This is a good place to watch."

"Isn't that the strangest thing you've ever seen?" Anna's voice reflected her awed reaction. "Amazing to think we're seeing new land being created."

But for the most part they were silent,

awestruck by a sight few people got to see. The streams of superheated lava glowed red-orange flowing toward the sea, then flashed a blinding yellow. It was mesmerizing, kind of like watching flames in a fireplace.

"The boat ride really was a good idea," Judy said. "I've been to see it during the daytime and it's just not the same. You only see the water and the huge steam plume from where the hot lava goes into the ocean."

As they milled at the railing, watching the lava, marveling at the heat felt even at such a distance, Edie glanced around. "What's become of Iris?" she whispered to Maggie.

Maggie looked around the deck. Edie was right; Iris wasn't there.

"I don't know what happened to her. She was here a minute ago. Is there a restroom inside? Maybe she went to use the facilities."

"I'll go look for her. She seemed rather taken with Sam. She might be upset."

Maggie nodded, and Edie walked off. The boat wasn't terribly large. Iris couldn't have gone far. No one had noticed because they were intent on the activity ashore.

It didn't take Edie long to discover Iris squatting in a shadowy corner, more or less huddled over her open purse. Hoping she wasn't interrupting a crying jag, Edie called her name softly. "Iris. Are you all right?"

To her shock, Iris jumped about a foot into the air. The huge but fashionable purse she affected tumbled from her arms and fell to the deck, spilling tissues and hand sanitizer, sunglasses and who-knew-what onto the deck.

"Edie!" Iris's voice was reedy with fright as she hurried to gather up her belongings. "What do you think you're doing, sneaking up on people that way?"

"Well, excuse me." Edie sniffed in irritation. She'd been trying to help, and this was the appreciation she got. Her voice stiffened. "I was afraid you weren't feeling well."

"I have excellent sea legs," Iris declared. "I never get seasick." As she spoke, she pushed the last of her things into her purse and stood up.

"That wasn't what I was concerned about," Edie explained. "I know you liked Sam, and I wanted to be sure you weren't here in the corner crying over his death."

"Oh, well, thank you, Edie." Iris did seem contrite, and Edie felt better. "I came over here to answer my phone. But it stopped ringing before I could find it in my purse.

I'm sure it went to voice mail. I'll check it later."

Edie nodded without comment, and followed her roommate back to the viewing area. She'd always thought Iris a little odd. The woman wasn't doing anything to make her change her mind.

CHAPTER 12

Quilt tour, day three. Thursday morning.

When the Quilting Bee women met for breakfast early the next morning, they were still commenting on the amazing sight of lava flowing into the ocean. The distraction of Sam's sudden demise could not detract from the beauty of nature — and its contradictory powers for both destruction and growth. They'd learned about the town of Kalapana, destroyed by the lava flow, but also of the over 500 acres of land added to the island. And then there was a new island being created southeast of the Big Island, the island of Lo'ihi.

The previous day had been so long and so filled with activities that everyone seemed to have slept well. Although they all commented on this as they met in the upstairs hall and on the stairs, Maggie noticed that no one mentioned it after they reached the dining room. They probably all felt as guilty as she did for enjoying such a pleasant night's sleep when their hosts had a sudden death and an upcoming funeral to worry about.

A subdued Manu brought out all the delicious food they had come to expect from him, but his solemn demeanor reminded them of the events of the previous evening. This new Manu was a far cry from the ebullient and friendly man they had come to expect. He kept watching the door as he worked, and Maggie knew his true focus was on Lurline and her well-being.

The mood of the group quickly turned somber. They were concerned for Lurline and how she might be handling her loss. Several of the women in the tour were widows, so they understood how difficult it was to lose a spouse. It could take days for the shock to wear off and reality to hit. That Sam had lied to his wife about his heart condition wouldn't help, as she had believed him in the best of health.

However, to everyone's surprise, when Lurline entered the room she flashed a bright smile, assuring them that their tour would continue uninterrupted. Manu hovered nearby, looking eager to offer comfort to his still-beloved ex-wife. Not that Lurline appeared to need it. Except for the tired look in her eyes and the circles beneath them, she seemed fine.

Victoria leaned in toward Maggie's ear. "If there's an upside to this, it's that she and Manu may be able to revive their marriage."

"He does seem much the better man, doesn't he?" Maggie agreed. "I certainly would never have chosen Sam over Manu."

Louise, on Maggie's other side, leaned toward them. "There's just no figuring who a woman might love, is there?"

All three agreed.

Manu, meanwhile, was being very attentive and extremely tender. He made up a plate for Lurline while the women offered their condolences, and had it ready for her before she even thought to sit down.

As they ate, Lurline informed the group that they would be having a short session on quilt design before leaving to tour a botanical garden and an orchid grower's facility. "Since the most common quilt designs are those from nature, what better jumping-off point than a garden to give you ideas? Flowers and leaves are especially popular for designs, so be sure to take notes. I hope you all brought cameras," she added, glancing around the table. "And your sketch pads?" Both items had been mentioned in the list of suggested items to bring on their tour.

Clare moaned. "I do have a sketch pad, but I can't draw at all."

Lurline merely smiled. "Don't you worry, Clare. You don't have to be an artist. You can use it to jot down ideas, and you can also trace leaves and flowers. Though you will have to be careful, since we'll be in a public garden. Please don't pick anything off the trees and shrubs. But, with help from your friends, you should be able to manage all right and be able to trace leaves without taking them from the plants. And there are often leaves or flowers that have dropped to the ground, so feel free to make use of those."

They had moved into the classroom to begin the day's lesson on design when a serious man wearing a rather conservative aloha shirt entered the room and approached Lurline. Manu stood in the doorway where they had entered, looking nervous. He held a dish towel in his hands, and was twisting it into a tight rope.

Maggie turned her attention from Manu to the stranger. He was about thirty-five, she thought, and quite nice looking. One odd thing: she noticed that his shirt was neatly tucked into khaki trousers, which she found unusual. Most of the local men seemed to wear their shirts untucked.

The initial silence gave way to a low-pitched rumbling of voices as she noted what the others must have already seen. The newcomer wore what appeared to be a fanny pack with a badge on it. Maggie had seen those packs in Arizona and knew it was a type of holster. She found herself smiling. She'd not seen a police officer carry his weapon that way before. Wait until she told Michael. He was sure to find it of interest.

"Mrs. Lurline Samson?"

"Yes?" She turned politely.

Maggie noticed that color drained from Lurline's cheeks and she clasped her hands tightly together the way someone did when trying to control a tremor. But she swallowed and continued to speak in a well-modulated tone of voice.

"It's Lurline Ilima, actually. I didn't take my husband's name because of my quilting business. I was already established under that name when we married."

Despite the signs of distress Maggie noted, Lurline managed to retain the upbeat tone she'd been using prior to the man's appearance.

Interesting, Maggie thought. Why would she be so upset about a visit from the police? Such a visit seemed like standard procedure after a death like Sam's — at least to Maggie.

"Detective Sousa, HPD," he said. "Could I speak to you for a moment, please?"

While his main focus was Lurline, he quickly took in the rest of the class and the women in it, all rapt with attention. "I believe all of you were present at the luau last night?"

There were nods from everyone and a few voiced yeses. Maggie could see Clare squirming with excitement. A police investigation could always pique Clare's interest. They were all mystery fans, but Clare was a fan *extraordinaire*. She especially liked to imagine herself an amateur sleuth like some of her favorite fictional characters.

"I'll want to speak to everyone eventually," he said, then turned back to Lurline. "But, for now, do you have a place where we could speak privately?"

To the dismay of the group, who were eager to hear what a police detective might have to say, Lurline led him inside. Before he followed her out, Detective Sousa asked everyone to refrain from speaking of the previous evening among themselves. Which, of course, just made them more anxious to do so. But since he left two uniformed officers in the room — "Didn't you feel like a kid in detention?" Clare asked afterward — the women were unable to do so.

As soon as her mother left, Makana moved into place at the front of the room. But she had lost her audience. Though prevented from discussing the previous evening by the looming officers, everyone was running through events in her own mind. Maggie could almost hear the hum of brainpower as the women deliberated over what had occurred the previous evening.

"Why do you think a detective is here?" Judy asked.

Makana shook her head, at as much of a loss as everyone else.

"I'm sure he has to investigate Sam's death since it was sudden, unexpected and in a public place," Maggie said. She looked toward one of the officers, but he remained stony faced, standing in a military "at ease" position and staring into the room. "I believe that's the usual procedure for an unexplained death."

"Even if he had heart trouble?" Makana asked.

Maggie nodded.

"They probably asked about his doctors last night and they'll check with them," Louise said. "But the police still have to investigate."

"What will happen to our garden tour?" Judy asked.

"We can still go," Makana replied. "Manu offered to drive the bus, and I can do it too. We'll manage."

"She calls her father Manu?" Edie's disapproving whisper was heard throughout the room, and Makana's cheeks turned pink.

"Let's begin designing our own blocks, shall we?" She immediately turned toward the board where Lurline had already drawn a large right-angle triangle and began explaining how one might arrange the elements of a quilt pattern in the space.

"As Mom explained the other day, folding is very important," she stressed, going on to demonstrate the technique once again. "If you've ever cut paper snowflakes, you'll know how to do it."

The fabric neatly folded into a right-angle triangle, she moved on to pattern design.

"We recommend an odd number of components in a pattern. Don't ask me why," she added as a hand shot upward. "It's just more pleasing to the eye, for some reason. This will be a repetitive design, too, so remember that it will repeat eight times. Or, you can fold your fabric into quarters and do a design that repeats four times." She opened one fold of her fabric triangle to show them the new form, a square. "Tahitian quilt patterns are usually done on the quarter. You can get in a larger leaf or flower that way." On the whiteboard, she demonstrated several different variations with the leaves and blossoms of a hibiscus as an example.

She had finished with the triangle, moving on to the square when Detective Sousa returned — alone.

"Ms. Ilima has offered us the use of several rooms, so we will begin the individual interviews now. Once those are done, you may go on with your planned day trip. These officers will conduct the interviews."

A group of uniformed officers appeared, six in all. They took half of the women into the house while the others remained to work at their designs. Some stitched at the pillow tops they had been given in class on the first day. They had all been delighted with the unexpected gift, and everyone had been working on their *ulu* pillow top as time allowed. Since Maggie had finished the appliqué, and as yet had no ideas for her own design, she proceeded to layer the pieces so that she could begin the quilting. Anyway, it would be too difficult to concentrate on original designs with all this interesting activity going on.

The individual interviews did not last long. Within fifteen minutes, the first women began filtering back, sending others in for their turns. Once everyone had been interviewed, Lurline and Detective Sousa returned to the classroom, accompanied by Manu.

"There's been a change of plan for today," Lurline announced. "I'll have to remain here with the police this morning, but the rest of you will continue with our tour. However, you'll be leaving immediately. Manu will take you to Rainbow Falls first — a last-minute addition to our schedule. You'll enjoy seeing the falls. Since we've had quite a bit of rain recently, there should be a lot of water flowing. Perhaps it will inspire your creative spirits. And early morning is the best time to see the rainbow at the base of the falls. Makana or Rita can tell you all about the goddess who lives there, in a cave beneath the falls."

As they filed out of the classroom, everyone was startled to see several police cars, vans and numerous personnel waiting outside. No one wanted to get on the bus and perhaps miss the next part of the little drama unfolding around them. But Manu urged them aboard. Still, until it was time to leave, his worried eyes stayed focused on the house and the police vehicles parked outside. Makana and Rita shared the front seat near the microphone that was usually occupied by Lurline.

Maggie, too, looked back at the house. She couldn't help noticing the exotic beauty of the old house, so lovely and peaceful with its long rows of blue agapanthus lilies planted across the front porch and all along both sides of the walkway that led up to the front door. The architectural style reminded her of the craftsman cottages so popular in areas of California. This place shouldn't have police scattered on the porch and on the sunny lawn; it should be peopled with stitchers relaxing in the rattan chairs on the porch and under the spreading branches of the trees on the lawn. Maggie could picture Hawaiian ladies of old sitting on mats beneath the large trees, working on their colorful quilts. Lurline had shown them a copy of an old photo depicting just such a scene. It showed her grandmother and her friends sitting on woven mats on the grass, huge hoops holding their quilts while they stitched. Maggie longed to be part of that scene. They could easily recreate it here, though she might be too old to sit on the ground for a quilting session. At her age, even sitting on a chair leaning over the quilt could become painful if she worked at it for too long.

With a sigh, she pulled her pillow top from her bag and prepared to begin quilting. Manu had said the trip might take fifteen to twenty minutes, and that was enough time for her to make a nice start on her pillow top.

As the bus left the driveway, Clare twisted in her seat. Her body fairly bounced as she strained to see as much as possible before they lost all sight of the inn.

"I can't believe we're missing all that," she said, though it came out closer to a whine. "Something is definitely going on, and we're missing it." Clare didn't seem to realize she was repeating herself as she turned toward Maggie and Victoria, seated behind her.

"I think they're serving a search warrant," Maggie said, pulling her needle through after taking several tiny stitches. "It's the only explanation for all those official people and vehicles waiting outside."

Edie agreed. "That's why they wanted us out of there right away."

Iris seemed especially distraught over the activity.

"Do you think they'll be going through

our things?"

Everyone shrugged. No one else seemed overly concerned about it.

"As long as they don't mess everything up, I don't mind," Victoria said. "Though I don't like to think of a male police officer going through my underwear."

"But it's so exciting to be part of an investigation," Clare said. "What did they ask you about during your interview?" She turned toward Maggie and Victoria.

Maggie wasn't the only one Clare queried. It seemed the police were most interested in the seating arrangements during the luau, and whether or not the quilt tour women had spoken to Sam — and when.

"Trying to determine the time of death," Edie declared.

"Of course!" Clare seemed ashamed not to have realized it instantly.

Maggie was surprised that it took Clare so long to tumble on the explanation, but she was most likely distracted by her excitement over being so close to a real investigation.

"Do you think Sam was murdered?" Clare asked, her voice dropping down to a near whisper.

"Don't be silly," snapped Iris, sitting across the aisle. "How could someone murder him right in front of all of us? He was sitting right in the middle of the table. Judy was sitting beside him." She nodded toward Judy, sitting just beyond her.

"I didn't do anything to him," Judy said. She seemed offended, as though Iris had accused her of something.

"I was on his other side," Lydia said. "And I didn't see anything. It must have been a heart attack. Isn't that what we said last night?"

"Yeah," Judy said. "Makana said something about a heart condition he was supposed to have checked out. Just like a man to keep putting it off."

"Well . . ." Louise's tone was speculative. She and Anna sat across from Edie and Clare, and they were as interested as the others in whatever was happening back at the Blue Lily. "We were all fully involved in watching the show, so I'm not sure we would have noticed if he was killed quietly."

"Wouldn't there have been a lot of blood?" Anna asked. "Or do you think he was poisoned?"

"That's what Captain Mai said last night, remember?" Clare's voice rose as she recalled this interesting tidbit. "Didn't she say some jealous husband or boyfriend must have slipped something in his drink?"

124

Even Rita and Makana were listening now. The entire bus was thinking, working out possibilities.

"The amount of blood depends on a lot of factors," Louise said. "I'm no expert, but I think it's possible to stab someone with something like an ice pick or a thin blade that would cause very little bleeding."

Victoria looked thoughtful. "Have you ever heard of the Empress Elizabeth of Austria? An assassin used a very thin blade to stab her in the heart as she walked along the Lake Geneva shoreline. She continued walking and talking and boarded her ship. No one knew she was hurt until she took off her corset and bled to death. The tight lacing contained the bleeding until it was removed."

"Oh, my gosh" and "Good grief" were heard in response to this piece of historical trivia.

"How on earth do you know that?" Judy asked, staring in amazement.

"She was a history teacher," Maggie said.

"I've always felt it's the interesting trivia that makes history memorable to the student. So I always tried to have special stories to tell my classes. It helped them remember people and events and made history more than just a dull series of wars, dates, and dead people."

But the momentary distraction of Elizabeth of Austria wasn't enough to keep them from their main topic of interest that morning.

"Well, Sam definitely wasn't wearing a corset," Edie remarked in a dry voice. "He had on a loose Hawaiian shirt and a light jacket."

"Can't really be sure about the corset," Maggie said with a grin. "No telling what he was wearing underneath that outrageous shirt."

Just as she'd hoped, everyone laughed. It was a good release of tension, even though Clare immediately returned them to the subject of murder.

"Don't people usually vomit or foam at the mouth or something when they're poisoned?" Clare said. "At least, they usually do in the mystery books, except maybe for Agatha Christie. She liked to use poison, but she didn't go into gory details."

"Well, he couldn't have been shot, not with all of us so close," Theresa said.

But Maggie wasn't ready to dismiss the possibility of a gun. "I don't know about that. It was terribly noisy with all those drums. My ears were ringing for a good while afterward. I doubt I would have heard a gunshot, even if it was so close."

"Wouldn't there have been a lot of blood if he was shot?"

Maggie frowned. "A good point."

"But . . . ," Anna almost sputtered. "You were right there, Louise. You checked his pulse. How could he have been murdered?"

While Clare wriggled in her seat over the various possibilities, Anna hugged her arms close, her entire body shuddering slightly as she spoke of murder.

"I suppose poison is the best possibility." Clare's voice remained skeptical. "With such a large group and all the distractions, it wouldn't be too hard to slip something into his food."

"Maybe." Louise thought for a moment. "But I doubt it. Sam looked peaceful, like he had a heart attack, or an aneurysm or something of that sort that kills quickly and quietly. You're correct about poison; it will often make the person vomit, or cause seizures or twitching, spasms — that kind of thing. And there was none of that. Someone surely would have noticed seizures."

Judy and Lydia both agreed they would have been aware of such unmistakable activity happening right beside them.

Clare got a gleam in her eyes. "Did you smell bitter almonds?" she asked Louise.

127

Louise barked out a laugh. "Honestly, I have no idea what bitter almonds would smell like," she said. "And you do know that only a small percentage of the population can even detect that smell?"

"Really?" Clare seemed disappointed to hear this.

But Louise wasn't finished. "A gunshot is still a possibility. There isn't always a lot of blood, you know. It would depend on the caliber of the gun, whether the bullet remained in the body, where he was shot. There are a lot of factors."

The conversation came to an abrupt halt when they entered the parking lot for Rainbow Falls. Maggie noticed with dismay that she'd barely taken a stitch. Once the conversation caught her attention, her pillow top lay untouched in her lap. She'd only managed about two inches worth of quilting stitches alongside one of the appliquéd breadfruits. With a small sigh, she put the pillow top back in her bag.

CHAPTER 13

Quilt tour, day three. Thursday morning.

Their arrival at Rainbow Falls State Park brought their discussion to a close.

As they gathered beside the bus, it was obvious to everyone that Lurline should be there to greet them and explain how this site could influence their creative spirit when designing. Instead, Rita greeted them, looking a bit guilty at not having used the bus ride to tell them about the goddess Hina and her dwelling underneath the falls.

As Rita began the tale, Manu watched sadly from his seat on the bus, his brow deeply furrowed. Everyone knew he wished he was back at the inn with Lurline.

"Hina was the mother of the demigod Maui. I'm sure you've all heard of Maui," Rita said. She looked from one to another of the women, most of whom nodded at her implied question. "He is a famous Polynesian demigod, and the island of Maui is named in his honor. Like many of the old-time Hawaiian women, Hina spent much of her day making kapa, which gives her a special affinity with quilters. Kapa is the name of the tapa cloth the Hawaiians made with the *wauke,* or mulberry, bark and is also what we call our modern quilts. Hina was famous for her beautiful white kapa cloth, but the sun moved so quickly across the sky every day that there wasn't time for it to dry. So her son Maui made a special lasso and captured the sun, making him promise to move more slowly across the sky so that his mother's kapa would have time to dry completely."

The mood of the group lightened with the telling of this old legend, and Rita summoned a smile. "Maui and the sun negotiated a compromise. That's why the days are longer for half of the year."

Victoria smiled. "An excellent story."

"So, we're here at Rainbow Falls, the home of Hina, and one of the loveliest spots on our beautiful island," Rita said. "When I was growing up, my parents used to bring us here whenever we came to Hilo, so it's one of my favorite places." A nostalgic smile lit her face. "The falls can be different each time you see them, since the water flow depends on the amount of rain heading downstream from the mountains." Rita continued speaking as she led the way to the viewing area. "As Lurline said, early in the morning is the best time to see the rainbow formed by the sun shining on the mist at the bottom of the falls, so we're here at a good time."

"Are we supposed to draw a waterfall to appliqué?" Anna asked.

There were a few titters of laughter from the group, but Rita took the question seriously.

"If you want to appliqué a waterfall, Anna, by all means feel free to do so. But I wouldn't expect to see one in a traditional Hawaiian quilt design. The Hawaiian patterns are much more representational," Rita told them. "Leaves and flowers are depicted on most of the old quilts we have. But many of the old quilt *names* depict a feeling, rather than a direct item. While there are many patterns called Plumeria or Lehua, there are also many with more esoteric names. For example, The Wind that Wafts Through the Valley and The Rain that Rustles the Lehua Blossoms. So listen to your creative side as you check out the sights, and use all your senses. You may get an idea just from the atmosphere, and that feeling may be translated into a quilt pattern." She held her smile as her gaze moved from one to another. "Perhaps one of you will be inspired to create a beautiful quilt pattern and call it The Mist at Rainbow Falls, or The Banks of Rainbow Falls."

Just then they heard the call of a cardinal.

"Or perhaps The Bird Song at Rainbow Falls," Victoria said with a smile. There were many appreciative chuckles.

"I'd like to do that," Anna said, ending with a wistful sigh. "But I'm afraid I'm not the creative type. Maybe you'll be the one to do it, Edie."

To her credit, Edie set about encouraging Anna, pointing out various plants and trees that might inspire her. As Maggie and Victoria followed them, they noticed that the smiles on the faces of the group members were no longer forced.

From Rainbow Falls, they proceeded to the botanical garden and then to the orchid grower. They finally returned to the inn after lunch at a cozy café that specialized in local cuisine. From a whispered conversation she overheard between Manu and Makana, Maggie got the impression that the police wanted them kept away from the inn until the early afternoon. It didn't matter, as the café was a good choice that they all enjoyed.

The rooms seemed bare and silent when they returned, especially the classroom. Lurline's large personality was enough to fill the room with warmth, and Maggie thought the place seemed cooler this afternoon without her genial presence. They filed in and found seats; Maggie noticed that they kept returning to the same places they took on that first afternoon, the day they first met Lurline. She seemed so much a part of their lives now. How could it be barely three days since they had met her?

Makana stood before them, her formerly smooth brow creased with newly present lines. She told them she'd just finished a cell-phone conversation with her mother.

"How are you?" Clare asked immediately. "And your mother?"

Maggie knew Clare had observed those worry lines too and intuited the cause. Makana was much too young for such obvious signs of aging.

"I'm okay, and Mom says she's fine. She told me she ate some lunch."

"You barely touched yours," Louise told Makana.

Makana seemed surprised that Louise had noticed.

"Me?" Her voice came out high and

squeaky.

"Of course, you." Maggie said. "We're concerned about all of you. It's not easy to cope with the sudden death of a family member. I hope you have something to eat soon."

"Oh." Makana still seemed amazed at this interest in her well-being. "I had a little something. I wasn't very hungry."

"You're not so sure that your mother is fine, are you?" Clare asked, putting her arm around Makana's shoulders and giving her a squeeze.

Maggie could tell that Clare wanted to wrap the young woman in a bear hug, but she limited herself to the half-hug around her shoulder and an affectionate pat on the arm. She could also see that Clare's gentle and caring voice brought Makana's emotions closer to the surface. A tear leaked from the corner of her left eye, but she swiped at it with one hand and pasted a determined smile on her lips.

"We should get on with the class Mom had planned."

Maggie patted her on the shoulder, hoping the small gesture would let her know that they were all there for her. But they weren't quite ready to settle down to quilting. "Where is Lurline now?"

"She went with Detective Sousa this morning. To his office. I'm sure there's a lot of paperwork involved in someone dying so suddenly, and in a public place and all. She thought she'd be back soon."

Maggie thought there probably was a lot of paperwork involved, but she didn't think dying in a public place required the lingering presence of uniformed police officers. Or the necessity of searching the family residence. And, when they arrived back, her sharp eyes had spotted a couple of officers sitting in their cars at the back of the inn. One to tail Makana, perhaps, and another for Manu?

"But wasn't there a search warrant served?" Edie asked.

Makana paled but didn't comment. Instead, she pulled out the volcano pattern Lurline had told them about, asking if anyone wanted to purchase a kit.

Since Makana was being so determinedly upbeat, no one attempted to broach the subject of Lurline again. Instead they commented on the pattern, and a few paid for kits to make it. Then they split into groups, some working on the quilt kits, some starting tentative sketches in the hopes of creating their own unique designs.

Maggie and Victoria both pulled out

notes, sketches and photographs and began to work on designs of their own. Lurline had suggested doing a design for a wall hanging the size of an opened sheet of newspaper. That way they could cut the snowflake design out of paper to see how it would look before ruining any fabric with something they did not like. So they carefully folded the newsprint until they had a triangle of the size they would fill with their design.

They had been working quietly for about an hour when Lurline returned, accompanied by Detective Sousa.

Lurline seemed to have diminished somehow. Maggie imagined a New Age person might say that her aura had dimmed. Her eyes looked dull; not from shock, Maggie didn't think. It seemed more like fear. Large dark circles underscored her eyes, and the fine lines around her eyes and mouth had become deeper and more noticeable. It was no wonder these latter were sometimes called stress lines, Maggie thought.

The Arizona women instantly surrounded Lurline, this nice woman who was so eager to share her culture with a group of strangers. *Haoles* she'd called them. Maggie had the impression that it was not always a friendly term, but the way Lurline said it was always kindly and welcoming.

Their warmhearted greetings and supportive hugs moved Lurline to tears.

"*Mahalo.* Thank you all so much. It's been a difficult morning." Her eyes strayed toward Detective Sousa.

"You need some hugs," Clare stated with confidence, proceeding to wrap her arms around the larger woman.

Maggie hung back as the others took turns hugging their host. She wanted the chance to observe Detective Sousa, hoping to get an inkling of why the man was still there. He was currently standing behind and to the side of Lurline, his hands clasped behind his back — basically doing as Maggie was: observing. He watched the women carefully. Maggie had the impression that he was putting them all into slots — the emotional one (Clare, of course), the timid one (Anna), the bold one (Edie), and so on. Maggie's eyes met his just as she wondered what *her* descriptor might be. He nodded politely. Was there a slight upward tug on the left side of his lips? Maggie wasn't certain but there was a definite twinkle in his eyes.

Maggie decided that she liked him — just as he gestured her forward.

CHAPTER 14

The time had arrived for the individual interviews Detective Sousa mentioned earlier that morning. As he told them all now, he had returned to the inn so that he could follow through with interviews of his own about the luau the night before.

"I'll begin with Ms. Browne, then I'll see you each in turn." He gestured toward the door, indicating that Maggie should go first. "Ms. Browne, if you please . . ."

Maggie walked out, following Detective Sousa to a room she realized must be Lurline's office. Barely larger than a broom closet, there was a desk, a computer and two file cabinets. The only feature saving it from starkness was the Hawaiian quilt wall hanging above the desk. Worked in bright red and yellow, it represented what Maggie realized was a royalty pattern of *maile* and Spanish-style hair combs. She felt proud that after only two days she was already knowledgeable enough to recognize it. She couldn't recall the name of the princess who favored the combs, but she remembered Lurline telling them about the popular pattern — and the popular princess.

Maggie seated herself in the straight chair beside the desk while Detective Sousa settled himself behind it. Despite her observation of the man, and her suspicion that he had a sense of humor, Maggie had not been able to divine any real cause for his presence or for the personal interviews. Police officers, and detectives in particular, Maggie knew, were experts at keeping a poker face. Therefore, Maggie felt certain that Clare was correct in thinking Sam's death was murder. Why else would there be all this activity around the inn, and questions about the luau and the seating arrangements. But the big question remained: how was he murdered?

Maggie's interview began with a surprise.

"I talked to a Detective Warner in Scottsdale this morning."

Detective Sousa might be a master of the poker face, but Maggie was not. She was sure he could see her astonishment — especially when he chuckled.

"We might be a small police force here, but we're very professional."

Maggie found herself returning his smile.

"I don't doubt it." Still, she felt slightly uneasy, wondering where this development would lead. Calling Scottsdale! Her son would probably be on the phone soon, asking her what was happening.

"Detective Warner tells me the St. Rose Quilting Bee has been involved in several of his cases. He mentioned you in particular, Ms. Browne. It seems you were quite helpful in a few instances."

Maggie felt heat on her cheeks and realized she was blushing. "We all like to read mystery fiction, so we end up analyzing and debating when there's a local incident. Since we knew all the people involved in the cases referred to, we had some insights that we hoped would help. And we shared those observations with the police."

"I'm glad to hear that you took those observations to the police. It can be dangerous becoming involved in a murder case," he warned.

Maggie sighed. "Believe me, I know. I hear those same words frequently from my son, who is a police officer in Scottsdale."

"Yes, Officer Michael Browne. Detective Warner mentioned him as well."

Maggie raised her eyebrows. If she wore

bangs, they would have disappeared beneath them.

"Are you warning me about this case? Sam's death, I mean? Is it a murder case?"

Neither Detective Sousa nor Lurline had mentioned Sam's official cause of death, or a reason for the police activity this morning. But Maggie did know the latter was highly unusual if they were talking about a natural death, even a sudden and unexpected one in a public place.

"You might as well know that we all suspect as much," Maggie told him. "The tour group, I mean. It was the main topic of conversation on the bus this morning — whether or not Sam was murdered, and if so, how. The how is what has us all stumped."

Detective Sousa shook his head, and this time Maggie was sure he was suppressing a smile. There was an odd sparkle in his eyes that seemed to be a cross between bemusement and distress over finding a group of nosey older women involved in his case.

"After speaking to Detective Warner, I'm not surprised to hear that."

He shuffled some papers in a file on the desk before him then looked back up at Maggie. "I understand that not all the members of your tour group are members of this Quilting Bee he mentioned."

"No. We have a small basic group at the Quilting Bee, and we asked if others were interested in the quilt tour. We did well to get a dozen people, especially with the economy the way it is. Iris did such a good job at controlling costs we were all able to manage it."

"So which of the women belong to the Quilting Bee?" He turned a sheet of paper toward her, and Maggie saw it was the guest list from the Blue Lily. The women's names were all listed in pairs, according to room assignments.

"Victoria, Anna, Clare, Louise, Theresa, Edie and I are the main Quilting Bee members. Iris has been coming to the Bee several times a week for the past year. She still works, so she can't always manage to attend. She sells real estate, you know."

Detective Sousa gave a small nod. Yes, of course he would be aware of that, Maggie thought. *She* didn't seem to be thinking. Not very well anyway.

She took a deep breath and continued. "Lydia and Bernie both belong to the St. Rose Senior Guild but not the Quilting Bee. They do other kinds of sewing for the group and wanted to come because they're interested in learning about quilting. Mainly, though, they signed up because they wanted to see their local friends." She went on to explain about Judy and Rita.

Detective Sousa was a good listener. He watched her face as she talked, did not fidget in his chair, tap his foot, or cross and recross his legs. He made a few marks on the sheet of names, and Maggie assumed he was marking the Quilting Bee members. She had a feeling he was a very organized man; she could just picture him at a big old-fashioned rolltop desk, all his papers neatly pigeonholed in their proper slots. She expected that his excellent listening skills brought forth a lot of information from the people he talked to. A strong desire to share information appeared when one had an interested audience.

He paused momentarily when she was done, rearranging his papers and making a few additional notes. Finally, he looked up, meeting her eyes.

He had exceptional eyes, Maggie noticed, the exact color of dark chocolate. He was quite an attractive man, and she found herself wondering about the lack of a wedding ring on his left hand. It seemed a shame that such a nice young man wasn't married. Of course, some men didn't like to wear a ring . . .

His next words, however, had her mind moving away from romantic thoughts and straight to murder.

"As you and your friends suspect, Mr. Samson's death was indeed a homicide."

Maggie nodded, not in the least surprised.

"The how is of great interest to me right now as well," he continued. "As you know, it happened right there at your table with over a dozen people present. That is why I am going to interview everyone myself, even though you'll all be going back over the same information you provided this morning."

Maggie nodded again. "I understand how these things work."

He frowned slightly, perhaps gauging her cooperation quotient. "Then you'll also know that I'll want your opinion on whether or not any of your tour companions have acted strange or out of character today."

As Maggie thought about that, he neatly steered her away from an answer for the time being.

"Just think about it for now, while I go through the events of last evening."

He had Maggie start out with a brief summary of the previous day, then asked for her impressions as they gathered to leave for the hotel.

"Did anyone act unlike him or herself?" he asked. "Anyone who is usually early, for example, but was late last night? Did anyone seem to be hiding anything?"

Maggie paused at this last. She couldn't help wondering what the murder weapon was and how difficult it would have been to hide it. A gun? A knife? She supposed you could hide almost anything beneath some of the loose flowing garments so many of them had purchased for the evening's luau. But that would be presupposing someone from their group had an interest in killing Sam. And while the muumuus could conceal a lot, there was the practical problem of access. How would you retrieve a weapon from beneath a full-length, voluminous garment without providing a peep show for the rest of the table? And how would you put it back afterward — to take it away again? A knife would be messy with blood; a gun would be hot from recent firing.

"We all remembered how cold it was during the night, so everyone took sweaters or jackets of some kind. That's different from how we travel during the day. Though I must say, some of the air-conditioned shops here really crank up the temperature — or I guess I mean they crank it down too low. They're very cold. We were talking about the need to tote along sweaters even for day trips."

Detective Sousa did not comment, though Maggie was sure she noticed a twitching of his lips at her comment about the air-conditioned shops.

He referred to one of his papers, then asked about their arrival at the hotel.

"How did you manage the seating at the luau? Were seats assigned in some way or did you just take a place at the table?"

"We just sat down. We all have our particular friends, so of course we tried to sit with them."

Detective Sousa pulled another sheet of paper from his folder and passed it to Maggie.

"This is a rough drawing of the table last night. The stage would be at the top of the sheet. This" — he pointed to a square with an X in it — "is where Mr. Samson was seated at the end of the evening. Could you please mark the square that would correspond with your seat at the table?"

Maggie examined the diagram. There was a long rectangle representing the banquet table, surrounded by squares indicating the chairs. Maggie stared at it for a full minute, trying to remember exactly where she sat in relation to Sam. She frowned at the page, mumbling about senior moments and dying brain cells.

"You'd think I could recall last night easily enough," she said, shaking her head. "I think I was here," she finally said, pointing to a square near one end of the table. "I wasn't quite opposite Sam, but I'm not sure how many others were sitting to the side of me." She shrugged helplessly. "I'm sorry I can't be more specific."

"Don't worry, we'll figure it out as soon as everyone else has a chance to look at this."

He shuffled a few more pages, then asked if she had spoken to Sam during the meal.

"I did say something to him during the meal," Maggie recalled. "Early on. He wasn't sitting there at the time, though," she realized, pointing to the mark on the seating chart. "He was closer to the other end of the table then, and called down the row to all of us. He made a remark about the *poi*. He was one of those men who thought he was very funny," she added.

"But only funny to himself, yeah?" Detective Sousa said.

"That's right." Maggie thought about the previous evening for a moment. "That's the only time I remember speaking to him. Once the show started, we were too busy watching the dancers to talk among ourselves. Also, the music and the drums were very loud, which made conversation pretty much impossible."

"Sam had quite a reputation with the ladies," Detective Sousa said.

Maggie tried to keep her voice neutral. "So I understand."

"Not your type, huh?"

Maggie suppressed an urge to grimace. "Definitely not my type."

Perhaps she wasn't successful in keeping her bias to herself. However, the detective's half smile endeared him to Maggie. She liked a person with a sense of humor, and this made several times now that the detective had allowed his true nature, rather than his stoic cop side, to show through.

"You're a widow, I believe."

Maggie nodded, then, remembering the recorder he'd started at the beginning of their interview, replied, "Yes."

"Did you notice if any of the women in your tour group were susceptible to his charm?"

Maggie felt uncomfortable by the question, and her face apparently reflected as much.

"No one likes to tattle on friends, Ms. Browne, but may I remind you that this is a murder investigation." Detective Sousa became all business. No more subtle smiles or twinkling eyes. This was serious. "So, tell me. Did any of the women in your group seem to succumb to his charm?"

"This is only our third day here . . . ," Maggie began.

"However . . ."

Maggie sighed. Why did she feel like a schoolchild tattling on her friends?

"He turned on the charm straight away. Anna complained that he kissed her on the lips when he presented her with a lei at the airport. She was uncomfortable about it."

Detective Sousa looked at her, one eyebrow raised, a silent question in the air.

"I received my lei from Lurline," she said. "With a light kiss on my cheek."

Detective Sousa nodded.

"Clare thought him charming, because she thinks he's the image of Cary Grant, who has long been her favorite movie star. But she's very happily married, and quite naive. Her responses to Sam's flirting were mostly blushes and giggles. It would never occur to her that he might want more than to enjoy a bit of repartee."

The detective jotted a note on the pad before him.

"Iris, who organized the trip for us, also

seemed taken with him. As well as the two local women, Rita and Judy. In fact yesterday someone mentioned she thought Judy acted as though she had met Sam before our tour. And, of course, Rita knew both Lurline and Sam before our quilt tour because she's also part of the local quilting community. And she helped Iris plan the tour for us. I mentioned that she's a cousin of Bernie's from the Senior Guild," Maggie reminded him. "Bernie put Iris in touch with Rita and they planned the trip together. I'm sure that's how Iris managed to get us such a good deal, having Rita here to negotiate."

When Maggie finished talking, Detective Sousa waited a moment to see if she had anything more to add. When she did not say more, he inquired, "Is that it?"

Maggie took a moment to think it over. "Most women can be flattered by the kind of attention Sam was willing to give. I'm sure some of the others smiled at his comments, or blushed over something he said. I believe even Theresa laughed over a comment yesterday. I'm sure I did too at some point. But for the most part, Victoria, Clare, Edie, Anna, Theresa and I were immune to him."

Detective Sousa studied her face for a moment, then nodded.

"And now, the question I asked you to consider at the beginning of our discussion."

Maggie had to smile at his description of their interview as a "discussion."

"You mean if I've noticed anything unusual among the tour women."

"Or the people running the tour," he clarified.

Maggie still shook her head. "I don't think so. Everyone is upset, of course, about the fact that Sam died right there in front of us. And that no one even noticed. And people were nervous this morning about the police presence, and thinking that you might be searching through our things. But I can't say that anything in particular stands out as unusual."

Maggie felt bad. She would have liked to have noticed *something* that could help. Especially if it was something that would turn attention away from Lurline. She really did like their hostess.

"If you think of anything, please let me know."

He removed a business card from his pocket and handed it over. Then he thanked her and let her return to the others in the classroom, asking her to send in Clare.

CHAPTER 15

Quilt tour, day three. Thursday afternoon.

As soon as she had sent Clare in, Maggie retrieved her phone. If Detective Sousa had called Scottsdale that morning, Michael would know all about the murder. He had probably tried to contact her too. Sure enough, there were two messages on her cell from Michael — and four missed calls.

Maggie was ready to press his number when the phone rang. It startled her enough that she almost lost her grip on the thin vibrating piece of metal, but she caught it before it fell and was destroyed. She checked the display. Michael.

Maggie put the phone up to her ear and took a deep breath before saying, "Hello." No telling what kind of mood he'd be in after hearing she was involved in another murder investigation.

Michael's voice roared through the receiver, causing her to pull the instrument away from her ear.

"Ma! What have you gotten yourself into over there? I thought you were on a quilting tour."

Michael was never happy when his mother became mixed up in a murder investigation, even though it always seemed to happen through no fault of her own.

"It's nice to hear from you, Michael. And I'm fine, thank you."

"Okay, I should have asked how you are." Maggie could hear the frustration in his voice. And his fear for her well-being. "But I already knew that you were okay. A detective from Hawai'i called Detective Warner and asked about the Quilting Bee members."

Of course Maggie already knew that Detective Warner had been consulted, but there was no need to tell Michael she'd just come from a private interview with said detective.

"I hope he assured Detective Sousa that we're all good, law-abiding citizens."

Detective Warner had been the detective in charge of the cases during which the Quilting Bee had information to provide to the police. Maggie wasn't sure how it happened that the Bee became involved, but somehow it did. In the first instance, it was because Maggie had known the victim and his family, and his body was found practically on the doorstep of the family's ranch. In her second contact with him, she and Louise had found another Bee member dead in her care-home bed. Maggie felt a need to investigate that case when Louise became the prime suspect. Then, just last year, Clare had gotten them involved in a cold case, trying to prove the innocence of a fugitive parish member suspected of killing his wife and children. And now it had happened again, and thousands of miles away from home. She was an innocent bystander — they all were — but Michael would still blame her for once again becoming entangled with murder. She knew it was only over concern for her safety, but it did make her want to rebel when he tried to tell her what she could and could not do. She was an adult woman, used to managing on her own — and quite capable of doing so. Besides, she used to change his diapers!

"I'm sure Detective Warner spoke well of you," Michael replied.

Maggie could hear her son sigh.

"He didn't know all the women who are on the trip. He took down all the names and came to ask me about them. Some of

154

your friends there are new to the Bee, aren't they?"

"Some of the tour members don't stitch with the Bee. We have a mix of people here, and even two local women. One of them used to live in Scottsdale, and the other is a relative of a Senior Guild member."

"And how well do you know these women who aren't part of the Quilting Bee?" he asked. "I was able to vouch for Theresa Squires. I reminded Warner that she was around for the Gilligan case, that she used to work for him."

"I'm glad to hear that," Maggie said. Michael knew all of the Quilting Bee members, but her closest friends were the ones he knew best — the core of the group, Louise, Victoria, Clare, Anna and Edie. The six women had been quilting together for years and had often joined Maggie's family for their traditional Sunday brunch at the Browne ranch.

"Are you sure everything is all right, Ma?"

"Yes, of course." Maggie didn't mind him asking, as she could hear the concern for her in his voice. She often worried about her sons; she surely couldn't object if her sons worried about her.

"What the heck is going on over there? Warner said the Hawaiian detective told him someone from the inn you're all staying at was shot and killed. But they didn't know he'd been shot until the autopsy. He seemed especially interested in someone named Iris Fleming. Isn't she the one who arranged this tour for you?"

"Yes." Maggie paused while she considered this new information. So Sam had been shot, and right in front of all of them. Wait until Claire heard that. "As for what happened, we don't really know. In fact, we've been talking about it all morning. Sam was an awful womanizer and was bothering some of the women in our group. But I can't imagine one of them shooting him over it. Clare felt that we should know what happened since we were all right there when it happened. But none of us do. Did. This is the first I've heard how Sam was killed."

"What?"

The explosive exclamation roared out of the phone, and Maggie pulled it away from her ear.

"What do you mean you were all there?"

"Goodness, Michael."

"You were 'right there'?"

"Yes. Didn't he tell you? Sam was killed during a luau our group attended. We were all seated at a long table watching a Polynesian show. Lots of drums and loud noises.

No one knew anything had happened until Sam didn't get up after the show."

Maggie heard Michael muttering something indecipherable, but she didn't think she cared to have him repeat it.

"It was all very strange, Michael. We were all together at the table — there were a lot of these long tables on the lawn of the resort. It was right on the beach — really lovely, though the beach here is rocky, not sandy. They had runners in native dress light scattered tiki torches. We had a wonderful time. We all enjoyed the meal, and the show was terrific. Then, when the show was over, Sam didn't get up. Sam was our bus driver and we had to get going to meet the boat for our lava-viewing excursion."

Maggie thought she heard something like choking from Michael's end, but when it didn't continue she went on.

"Lurline — that's his wife — poked him in the shoulder and told him to wake up, it was time to go. But instead of opening his eyes, he slumped over. Just keeled over onto the next chair. Louise said he was dead and we called nine-one-one. We thought he had a heart attack. If he was shot, it must have been a small-caliber bullet that didn't exit the body."

Maggie heard Michael emit a long exhale.

"You seem to know a lot about it."

"Michael, what do you suppose we've been talking about all morning? This is big news for our little group." She shifted the phone from her left ear to her right. "Not that the police told us anything, only that he was murdered. You just told me he was shot. There was a lot of loud music and even louder drums, and no one heard anything. We think they served a search warrant this morning — they sent us off early on a tour we had lined up, and with another local woman, Bernie Hernandez's cousin, as escort. We've just put together some of this information from what little we know. No one noticed any blood, for instance, so it had to be a small-caliber gun, and the bullet must have remained in the body."

"You watch too much TV," Michael mumbled. But Maggie knew not to take his stern act seriously. He was fond of telling people that one of his mother's favorite television shows was *Forensic Files.*

"Is anything I suspect wrong? Can you think of another way it could have happened?"

Michael seemed reluctant to answer, but finally admitted her theories were correct. "The killer probably got right up to him, put the gun against his rib cage and pulled the trigger. Something small, like a twenty-two."

"What I can't figure out is how the person got the gun there and pulled it out without anyone seeing it," Maggie said. "Most of us were wearing very loose muumuus, and you could hide a lot under one of those things. But you couldn't pull something out from underneath one of those ankle-length dresses without creating quite a scene."

"Wait until Hal hears about this. He's not going to be happy. He'll be on the phone telling you to come home too."

Maggie couldn't believe he was threatening her with her eldest son. Hal might be a lawyer, but she could handle Hal better than her police-officer youngest son. "I'll call him. He'll be fine. I'll assure him that all is well here."

Michael knew there was no arguing with his mother when she used that tone of voice.

"So who is this Iris Fleming? I know she's the one who arranged the trip. Has she been at St. Rose for very long?"

"I don't know why he would be interested in Iris in particular, unless it's because she arranged the trip. She's a new member of our group. She moved to the parish about a year ago and joined the Quilting Bee almost immediately. She's not retired like the rest of us. She still sells real estate, mostly high-end homes, but she comes three or four mornings a week to quilt."

"So what do you know about her?"

Maggie thought for a minute. "Not that much, really. She used to own a travel agency. She mentions that a lot. Her ex-husband ran out on her and managed to destroy the agency at the same time." She paused and her voice became thoughtful. "Now that I think about it, while she talks a blue streak every morning, she doesn't really say much."

"Pardon?"

Maggie wasn't surprised that Michael found that confusing.

"She talks and talks, but she never really gives out much information about herself. She complains all the time about this awful ex-husband of hers, but she never gives details. That kind of thing."

"So, was this Sam targeting Iris as his next conquest or something?"

"I don't know," Maggie admitted. "He seemed to flirt with every female he came in contact with. Some men are like that, you know, and he definitely was. He did flirt with Iris, and she flirted some back. But so did a few of the others on the tour. Judy, the local woman, for one. And her friend

Lydia too. I had the impression Judy knew Sam somehow, but didn't want to admit it to any of us."

"So did Iris encourage him?"

"Maybe a little. There *was* something strange about the way Iris and Sam interacted, but I haven't been able to define it. She seemed very nervous on the bus this morning, but then most everyone was. There were so many police vehicles here, and they pretty much shoved us out the door. We figured they had search warrants, and Iris seemed especially irritated thinking they might search the guest rooms." Maggie paused but could think of nothing else that seemed important. "We spent the whole bus trip trying to figure out how Sam was killed."

"Ma!"

Maggie heard the warning in her son's voice. He was constantly telling her to stay out of police business, and he hated it when she ignored him.

"Ma, please. Be careful. I hate having you so close to a murder, especially when you're so far away."

"I doubt if any of us are in danger, Michael. It's got to be a jealous husband or something. There's something very personal about this whole thing."

161

"Did you and your group of gossipers figure out if Iris is involved in this?"

"Group of gossipers! Honestly, Michael!"

"I call it as I see it."

"Well, no, we could not figure out if Iris might be involved. Sam, the victim, was an awful womanizer, so it looks to us like the police are focusing in on his wife. She, her ex-husband and their daughter, all work here at the inn."

She heard Michael blow out his breath at this information. "That was a situation waiting to explode."

"Some of us said the same thing when we learned the cook-slash-gardener was the ex-husband."

Michael sighed. "I wish you would come home, Ma."

"I know you do. But I'm sure there's no danger."

"You can't be sure of that. I know you and the Quilting Bee. You'll start poking around, and you could become targets." He paused. "You don't know those other women in the group, not like you know the other Bee members. How can you be sure one of them didn't do it?"

"Well, none of us who came here from Arizona could have brought along a gun. There's no way to smuggle that kind of thing through the TSA these days."

"It is a dangerous situation, whatever you might think," Michael insisted. "So be extra careful. And someone in your group could well have a gun."

"What do you mean? How could someone sneak it past the TSA?"

"You don't sneak it past. You pack it in your luggage. There's some paperwork involved, but as long as you have a legal license, it can usually be done."

Maggie was quiet for so long, Michael had to ask if she was all right.

"Yes. I am." She swallowed hard. "Michael, Iris has a permit to carry a concealed weapon. She got it because she sells real estate, and you remember how some women were attacked at open houses some years ago."

"That's it, Ma. You need to come home. I'll pay the extra charges for you to change your ticket."

"Don't be silly, Michael."

Maggie heard her son blow out his breath in sheer frustration. "Why did I know you would say that?"

"Our tour has barely started. There's still a lot I want to see. I've made a good start on a design of my own, too. Despite Sam's death, I'm enjoying the tour. And I like

Lurline. I can't see her killing Sam, despite her being the most obvious suspect."

Before her son could caution her yet again, Maggie said good-bye and disconnected the call.

CHAPTER 16

Quilt tour, day three. Thursday afternoon.

Once the interviews were over, the women were quick to compare notes. As with the earlier interviews, Detective Sousa's main areas of interest seemed to be the seating arrangement and whether the women had spoken to Sam — and when. Among the Quilting Bee's core members, all diehard mystery fans, there was no question about why he wanted this information.

"Determining the time of death is much trickier than the average TV show depicts," Louise said. "He's trying to get a better idea by finding out who was the last to speak to Sam and what time that was."

"And I'm sure he was checking what we said against the first interviews," Edie said, "looking for any inconsistencies."

"Did he ask if anyone acted uncharacteristically today?" Clare asked.

There were several murmurs of assent.

Maggie, uncertain of whether or not he'd told everyone it was a murder investigation, kept that information to herself. Before she could tell them about his call to Scottsdale and her subsequent talk to Michael, Lurline broke the news.

Still standing at the front of the room and listening in on the various conversations, she probably thought it was the only way to get past this and move on to quilting once again.

"You'll all know soon enough, so I might as well tell you. Sam was murdered."

Her voice was flat, her expression unreadable, and the comment dropped into the room like a ball of lead in a small pond. She certainly didn't seem to be emotional about what should have been a debilitating revelation, Maggie thought. Then was immediately ashamed for thinking it. The poor woman was newly widowed and probably still in shock.

The reaction of the others, however, was nothing even close to calm. Apparently Detective Sousa had not mentioned the murder investigation to anyone else. Wait until they heard he was shot, Maggie thought.

Clare, beside herself, exclaimed in a high-pitched voice, "Murdered! I knew it!" Then, perhaps feeling that her outburst sounded shameful at best and coldhearted at worst, she added, "How awful!"

Despite her final words, however, Clare's eyes sparkled with interest and anticipation. Maggie knew Clare's excitement came from being so close to a police investigation, but Maggie also wondered what people would think if they didn't know Clare well. Would the Ilimas think she was ghoulish, perhaps?

Clare, meanwhile, was still trying to make Lurline feel better. Unsuccessfully. "Maybe we can help. We have some experience with this kind of thing."

"You're a detective?" Makana asked.

Maggie almost laughed. Makana's face sported a look of puzzled amazement that a pudgy older woman might be a real detective.

"Oh, no." Clare wasn't the least put out by such surprise. "We're just amateurs, like the detectives in books and television shows. Like *Murder She Wrote,* you know."

Makana's expression remained blank and Maggie knew she'd never heard of the show. It had been on television too long ago for a person as young as Makana to remember, even if they did play the reruns on cable. Sometimes Maggie felt every one of her years.

"Yes," Clare continued. "We've helped solve several murders. Maggie is really good at figuring things out."

Lurline looked startled rather than interested in the help of the Bee women. "You've solved several murders? *Several?*"

Maggie waved her hand in dismissal. "There was a former neighbor, then some people associated with our church." She minimized her own part in it even as she shrugged her shoulders. "We were able to help the police because we knew everyone involved. This is a completely different situation, Clare."

Clare, however, didn't care to be deterred. "But, Maggie, if we could help Lurline here, we should. You know the spouse is always the chief suspect in a murder case," she informed Lurline.

Lurline swallowed hard. "I did get that impression from the sort of questions the detective asked."

"Really?" Clare asked, always interested in all aspects of an investigation. "Like what?"

The others might be thinking that Clare was butting in again, Maggie thought, but they were too interested in hearing Lurline's answer to bother telling her so. Those doing the appliqué on their pillow tops continued with their work, but the women attempting to create new patterns paused to listen. Creative endeavors took full concentration.

"He asked a lot of personal questions about our relationship," Lurline finally admitted, sinking down into her chair. Shoulders slumped, she was the picture of despair. "I guess you all noticed what a flirt Sam was." That understatement drew a snort from Edie, which Lurline politely ignored. "Our relationship has always been rocky — or at least it got that way within six months of our marriage. I've often been sorry I married him at all. We could have had some good times together without bothering with a marriage license. There was so much passion in our relationship that we were often fighting. But making up was always good," she added with a sad smile.

She sighed, and her eyes moved toward Makana who stood silently at the side of the room. "It's been worse lately, since Makana moved back here from Honolulu. She's been at the UH campus in Manoa for the past four years, but she's done now and wants to get into the business with me. I'm really happy to have her join me, but it's been rough having Sam flirt with her like she's not a relative let alone his stepdaughter. The age difference was bad enough, but the fact that she's his stepdaughter . . ." She was getting quite agitated. It was obvious that even with Sam gone, there was still a lot of passion in their relationship. Lurline took a deep breath. "I've been threatening divorce."

"It takes two to create a problem of that sort," Edie said.

Maggie wished she hadn't said that. The poor woman had just lost her husband, even if she did seem to be taking it terribly well. Telling her that her daughter was partially at fault for maintaining a flirtation was insensitive. But then, no one ever accused Edie of being sensitive.

Makana gasped, threw a pleading look toward her mother and slammed out of the room.

Lurline didn't get upset or angry. She merely looked after her and sighed heavily.

"Makana is young, and she was hurt recently by a longtime boyfriend. I think it made her feel young and desirable again, having Sam flirt that way. I could handle Sam's flirting up to a point." She looked around the room, and her gaze rested for a moment on Judy before she turned away. Anger flashed in her eyes, then was gone. "And Makana had been working on it. I've noticed her going out of her way to avoid

Sam since she came back last month."

Lurline stood, walked briskly to the front of the room and turned to face them, her expression all business. "But let's not let this get in the way of our creative spirit. I know you spent the morning exploring. Has it given you wonderful ideas?"

But Edie wasn't ready to let her off the hook so easily.

"But what killed Sam? There didn't seem to be anything wrong with him last night. Except for the fact that he was dead."

Maggie thought that Edie's phrasing would have been funny if not for the seriousness of the situation. In any case, no one even cracked a smile.

"That's true," Louise said. "I thought it might have been a heart attack or a brain hemorrhage. Why are they calling it murder?"

Lurline took a deep breath. Anyone could see she did not want to discuss the matter further. But it was equally obvious that the others were not ready to let it go. If she wanted the class to do any quilting work at all, she would have to answer their questions. So, with a deep sigh, she did.

"It seems someone shot him. It must have been a small-caliber gun. Detective Sousa didn't say exactly, but apparently no one realized he'd been shot until the autopsy this morning."

Clare gasped. She always was the dramatic one, Maggie thought. But Maggie knew how Clare loved to imagine herself living the life of an amateur sleuth in one of her beloved murder mystery books. So, even though Clare had thought Sam handsome and debonair, she would find investigating his death more exciting than having dinner with a Cary Grant look-alike. After all, she'd barely known him. It was easier for her to sympathize with Lurline on her loss than to pretend she'd been affected.

"Did he ask if you own a gun?" Maggie asked.

"I don't. And he did ask. That's what they were looking for this morning." Lurline frowned then apparently came to some conclusion and continued. "Sam had a little pistol. It wasn't registered locally, so he usually kept it hidden in a drawer." Lurline heaved a huge sigh. "But it seems to be missing." She, as well as the others, realized that this was not a good thing. Silence fell over the group.

"When did you see it last?" Maggie asked.

"I don't remember. I told Detective Sousa that."

"You have to try harder to remember,"

Edie told her. "If you can figure out what happened to it, we might be able to determine who killed Sam."

"That's assuming the person used Sam's gun," Louise said.

"Wouldn't that be perfect, though?" Clare said. "Using the victim's own gun. It's the kind of thing they always do on television and in movies, a kind of poetic justice."

"Do you have any idea at all the last time you saw the gun?" Victoria's soothing voice was a gentle balm after the rapid questions of the others. It was just enough to break down Lurline's reserve.

"Okay. I didn't tell Detective Sousa this. But I do know when I saw it last. It's just that it won't sound good. He already seems to suspect me, and I didn't want to give him more ammunition. So to speak." She winced at her unintended pun. But no one laughed. This was too serious for laughter.

"I know the gun was here on New Year's Eve. Sam and I had a few drinks to celebrate and we ended up having a huge argument. He took out the gun and waved it around. It scared me and I threatened to call my lawyer first thing in the morning. But of course the next day was a holiday."

She paused and seemed to be looking back at what had occurred a mere two weeks earlier.

"Sam left the inn after our fight. Stormed out, actually. Luckily there weren't any guests that night. And a good thing, too. We might have scared them off. Of course, we might never have had such a big fight if there had been outsiders in the house. We probably wouldn't have had any drinks either — or had just one apiece."

"What happened?" Anna asked. "You obviously made up since you were both here to greet us."

"Sam returned on New Year's Day, in the afternoon. He had an armload of orchids — all kinds, all colors." She sighed, remembering. A tear rolled from her eye and began a track down her cheek. "He had a two-pound box of chocolates and a bottle of champagne." She wiped the tear from her cheek just before it reached her jawline. "By the time we went to bed that night, I'd forgotten all about the fight. Or calling my lawyer."

"This could be important," Maggie said. "Did Sam take the gun with him when he left that night?"

Lurline gasped, realizing immediately the importance of this. She furrowed her forehead as she thought back to that evening. But it was no use. "I don't know. He might have. I don't think I saw it again after that night."

"Do you know where he went that night?" Maggie asked. "Did he go to a friend's? Sleep in his car? Sit at the beach and moon over you?"

Lurline smiled at this last, but it didn't help answer the questions. She shook her head slowly from left to right. "I never asked. He came back contrite and bearing gifts. He could be so charming." She sighed, and Maggie could finally see the regret and sadness she had expected that morning. "We always had great chemistry between us."

"Can you guess at where he might have gone?" Louise asked. "A friend's, maybe?"

"He never really made any close friends here," Lurline said. "He blamed prejudice against *haoles,* but he just wasn't very good at making friends with other men. He didn't seem to have any close friends on the mainland, either; at least, he never called anyone."

"I hate to ask, but could he have gone to a girlfriend's?" Maggie asked.

"I hate to admit it, but that's a possibility. I know he was unfaithful. He denied it, but I could tell. That's why I was threatening divorce, but he was such a charmer he could always talk me out of it."

"And you never saw the gun again after New Year's Eve?" Maggie said.

"No."

"Didn't you have to go into that drawer where he kept it, to put away clothing or something?" Edie asked.

But Lurline shook her head. "I knew he kept it hidden in that drawer but I just avoided rummaging in there. I didn't want anything to do with a gun."

Clare decided Lurline had been out of the loop long enough. "Detective Sousa asked me about Sam's flirting with members of the group."

The other women all nodded. Apparently that topic had been covered in all of their interviews.

"He asked all of us. He seemed very interested in that," Theresa admitted. "Did Sam flirt with anyone in particular? Did anyone seem especially taken with him? You'd think one of us killed him."

Judy and Anna gasped, and Iris looked very uncomfortable.

"Detective Sousa might think so," Edie said. "He probably suspects everyone at this point."

"I had no idea the Quilting Bee was so exciting," Bernie said. Lydia quickly agreed.

Neither of them looked particularly happy about the fact.

"I had to tell him that you seemed to know Sam already," Maggie said, turning toward Judy and Rita.

Rita nodded, but Judy seemed shocked.

"You told him I knew Sam before this tour?" She stared aghast at Maggie.

"Didn't you?" Unblinking, Maggie met her stare. The look held for a few seconds that felt to Maggie like several minutes.

Judy dropped her gaze first. She had the grace to blush, look down, and mumble a low-voiced "sorry."

"Did you lie to the police about that?" Edie's voice dripped her disapproval. "If you did know Sam personally before this tour, Detective Sousa will learn about it quickly enough, you know."

Judy looked ready to cry. "I knew I shouldn't lie to the police. But I didn't know what to do. I was so scared that if I told the truth about knowing him before, my husband would find out."

"You mean you had a fling with him?" Lydia seemed surprised by the news. The two of them had flirted with Sam together, but it seemed Judy had not shared all of her secrets.

Lurline's lips tightened and Judy's eyes

shifted toward her.

"We just met at a party over the holidays." She took a deep breath. "It was a gallery opening. I love art, my husband doesn't. And he was working that night — most of his work is done at night, of course — so I went alone. Sam was also there alone. He told me you were working too," she said, addressing Lurline. "I haven't made a lot of friends here, and it was so nice to have someone to talk to. We had a lot in common. Or at least, we seemed to. Both of us from the mainland and without local friends. Both interested in art."

Judy pushed her hair away from her face and took a deep breath. Perhaps she realized that much of what she was saying could easily be fabrication, Maggie thought. Any man could claim an interest in art when he wanted to pick up a woman. It was the kind of line that would appeal to a woman, one that she would be eager to believe. It made the man appear gentle and safe.

"Anyway," Judy continued, "we had some wine at the gallery, then went to a restaurant for a late supper. We had wine with dinner. By the time Sam suggested he drive me home, I was in no condition to refuse. And it seemed so sophisticated, so urbane, to let him drive me home and then to invite him in." She sniffed. "We were two misplaced mainlanders stuck here in Hilo for the holidays, alone. It's lonely when Josh is working up on the mountain. I'm alone a lot." Tears filled her eyes as she looked at Lurline. "I'm so sorry. I never meant for anything like that to happen."

"Shame on you," Edie scolded. But her voice was gentle, without malice.

"I went to confession," Judy admitted in a meek voice.

"I'm sure God forgives you," Anna said, patting Judy on the arm. Judy threw an appreciative glance toward Anna, her eyes softening beneath the shimmering tears.

"You weren't the only one." Lurline sighed. "I can't be angry at everyone he managed to seduce."

"You'd better call Detective Sousa and own up," Edie advised. "That sob story about your indiscretion and worry over your husband finding out should be enough to keep you out of trouble if you tell him right away."

"Do you have Detective Sousa's card?" Maggie asked. "If not, he gave me one."

But everyone had one of the detective's cards, including Judy.

Judy nodded miserably. Pulling her cell phone out of her pocket, she moved into the next room. Maggie was glad to see Lydia approach her friend, put her arm around her shoulders, and hold her while she dialed.

While Judy called, Clare turned to a fresh page in her sketchbook. "We should make up our own seating chart," she said. "It's no wonder he wanted to know where we were all sitting. And who talked to Sam when. Imagine — he was shot." She sounded amazed at this surprising news.

Maggie knew where Clare would be going next, long before she said the actual words.

"If we have our own diagram, we could see just where everyone was and try to figure out who had the opportunity to get close enough to Sam to shoot him." Clare paused for a minute as her excitement built. "The killer must have gotten right up close to him, don't you think? Otherwise, someone would have seen the gun, noisy show or not."

At her use of the word "killer," Lurline started. It was as if Sam's murder didn't seem real somehow, but hearing the actual word forced her to face the truth. Someone had killed her husband. And the police thought that someone was her.

"Clare." Maggie's sharp voice cut off

anything else Clare might have said.

Really, Maggie thought. Clare might find murder mysteries highly entertaining reading. She did too. They all did. But she should try to be more considerate in a real case like this. Lurline's husband was so newly deceased. And, much as they liked Lurline, did they actually know anything about the woman? Maybe she had killed him. There was a reason the spouse was always the first one looked at in a murder case. Statistics bore out the logic of such suspicions. And Lurline *was* sitting right beside him at the luau.

But Louise offered a different perspective.

"The person who killed him didn't *have* to sit right beside him. I would think it could be done by someone leaning in between two people." Louise demonstrated by approaching Maggie and Victoria who were sitting together. She then bent forward almost squeezing in between them, as if whispering something close to Maggie's ear. What the others couldn't see was that her hand had come down between the two women, and she'd poked Maggie in the ribs with a "pistol" formed by her fingers.

"Okay," Maggie conceded. "That could work."

"Well, thank you for that," Iris said. "I was

sitting beside Sam for much of the night, you know, so I'm glad to hear you aren't calling me a killer just because of an accident of seating." Her voice reeked sarcasm. "Or accusing our kind hostess," she added, "who sat on his other side."

Lurline shot her a grateful look.

"No one is accusing anyone," Maggie said, "which is why I don't think a chart is a good thing."

But it was too late to keep everyone away from such a diverting topic. Theresa was already sketching out a large diagram of the seating at the previous night's luau, penciling in a few names. Like the seating chart that Detective Sousa had shown Maggie, Theresa's chart consisted of a long rectangle surrounded by small squares.

"Okay, I've started a diagram. Where was everyone sitting? Put your names in and let's see what we've got."

So much for keeping their sanity in a difficult situation.

Led by Clare, an eager group gathered around Theresa's table. Clare took the sketch pad from Theresa and wrote in her name, then passed it along.

"I don't know what good that is going to do," Edie said. "We all know who was sitting on either side of Sam, because they were there all night."

"No, we moved around a bit," Lurline said. "Once the show started, a few people complained that they couldn't see the stage very well. Sam moved down a few places then, so he wasn't sitting right beside me after the first number."

"Oh?" Maggie did find this interesting. During the meal, Sam had sat beside Lurline, with Iris on his other side. She'd thought it a shame Iris had encouraged him that way, as it would have been easy enough for her to sit elsewhere.

But hearing of the musical chairs, she was more interested in Theresa's chart. As she penciled in her own name beside Victoria's, she realized that Sam had ended up sitting just across from her.

"Sam ended up beside you, Judy?" Maggie asked.

Embarrassed after her recent disclosure about Sam and herself, Judy turned a rosy pink.

"And I was on his other side," Lydia said. She at least was unapologetic about sitting beside their playboy driver; because Lydia really was just indulging in a bit of vacation fun, Maggie realized.

"So, did one of you shoot him?" Louise asked. She softened her remark with a smile so that they knew she wasn't accusing anyone. Still, Judy blanched and Lydia looked startled.

"You were sitting next to him too," Judy suddenly said, pointing at Iris. "But you moved during the show. You were always flirting with him too. Did you kill him because you realized he was just trying to be nice to you and you couldn't take his pity?"

Iris held herself straight, as though she was above this kind of catty bickering. "That's the most ridiculous thing I've ever heard. I just enjoyed flirting back. Having a little vacation fun. I knew it was just his way of getting better tips off the older women."

"Better tips!" Judy looked ready to fly across the table and slap Iris, just to wipe the smug smile from her face. But Lydia grabbed onto her friend's arm and held on.

"Don't be silly." Edie's scolding voice brought a bit of sanity and more than one sheepish expression. Maggie thought that the two women involved now felt silly for yelling at each other, and the others felt bad for not stopping it — for watching in guilty fascination to see how it played out. "Tele-vision is doing this to us," Maggie told Victoria later. "We've become a nation of voyeurs."

However, while the women might be feeling embarrassed about poking into the private lives of some of the group members, there wasn't enough guilt to cause anyone to back off. They still wanted to solve the mystery, they were still curious, and they meant to see what conclusions they could draw.

"How could Iris get a gun?" Edie asked. "Better to say that you did it, since you're a local. It would be easier for you to have access to a gun than a tourist on a ten-day visit."

Maggie had to smile — both at Edie's calm thinking about the impossibility of bringing a gun in on the plane and at the outraged expression on Judy's face. If Judy hadn't already admitted knowing Sam — and "knowing" him in the Biblical sense — they all would have recognized that truth now.

"No one had to bring in a gun," Anna said, her logic impeccable. "There's a gun missing from the inn, remember?"

Anna's words produced a silence so deep they could hear cars passing on the outside road. Since the house was set far back on the lot, the guests inside the inn had rarely

185

noticed any traffic noise.

"Honestly, what's wrong with all of you?" Maggie said. "You're acting guilty, and we know no one in our party killed Sam. No one really knew him. A death like that isn't something done on the spur of the moment. It took planning. If one of you got offended by his flirting at the table, you would have taken a knife off the table and stabbed him."

"There weren't any knives on the table, Maggie," Clare said, causing Maggie to release her breath in exasperation.

"For goodness sakes, Clare, I was speaking metaphorically," Maggie said. "I just meant that shooting someone in such a way that no one even notices until the autopsy is a rather specialized way of killing someone. It requires planning and preparation. If you kill in a fit of passion, you would use whatever was to hand."

"One of those great knives the dancers were using," Clare said with a smile. "Wouldn't those make good murder weapons?"

"You could probably do a beheading with one of those," Louise remarked.

There were a few tentative giggles, which was enough to get them back to the subject at hand.

"So you're back to me, aren't you,"

Lurline said. Her voice was incredibly sad when she said it. "Someone close to him." She sighed again. "Half the arguments we've had lately have had to do with Makana and the way Sam acted around her. I guess that makes me a good suspect, even though I don't own a gun."

Maggie hesitated to mention the missing gun that had apparently resided in a drawer in her bedroom. Like the others earlier, Lurline seemed to have forgotten that there was a gun handy right there at the inn — right in her own bedroom.

CHAPTER 17

Quilt tour, day three. Thursday afternoon.

The St. Rose women returned to quilting and design as the seating diagram was pushed to one side. However, it didn't take Clare long to return to her favorite topic. Unlike Maggie, she was not attempting to design her own block, so it was easy for her to multitask — to work and to talk. She had purchased a kit for the volcano block from Lurline and was working on the appliqué. The vivid red of the background fabric — it was worked as reverse appliqué with black on the top — reminded Maggie of blood.

As soon as Lurline stepped outside to take a phone call, Clare turned to Maggie.

"Do you think we'll be able to help Lurline prove her innocence, Maggie?" Clare looked up, her needle with its black thread held several inches above her work.

"We can begin with the seating chart we started," Theresa suggested. "I've been working on it and I think it's finished." She held up the sheet of paper. "After I heard about people moving around, I started another diagram — before, during and after, I guess you could say." She held up another sheet of paper. "So now I have three separate diagrams — one for where people sat during dinner, one for when the program began and another for where you were when the program ended." She shook her head. "I had no idea there was so much shuffling around. I stayed in the same place the entire time."

She handed the paper to Clare, who studied it then passed it to Maggie. "What do you think, Maggie?"

Maggie and Victoria poured over the diagrams.

"According to this, Sam sat near the end of the table during the meal, with Lurline and Iris on either side of him. Then he switched places with Anna when the show started, so she could see better. But not in her exact place. He sat between Lydia and Judy rather than beside Judy. And at some point, Bernie wedged her chair in at the end of the table — also to see better — and everyone squeezed closer together. It was so tightly packed at that point; that must be what kept Sam upright after he was shot."

Maggie looked at the names and frowned. None of the women, except perhaps for Lurline, whom she did not know well, seemed logical as suspects. They had all just met Sam. How could one of them get so upset with him so quickly — quickly enough to want him dead and to actually do the deed? It didn't make sense. And how would any of the tour group know about the gun in Sam's drawer?

"Right now, the police are working on the premise that whoever sat beside Sam shot him. We have to prove someone else had an opportunity." Maggie thought for a moment. "For example, were there any old girlfriends of Sam's working there? He seemed to get around. He knew women at all of the stops we made yesterday, though of course that could be because he takes other tour groups there all the time. But the same could be said about the hotel."

"But how can we know who knew him there?" Clare asked, a helpless tone to her voice.

"That's the problem exactly," Maggie said. "There's no way for us to know, or to know who in town might own a gun. But the police can get that information. That's why we have to let them do it and stay out of it," she concluded.

Clare looked extremely disappointed. "But we know about Sam's gun being missing from its drawer."

"However, we don't know who took it. Sam may have removed it himself."

"You mean committed suicide?" Anna asked, wide-eyed. "In front of all of us?"

Maggie sighed. "No, that's not what I mean. We don't even know if it was Sam's gun that killed him. I'm just saying that Sam might have scared himself as well as Lurline when he waved that gun around during their argument. He may have disposed of it, or given it to a friend for safekeeping."

Everyone agreed that this seemed a reasonable explanation for the missing gun.

Maggie shook her head, still unhappy with their involvement in this mess. "The motive is what's going to solve this case. Trying to determine who had the opportunity is all well and good, but it seems a lot of people were in a position to shoot him." Maggie paused as she looked over the seating chart again. "It is an excellent puzzle. Still, I don't think we have enough pieces to put it together. And since we don't know the people involved here the way we did with those past cases in Scottsdale, I don't see how we can ever assemble enough of the pieces to create a full picture."

"A lot of people besides the immediate family have motive," Clare said. "He wasn't a very good husband. It seems like any number of old girlfriends or husbands of old girlfriends could have done it. Remember, Captain Mai on the boat that night said right off that it must be the husband of one of his conquests."

"We can rule out our tour group at least." Theresa said this with a sigh of relief.

But Edie wasn't having it. "How do you figure that?"

"Because we all flew in. Someone said it before," she said. "None of us could have brought a gun on the plane. They're very strict about that kind of thing. None of us would have known Sam had a gun on the premises. And which of us would know where to purchase a gun in a small town like this, in an unfamiliar state and all. Everything is so different here."

"She has a point," Victoria said. "Everyone here in Hilo is very friendly, but I'm sure their helpfulness would stop short of helping a tourist procure a gun."

"Besides, we've all been together the whole time we've been here. No one has gone off on their own for shopping, so how could one of us have bought a gun?" Lydia asked.

"I know," Clare finally said with a triumphant grin. "Let's do it like a puzzle game."

"It isn't a game, Clare," Anna said quietly.

"I know that." Clare almost snapped. She was impatient to tell them her new idea, but they weren't giving her a chance. "Just listen for a second. That was a poor choice of words. What I *meant* was, let's puzzle it out."

Maggie looked thoughtful.

"How do you mean?" Edie asked.

Clare took a quick glance around the room, checking to be sure it was just the tour group women in the classroom. Then she lowered her voice. Everyone leaned in closer.

"You mentioned that the police always suspect the spouse first," she said, looking over at Maggie, who nodded. They all knew that was true. "Suppose we start with Lurline and see what we can come up with. We could make columns — one side with things that might prove she did it, one with things that prove she didn't. Then we could do Manu and Makana."

"That's not a bad idea," Edie told her. High praise indeed from that quarter.

"I agree," Louise said. "The only question is whether or not we can get enough information about them. At home we know everyone in the parish and that's what has helped us discover the truth."

Maggie nodded slowly. She still wasn't sure she wanted to be involved, but she could see that everyone else was entranced by the idea of trying to solve the mystery. And of course, the quicker it was solved and Sam's murderer arrested, the sooner their quilt tour could get back on track. Unless Lurline really did kill her husband.

"Okay," she said followed by a heavy sigh. "Don't any of you mention this to Michael."

Clare nodded, suddenly all business. "We'll start after dinner — as soon as we can be alone in the classroom."

CHAPTER 18

Quilt tour, day three. Thursday evening.

Dinner was a subdued affair. Lurline had been whisked off to the police station yet again for more questioning. Makana was so upset, she barely touched a bite. Manu hovered, checking serving platters that did not need checking and starting to clear plates before the women were finished.

Finally the meal was over. Manu disappeared into the kitchen, his expression such that Maggie would not be surprised to find him crying over the dirty dishes. With the long look on his face, and his distracted air, they were probably lucky their dinner had been up to its usual standard.

Makana remained in her seat, a dejected expression on her face. Tears seeped from her eyes and she periodically swiped at them. She'd barely touched her meal, and any comment about her mother brought new tears.

"Come now, tell us what's wrong," Victoria urged. "This isn't just about your mother being questioned by the police, is it? It might help you feel better if you talk about it." Victoria's soft voice and gentle manner were often enough to have someone spilling their life story.

Makana was no exception.

"It's all my fault, all this trouble Mom is in."

"Why, did you kill Sam?" Edie asked in her forthright way.

"No, of course not." She answered quickly, denying her involvement. But then she moaned. "But I might as well have." Her voice was pitched so low, those at the other end of the table could barely hear her.

The tour women exchanged worried glances. Did that mean she *had* done it? Or did she suspect her mother had?

"Come now, you don't mean that." Maggie tried to keep her voice neutral. She didn't want Makana to think she was scolding her or, heaven forbid, mocking her.

"Oh, but I do. I've been a terrible person," she cried. "Letting Sam flirt with me, making Mom really upset. I know that most of the arguments they had recently were about Sam's attitude toward me. He was always making inappropriate comments, and for a long time I let him. He was a jerk, but Mom loved him."

"I think you're giving yourself too much credit," Louise said. "You're still a young woman — young and inexperienced, I would guess. Sam was a player, a man of the world. I doubt that anything you said would have stopped him."

"I could have slapped his face. Like they do in those old movies. You think that would have made a difference?"

Beseeching eyes sought assurance from one then another of the older women, but they were unable to help her.

"I don't think that would have made much difference," Victoria admitted.

"Do you think your mom killed Sam because of the way he acted around you?" Edie asked.

But Makana didn't answer. Maggie wondered if she'd even heard anything they said. She seemed completely wrapped up in her misery and loath to release it. Instead she rose up from the table suddenly, setting her chair rocking as she rushed from the room.

"I have to make this right," she said.

"What on earth . . . ?" Lydia watched in astonishment.

"I hope that girl isn't going to do something foolish," Victoria said. Her lips tightened as her gaze remained on the door where Makana had fled.

Manu entered just in time to hear Victoria's softly spoken words.

"I thought I heard something," he said, his anxious eyes glancing quickly around the room.

"Probably the chair banging," Edie said. "Makana got up so quickly, her chair almost fell. It rocked back and forth."

"Where is she going?" Manu asked.

The women exchanged worried glances, but didn't know the answer. There were several shrugs.

"My best guess . . . ," said Maggie. "I think she may be going to the police station to see her mother."

"She said something about being responsible for all of Lurline's problems," Louise added.

Manu let out a word that turned Anna's cheeks red.

"I'd better go after her. I hope she's not going to do something foolish. I know Lurline didn't kill Sam. It's not in her nature. And Makana didn't either."

Maggie thought he added the last almost as an afterthought. He was already turning toward the door, and he, in his turn, stormed from the room. The women remaining watched the door slam behind him, not sure what to do. The table was still set with coffee and dessert, though they were pretty much through with eating.

"I hope *he* didn't do it," Edie murmured.

"Don't you think that, of them all, Manu has the best reasons to have resented Sam?" Iris looked around the table. "I don't know how he put up with it for so long. If I was him, I'd have poisoned Sam's food long ago."

There was a gasp from Anna, and Victoria tried to tell Iris that she didn't mean that.

"Oh, but I do. Manu does all the cooking. It would have been very easy for him."

"And very easy for the police to find and arrest him." Edie's droll words brought several nods of agreement.

"That may be why he used a gun." Iris wasn't willing to let go of her favorite theory. "He's right here all the time, *and* he still seems very close to Lurline. He could have known about the gun. He certainly would have access. He's often here alone while the others are out with the tour groups."

"And if Sam had been poisoned, Manu would be my first choice for the killer," Maggie said. "Unfortunately, that is not what happened. And while your theory is very interesting, Iris, there's no proof. However, we can keep your scenario in mind while we consider alternatives."

Iris didn't look happy at this proposal, but she didn't argue with it, either.

"She barely ate a thing," Louise said, looking very concerned.

"You mean Makana?" Clare asked.

"She never does seem to eat much," Victoria said.

"You're thinking she has an eating disorder?" Maggie asked.

"I don't know. I haven't noticed any other symptoms, but there is something odd about the way she eats." Louise continued to look worried.

"She just drinks tea for breakfast," Lydia said.

"She seems to eat better at lunch," Theresa remarked.

While Maggie did agree that Makana had a strange appetite, she wasn't sure where Louise was headed.

"Why don't we finish cleaning up here?" Victoria said, indicating the disheveled state of the dining room table.

"Clean up the dishes? In a hotel?" Judy seemed shocked at the suggestion.

"I'd hate to leave all this for Manu to find when he gets back," Victoria insisted. "We can at least take it all into the kitchen."

The others agreed, Maggie and Louise among others taking a few dishes and heading into the kitchen. Reluctantly, Judy picked up her dessert plate and coffee cup and followed. Victoria piled all the dirty dishes into the sink then filled it with soapy water.

"Why don't we head into the classroom and see about working on our designs," Rita said, as they headed out of the kitchen. "We'll be visiting some quilt and fabric stores tomorrow, so you should decide on designs and what kinds of fabrics you might want to look for."

Maggie was glad that Rita took over. The distraction was more than welcome. It would be too easy to spend the night debating suspects and motives. This was supposed to be a vacation, a tour to learn about a different style of quilting. Perhaps it could still be salvaged. Hoping she wasn't deluding herself, Maggie headed out to the classroom. At the gardens that morning, she'd had an idea for a design. The interviews with the police that afternoon had been very distracting, but she had managed a beginning sketch. The idea of perfecting that design now was appealing. So she hurried after Rita.

Thinking to start on a small scale, Maggie opted for an anthurium design for her first attempt, and a wall hanging the size of an opened sheet of newsprint, per Lurline's practical suggestion.

For the first minutes in the classroom, Maggie worked diligently. The large heart-shaped leaves were easy enough to draw, and she'd been especially taken with the large, almost misshapen spathe of the *obake* variety of anthurium. The spathe, she'd learned, was the correct term for the large, usually red heart-shaped "petal" of the anthurium blossom. The *obake* blooms were large and interesting, so she hoped it would make a pretty pattern.

But Clare wasn't nearly ready to leave the topic that gripped her. Working at the table beside Maggie's, it was easy for her to sidle over.

Clare was still fretting over their lack of knowledge about a crime that occurred mere feet from where they were sitting. "We were all right there when it happened. You'd think we'd be able to say so-and-so did it."

Maggie could see the frustration on Clare's face. All those mystery books she read, all the mystery programs on television — and now here she was, actually present at a murder, and she hadn't even known a murder had occurred. But Maggie was experiencing some frustration of her own. She was cutting her drawing from folded newspaper at the moment, and hoping it would look as good in reality as it did in her mind. She didn't want to return to talk of murder. Especially such an impossible situation as that in which Sam had been killed.

"There must be some way we can figure it out," Clare insisted.

Lydia was not a member of the Quilting Bee so had not participated in the solving of previous murders, but she was willing to participate. She had already told them how much she liked mind puzzles. "We could start by asking ourselves who had the opportunity to actually shoot him."

"We're doing that with the seating chart," Clare said, "trying to clarify who sat beside him. Especially since the police were also interested in the seating arrangements. Where's that chart, Theresa?"

The chart made its appearance once more. Scribbled on and scratched out, with arrows pointing to various spots, the thing was a mess. Still, half-drawn designs and cut-out pillow tops were abandoned on the tables as, for the second time that day, everyone gathered around Theresa's table. Maggie set down the paper and scissors, giving her project one last regretful glance as she too moved from her table.

Clare stood beside Theresa, the seating chart spread out before her. Lydia and Judy peered over her shoulders.

"Well, Lurline did sit beside him most of the night." Judy's tone made this sound like an accusation. "That gives her opportunity."

"And it would be simple enough for her to take Sam's gun from the drawer," Lydia added, supporting her friend's theory.

"Who else sat beside him? Besides me, I mean." Her cheeks flushed a bright pink, Judy seemed to remember that the group was actually trying to prove Lurline did *not* commit the deed.

Clare thought for a moment. "Makana did for a while, but that was during the meal."

"Manu left once he'd eaten, so we can cross him off." Victoria looked over the confusing chart. "We know Sam was still alive when the show started because he switched seats with Anna."

"Good point," Maggie said. "Does anyone know where Manu went? Did he come straight back here?"

"Oh, no," Edie said. "He showed up when we discovered Sam was dead, remember? He was right there to comfort Lurline."

"I saw him sitting in the bar when I went

inside to use the restroom," Anna said.

Maggie frowned. "Was that during the meal or during the program?"

"During the pause between the two halves of the program. I thought there was going to be an intermission when they finished with the Tahitian part of the program and said they were moving on to Hawai'i, so I rushed off to use the facilities. But I could hear the music start up before I even reached the restroom, and the dancers were halfway through a number when I got back."

"Sam must have been dead by then," Louise said. "He'd been dead for a while when I tried to find his pulse, and the likeliest scenario has the shooter doing it during the heavy drumming in the early part of the program."

"Do we know if Manu came back to the table during that part of the program?" Theresa asked. "Louise is right. Sam had to have been shot during the Tahitian numbers or it's more likely everyone would have heard the shot."

"Unless they had a silencer." Clare seemed quite pleased with this new idea.

"They're called suppressors — sound suppressors," Edie said.

"And it's illegal to even own one," Maggie reminded them. "How would one of the family, or one of us, come into possession of such a thing?"

"And homemade ones like you see on television," Edie said, looking pointedly at Clare, "wouldn't have worked, because things like pillows or liter soda bottles are too big to hide in a crowd."

Maggie looked around the room. There were no other comments about sound suppressors — thankfully. But on the other hand, no one could say if Manu had returned or not. She sighed.

"Let's try a different tack," Theresa said. "I for one didn't take anything with me to the luau. There was a pocket in the side seam of the muumuu I got, and I just tucked my camera in there. I didn't think I'd need anything else."

"That's a good idea, Theresa," Maggie said. "Detective Sousa asked me what everyone took with them that night."

"I suppose he's trying to figure out who might have been able to smuggle in a gun," Edie said. "I didn't, of course, I don't have a gun. But I did take my purse. I just don't feel right without it over my arm. You had one too, didn't you Iris?" she asked her roommate.

Iris nodded. All the others admitted to taking a purse, except for Maggie, Victoria and Louise. Like Theresa, they all had pockets in their new clothes and had decided not to carry bulky purses.

"Okay," Clare said. "We'll cross you four off the list of suspects since you had nowhere to hide a gun." Clare smiled, but no one else found her comment humorous.

Iris and Judy in particular looked ready to argue. They ended up nodding vigorous agreement when Lydia made a rather wild suggestion.

"Those muumuus are so loose," she said, "it would be easy to hide a gun underneath. And no one would ever know it was there, because of all the material."

"But then you'd have to be prepared with a holster, or even some duct tape," Maggie said. "Some way to hold it under your clothes."

"And how would you get it out or put it back, without everyone noticing," Edie added. Exactly the point Maggie had made with Michael.

Reluctantly, everyone had to agree that she was correct. Trying to retrieve a weapon from beneath a muumuu would be an impossible task. And putting it back even harder.

"This is getting us nowhere," Edie said.

Maggie agreed, but Clare urged them all

to keep trying.

"We were all right there," she repeated. "There must be some way for us to figure out what happened."

Clare was beginning to whine, and Maggie felt sorry for her. Clare desperately wanted to feel she hadn't missed out on the most exciting event to happen on their vacation. Even if they hadn't been present, she would have wanted to figure out the whodunit. But having been so close, it frustrated her to be so clueless.

"What about motive?" Maggie suggested. "Maybe we can try to work that out."

"We don't know enough about Sam to figure out a motive," Iris said in disgust. "Why don't you leave it to the police? It is their job, after all."

But Clare was already looking straight at Rita.

"We'll have to start with you, Rita."

Rita looked startled. "Me? Why me?"

"Because you're the only one among us who knows Lurline and knew her before all this started," Louise stated matter-of-factly.

"Oh."

"What do you know about Lurline's and Sam's marriage?"

Maggie could see that Rita was still nervous. Why was that? she wondered.

"I already told you how they met when Lurline was on the rebound. And everyone agrees they had this really passionate early marriage."

"The thing is," Louise said, "as Lurline said earlier, that kind of passion can make for a tempestuous relationship."

"Oh, they had that all right," Rita said. "I doubt there's a person in the quilting community here who hasn't heard them yelling at one another. But they always made up and were as loving as ever."

"How long have they been married?"

"Six or seven years, I think."

"Oooh," Clare said. "The seven-year itch." She nodded sagely, as if this explained everything.

Edie didn't dignify Clare's new theory with a comment. "Has Manu always hung around Lurline and the inn looking like a lovesick puppy?"

Judy jumped in with a reply for this question. "Sam told me that Manu and Makana looked after the inn while he and Lurline honeymooned in Fiji. Makana was still in high school then."

"I do know that Manu refused to give up his interest in the inn," Rita said. "Since they started it together during their marriage, one of them would have had to buy the other out. Neither of them would give it up, and neither had the money to pay out half the value to the other. So they had to agree to operate it together. There was a lot of talk about that in the quilting community."

"I'll bet," Edie murmured.

"Lurline tried to argue that she deserved to have it because this was her grandparents' home and then her mother's. But I guess that argument didn't work in court. They turned it into a bed-and-breakfast together while they were married, so I guess that trumped her argument about a family estate."

"Manu really has the best motive, doesn't he?" Iris said, returning to her pet theory. "It's pretty obvious to all of us that he's still in love with Lurline. Maybe he just finally snapped."

"But don't you think Makana might have told him about Sam's health issues, even if she didn't tell her mother?" Louise asked. "Manu could have just waited. Sam didn't strike me as someone who took care of himself. Eventually his bad habits would have gotten him, while Manu looks to be in excellent health even if he does carry a few extra pounds. He appears much younger too. He had every reason to believe he would outlast Sam and be able to win Lurline back."

"I agree," Victoria said. "I think it's likely that Makana shared that information with her father. She and Manu have a close relationship — that's easy enough even for strangers like us to see. He could have just hung on and waited, especially since he knew Sam wasn't taking care of himself." She smiled, mischief dancing in her eyes. "He could even have been subtle about it and provided a diet that would have exacerbated Sam's problems."

Grateful for the levity, everyone smiled.

"What a shame we aren't in Scottsdale," Clare moaned. "If we were, Maggie could talk to Michael and get some decent information for us."

"I doubt it," Maggie replied. "You know how Michael hates it when I try to 'butt in,' as he puts it. He's already called and warned me off."

"Could we go back to see the hotel, do you think? You two have cars here, don't you?" Clare asked, turning to look at Rita and Judy.

"What good would that do?" Iris asked. She seemed truly puzzled.

"It's always good to get a real sense of the crime scene," Clare said.

"But we were all right there. Last night," Judy said with a shudder, not anxious to return to the scene of the crime.

"Do you think the hotel has security cameras?" Theresa asked. "Though it seems doubtful they would have them outside where the luau was set up."

"Cameras? Here in Hilo?" Rita with a laugh. "I sincerely doubt it. Hilo is seriously behind the times. My father is from Maui, and he's always said how backward we are here compared to Maui County. There's still a small-town mentality here. And none of the local hotels are affiliated with a big chain that might have that kind of security as a matter of course."

"There was going to be another big luau tonight," Maggie remarked. "I heard some servers talking about it, about there being luaus two nights in a row. I guess they usually have several days in between, but tonight's was for some big convention group. A lot of the same people will probably be there serving. Maybe we could talk to some of them once the party is over."

"That's a good idea. We were done by eight last night." Theresa checked her watch.

"But we can't just go barging in on a luau that's already started. They sell tickets to those things," Iris reminded them. "Expensive tickets."

"No problem." Theresa grinned. "We'll go into the bar, say we're having girls' night out. Anyone can do that, and the bar looks right out over the lawns where they do the luaus."

"That's where I saw Manu sitting last night, when I went to the restroom," Anna reminded them.

"Then we'll start there," Maggie said. "We can see if the same people are working tonight and ask them if they remember Manu."

"I have a picture of him," Clare told everyone, a smug pleasure in her voice. "It's right here on my digital camera." She brought up a photo she'd taken of Manu serving her breakfast of macadamia nut pancakes, a wide grin on his face. We can show them who it is we're interested in. I have pictures of Lurline and Makana too."

Maggie shook her head at the photo, but if it was all they had it would have to do.

"Great," Bernie said. "This sounds like fun. It's been much too depressing today — all this talk about murder. I know it's a terrible thing, but we barely knew Sam. I hate that his death is ruining our vacation. I'd love a girls' night out."

"Let's do it," Rita agreed, grinning at her

cousin. "Class dismissed," she announced to the group at large.

Being back at the hotel was a grim reminder of the event that had ended their previous evening out. The party atmosphere that prevailed in the cars on the drive over quickly dissipated. As they pulled some tables together, Maggie had to remind everyone that they should be having fun. The gloom that permeated the group as they looked out at the luau grounds was more appropriate to a funeral home than a resort bar.

A few smiles appeared as their waitress approached. The few generated several more, and within minutes the atmosphere had lightened. Judy started them off by ordering a mai tai, and Lydia and Bernie quickly followed suit. Within minutes they had a table full of prettily colored drinks decorated with pineapple slices, cherries, and little paper umbrellas.

Maggie, not in the mood for alcohol and thinking she might have to drive one of the cars back to the inn, accepted a coconut smoothie from the waitress and gave her a generous tip.

"I heard a man died at the luau last night," she mentioned, trying for a casual, gossipy tone.

"I know. Isn't it terrible?" The young woman accepted the tip money with a gracious smile, but didn't elaborate about the previous evening.

Maggie decided to try again. "Was it a heart attack?"

Accepting an equally extravagant tip from Victoria, the girl leaned down. "We're not supposed to be talking about it," she told them. "But my uncle is a cop, and he told me the guy was shot." They could hear the awe in her voice. "Can you imagine? Right outside there. They think it happened during the Tahitian part of the program when the drums are really loud."

"Did they catch the person who did it?"

"No. They have no idea who did it, but my uncle thinks the wife or the stepdaughter looks good."

Clare, listening raptly from the other side of Maggie, emitted a squeak of surprise, but managed not to say anything else. Once the waitress had moved on, Edie turned to Clare.

"I don't know why you're surprised, Clare. Isn't that what we all thought? That the police suspect Lurline killed Sam?"

"Why don't you take that photo of Manu up to the bar," Louise suggested. "You can ask the bartender if he worked last night, and if he did, ask him if he remembers seeing Manu."

"But what good will that do?" Anna asked. "I told you I saw him. He was sitting right there at the curve in the bar, looking out toward the lawn."

"We want to know when he left," Maggie reminded her. "And if he was here for the entire show. Whether or not he went in and out. Any or all of that."

"I'll do it," Edie said. "Let me have the camera, Clare."

Clare gave up the camera, but reluctantly. In the end, she followed Edie up to the bar, where Edie ordered another ginger ale. Edie always had nonalcoholic drinks.

"Do you work every night?" she asked outright. Clare poked her in the side, astonished at such directness.

"Sure. Make good tips here and I got three kids," the man replied.

"I wonder if you'd look at a photo for me. I'm hoping you noticed this guy here last night."

She took out the camera, pressed the on button, then checked that the photo of Manu appeared on the viewing screen.

The bartender looked at the camera. Then he looked at Edie.

"What's this about?" He no longer appeared as friendly as he had a moment earlier.

Clare sighed loudly, and this time it was Edie who poked Clare.

"I take it you know Manu." The bartender didn't respond, but merely stared silently. "We were here for the luau last night, with the group from the Blue Lily Inn. We were sitting right beside Sam and didn't even know a crime had been committed. We've only been here a few days, but we really like Lurline and Manu, and we're concerned that the police are focusing on Lurline as the prime suspect in Sam's murder." Edie paused, looking intently into the bartender's face. "You do know Sam was murdered last night." It was a statement, not a question.

He gave a short nod. "Word traveled fast. We're like family here in the hotel. Most of us have worked here for years. We all knew Sam, too. They bring the Blue Lily guests here for the big luau all the time. So, yeah, I know Manu. Went to school with him. He's a good guy."

Edie and Clare wondered if he would say the same about Sam but he did not. No surprise there, Edie thought.

"See, we thought that Manu could be eliminated as a suspect because he didn't stay for the entertainment. I thought he left after he ate, and planned to come back to get us." Clare put as much sincerity into her voice as she could. "But then our friend Anna came in to use the restroom and saw him sitting here, staring out at the lawn."

Once again the bartender gave a short nod. "Manu, he's still crazy over Lurline. Yeah, he was here, right there where you say, staring outside. Watching Lurline for sure."

"Mooning over her, more like," Edie muttered.

The bartender shrugged.

"But Manu, he didn't go out once he got here. He sat there, had a couple beers. He ran out when he saw the commotion after."

"Thank you," Edie said, and Clare was shocked to see the size of the tip she placed on the bar. Edie was notoriously thrifty, but she was certainly showing her appreciation for the information.

"By the way," Edie added, turning back momentarily. "We don't notice any surveillance cameras. I don't suppose you have any hidden ones?"

The bartender laughed. "No. We not that fancy here in Hilo."

Edie thanked him once again, and she and Clare hurried back to the others to let them know what they'd learned. Clare couldn't wait to tell them what he'd said about security cameras.

"He said they weren't that fancy here in Hilo," she said. "It didn't seem to bother him that they don't have them. And he has to work here. They're very laid back, aren't they? Do you think that will keep the police from finding out what really happened?"

"Detective Sousa struck me as very professional," Maggie said.

Victoria and Louise agreed. "He seems like a good investigator to me too," Louise said. "I don't think you have to worry."

"I just don't want them to settle on someone and stop investigating," Clare said. "In books, the police do that all the time, especially in small towns. That's why the amateur has to find the killer."

Victoria was quick to point out, "Those are fiction, Clare."

Maggie was relieved. She'd had to suppress an almost irresistible urge to roll her eyes.

"Maybe we should spread out, talk to various people. See what we can learn." Louise stood, looking around the table to see if the others agreed.

Maggie, Theresa and Clare also stood; Lydia and Rita a bit more reluctantly. Maggie knew Anna was too shy to approach strangers on her own, but was surprised that Iris did not get up. Instead, she raised her drink in a toast. "I think I'll have another of these," she said. "Then maybe I'll join you."

Lydia and Judy quickly sat back down, happy to keep Iris company. Bernie and Rita also remained at the table.

The Quilting Bee women spread themselves around the resort, speaking to anyone who would talk to them. But after an hour, they trudged back to the table, comparing their meager results. They had not learned anything new. But they all agreed that the evening had not been a waste.

"This is a nice place," Bernie announced, toasting the room at large with her third mai tai. "The live music is real good," she added, sending another toast in the direction of the trio of performers.

By the time they returned to the Blue Lily, they were all feeling the effects of the drinks they'd had. While they had begun by pretending to have a good time, they had proceeded to do just that. Edie and Maggie took over the cars to drive back since they had stuck to nonalcoholic smoothies or sodas while the two local women had each had several drinks. There was a lot of laughing and giggling as they walked from the cars to the inn. Anna and Bernie nodded sleepily, while Clare and Edie were enthusiastic and eager to get on with things. In the end those who felt invigorated retreated to the classroom to work on their designs and stitching while the sleepyheads trudged upstairs to bed.

Maggie and Victoria sat up for a while, discussing what little information they had managed to accumulate.

The three Ilimas were still missing in action when the last of the tour group retired for the night.

CHAPTER 19

Quilt tour, day four. Friday morning.

Manu was back in the dining room the next morning, presiding over breakfast as usual. Everyone was delighted to see him, and warm hugs were exchanged all around.

There were even more delighted exclamations and more hugs when Lurline and Makana entered the room together. The noise level flew up as thoughts of food were abandoned and voices from all sides tried to ask what had happened.

Lurline, dignified as always, urged her students to fill a plate and sit down. Once that was accomplished and they were all seated around the long table, she cleared her throat and thanked everyone for their concern.

"It was quite the night, last night," Lurline said.

"Yeah, for some of us too," Lydia quipped, gripping her head with both hands. Beside her, Judy popped two aspirin into her mouth and swallowed them down with some water. This morning, guava juice or even orange juice seemed too exotic a drink for her.

Lurline gave them a quizzical look. "Did you go out partying last night?"

Her voice remained neutral and Maggie knew she was trying hard to be nonjudgmental. But it was apparent to all of them that she thought such festivity out of place while she struggled for her very freedom.

For a moment no one answered. Then Iris stepped in for them. "We just went out for a drink, listened to a little live music. Some of those fancy drinks really pack a punch."

Judy and Lydia shot her a look of gratitude. Maggie too was relieved. No use telling her about their investigations yet.

"We had a good time," Theresa said. "A few drinks and some real nice live music."

"Well, good," Lurline said.

"So . . ." Clare glanced anxiously at Makana. "Last night . . . Makana ran out of here without telling us where she was going. She was very upset. We were relieved that Manu went after her."

Lurline reached over and covered her daughter's hand with her own. "Makana was very brave. Dumb, but brave." She smiled weakly at the younger woman. "Detective Sousa had me in the interrogation room, asking his questions for the umpteenth time, when Makana here came tearing in, a uniformed officer on her heels. She screamed at him to stop harassing me and claimed *she* had killed Sam." Love shone in her eyes. "And right after her came that idiot over there," she said, gesturing toward Manu. But her eyes were still soft and warm and filled with love. "He said, no, Makana did not kill Sam, *he* did. Both of them wanted to save me, and tried to confess to something they didn't do."

"So what does this *lolo* do," Manu said, pointing to Lurline who the visitors later learned he'd described as crazy. "She goes and tells that detective that she did it. *She* killed Sam."

Maggie couldn't help it. She laughed. And that set off everyone else. Soon the entire room was laughing out loud at the insane scene Lurline had just described.

"What did that poor man do," Maggie asked, "with all three of you saying you did it? I assume you all claimed to have acted alone."

"Of course," Manu said.

"Well. I stayed in that room with Detective Sousa, but other officers took Makana and Manu to other rooms. They didn't want us all together to compare stories, I guess." Lurline smiled, still bemused by the situation.

"They grilled us," Manu claimed.

"It was frightening," Makana added, wrapping her arms tightly across her upper body.

"That's what you get for lying that way," Lurline scolded, but they all knew she was not angry at her daughter.

"But they obviously let you all go," Maggie said.

"Detective Sousa finally said that we were all nuts and to go on home," Lurline said. "He said he would know where to find us."

"I guess on an island like this," Maggie said, "there's no danger of you taking off. Not like in Arizona where the Mexican border is so close."

Edie nodded. "And I'm sure he's alerted the airlines in case any of you try to leave."

Lurline blanched. It seemed the seriousness of the charges against her had still not penetrated fully. Makana emitted a nervous giggle.

Happily, Victoria came to the rescue, managing to return the mood in the room to its rosier state before Edie's awkward remark. "We're glad to have you back," she said, in her kind, soft voice. "Not that Rita wasn't doing an excellent job," she added, with an apologetic nod to Rita.

Rita acknowledged the compliment with a smile. "I'm just glad to be here with Bernie and happy to be in a position to help out. I know you all signed on for Lurline's excellent sessions."

The murmur of appreciation that followed was lost on Lurline, however. Her attention was caught by a car pulling into the driveway outside the window.

"Goodness, I hope that's not Detective Sousa back already." She squinted at the window, trying to get a better look at who might be coming in.

"It's a man." Theresa sat near the window and had a good view out to the driveway. "Not Detective Sousa," she added as the driver emerged from the car.

"Oh, my gosh," Lydia exclaimed, lowering her head to peer out the window. "Judy, isn't that your husband?"

Judy's face lost all color. She stood, though a bit unsteadily, and started for the door. But before she was able to move more than a step or two, the man had burst through the rear entrance and found them in the dining room. His face was stormy, but Maggie thought it was more fear than rage. In any case, he rushed up to Judy, wrapped his arms around her and held on tight. He rested his head on the top of her hair and breathed a sigh of relief audible to everyone in the room.

Maggie watched with interest. So this was the often-absent astronomer. He was a good-looking man. Not as tall or as sophisticated as Sam; there was something of the science geek in his appearance. But he had clear blue eyes currently filled with concern for his wife, and a head of thick, wavy, straw-colored hair. He looked like a nice Midwestern farm boy, Maggie decided.

"I just heard!" he said, pulling back from the hug far enough to look down at her. "A police detective came to the house. Are you okay? Why didn't you call me?"

His words rushed out, full of emotion, full of concern — and more than a little anger. The tour group women listened eagerly. Even though we all know we should leave and give them some privacy, Maggie thought.

Judy was clearly mortified. Maggie didn't understand why. She agreed with Victoria, who had whispered, "Isn't that sweet?" in her ear. Why should she be embarrassed? She should be proud to have a spouse who showed such love and concern.

He pulled far enough back to peer down at his wife's face. "Get your things. You're coming home with me right now."

"Don't be silly." Judy giggled nervously as she pushed away from him. "I did try to call you, but I got the voice mail and I didn't want to just leave a message about something like this. I didn't want you to worry," she added.

He looked embarrassed. Maggie thought that interesting. It appeared that Judy had a legitimate complaint when it came to him being gone at work all the time.

"I was working," he stammered, confirming Maggie's theory. But he recovered quickly, and anger took over. "A police detective came to see me this morning!"

His indignation had Maggie rapidly feeling less sorry for him. He seemed more upset for himself than for what his wife had experienced.

"Josh, please." Judy tried to inch toward the door to the sitting room but wasn't having much luck at covering the ground. It was a good ten feet away and Josh showed no inclination to follow her. Maggie felt sorry for her. She was sure Judy didn't want to have this discussion in front of the entire group — all of whom knew about her one-night stand with Sam. Was she concerned that someone might blurt that out in front of him? Even Edie wouldn't be that crude.

But not only was Josh resisting his wife's efforts to lead him out of the room, he wasn't listening to her, either.

"He asked all kinds of questions about you." His voice rose as he seemed ready to lead into whatever kinds of questions he'd been asked.

"Not here, Josh." Judy's voice was no longer palliative. Nor did she try to soothe him by letting him think he was in charge. She made her statement with authority, and followed up by literally pushing him out of the dining room and into the empty classroom.

Unfortunately for Judy, but to the delight of the eavesdropping crowd, their every word could still be heard from the breakfast table.

"He wanted to know about your friends, Judy. As though he suspects you have *men* friends here," he finished, emphasizing the word men.

"It's a murder investigation, Josh. Of course he's going to try to get all kinds of information about everyone who was there."

"Well, this is ridiculous. I said so when you first talked about it. Paying to stay at an inn right here in town, ten minutes from home. You need to give up this foolishness and come home. It might be dangerous here."

Well, at least he seemed concerned for his wife, Maggie thought.

"It's perfectly safe," Judy said. "And I explained about the fee. It's for the classes and the tours and everything. Room and meals here were included. Besides, Lydia and I are having such a nice visit. And I'm learning to quilt. You wanted me to get a hobby and I think I'm going to like stitching. It's very creative, like painting. Except for Sam's death, I'm having a good time."

Maggie noted that her voice had lost its firmness now, and turned wheedling. Typical man/woman stuff, she thought. She wouldn't be surprised if she was looking up at him from beneath her eyelashes. Perhaps even fluttering them. She'd seen Judy use some of her wiles on Sam before his death.

"I've never known anyone who was murdered," Josh said. He seemed insulted that he was now associated with someone who did.

Lurline chose that moment to make an attempt at distracting the group, but a few quick shushes led her to abandon the try.

"Is there any truth to what this detective was indicating? Did you know the man who was murdered — I mean before this damned quilt party?"

"Josh!"

Judy's voice dropped, as though she realized everyone must be trying to overhear them. However, they still managed to make out her reply.

"I had met Sam at an art gallery opening last month. One of those holiday parties you were too busy to attend."

"Whoa, zinger!" Theresa whispered.

Maggie smiled.

"We can discuss this further when I get home next week," Judy said. "You're just making a spectacle of us. You realize everyone in there is listening carefully, trying to hear what we're saying."

There were a few blushes at that, Maggie noticed. But for the most part, no one was terribly ashamed. No one resumed eating. Ears remained alert.

"Now, stop making a fool of yourself and come in and meet the others. I'm not going to leave, and that's that. It's so good to see Lydia again, and I refuse to cut short our time together."

As everyone turned back to their food in an attempt to cover the eavesdropping, Judy and her husband returned to the dining room. She stopped just inside the door and raised her voice. Although the regular noise of flatware clicking against plates and ceramic pieces clacking together had returned, there was no overriding chatter.

"Everyone, this is my husband, Josh."

"Ah . . . hello." He looked fairly embarrassed to be greeting the entire group, a group he'd just been urging her to abandon. And he had to know they had all heard him doing so.

She went around the table, introducing everyone by name.

"She's right, you know," Lurline assured him, "about it being safe for her to stay. There's no danger here. Someone targeted my husband for some specific reason. I'm sure no one else is in any danger."

"I didn't see the news last night. I was working. Then this morning . . ." He pushed his hand through his hair once again. "It scared me, knowing that she was right there when it happened."

"Please let her stay with us," Lurline began.

Maggie smiled. Smart of Lurline to pretend they hadn't heard Judy say she was staying no matter what. Let him think they had only heard his initial comments about coming to take her home.

Her friend seemed to have caught on too.

"Oh, yes," Lydia said. "Please, she can't go. I came on this tour especially so that we could spend time together, learn to quilt together. It's been so long since you moved," she added, "and I've missed her so much."

"It's not up to him," Edie said, disgust plain in her voice. "Judy's an adult. She can decide for herself."

"Besides," Maggie added, "I'm sure Detective Sousa appreciates having all of us here in one place. It makes it easier for him when he wants to check on something about that night."

Josh seemed surprised to hear that, and he didn't look happy about it, either.

"We have a special surprise planned for today," Lurline went on. "It's been cleared with Detective Sousa and everything. You really don't want to miss it," she told Judy.

Judy squared her shoulders and looked her husband in the eye. "Edie's right. It's not up to you to decide what I can do, Josh. I appreciate that you were frightened for me, but I want to stay here with Lydia. And learn to quilt. I think I'm going to enjoy having it as a new hobby. Something to do while you're on the mountain," she added.

Whoa, Maggie thought. Another direct hit. Maggie could see how that final barb hurt Josh. They obviously had issues regarding the long hours he worked. Maggie had a feeling that Judy also resented Josh bringing her to such an isolated spot to live. Perhaps she was finally taking responsibility for her own life — and the way she filled it. Maggie didn't have much patience for whiners, but it looked like Judy might be learning to create her own happiness. Good for her.

Judy practically pushed Josh out the door, returning to her now-cold breakfast and a quick hug of support from Lydia. And to Lurline's explanation of the planned surprise.

"All of this was already on the schedule, just not for today. But this did seem the perfect time for an all-day excursion. We'll be starting out at the Mauna Kea Beach Hotel which has a beautiful collection of Hawaiian quilts commissioned by Laurance Rockefeller when he built the original resort hotel in nineteen sixty-five. We'll then stop at the King's and Queen's shops in Waikoloa for some shopping. There's a small quilt shop there that you might enjoy, and lots of other interesting shopping. There's a wonderful store there if you want to get gifts for your grandchildren. Then we'll have a picnic lunch at Hapuna Beach Park. This is a beautiful white sand beach, one of the prettiest in the islands. And Manu has packed a mainland-style picnic lunch today."

Maggie noticed several sighs of relief. While the bento lunches had been interesting, everyone was pleased that they wouldn't have to deal with more unusual foodstuffs.

"We'll finish up at quilt and fabric shops in Waimea and Honokaa," Lurline said. "It will be a long day, but I think you'll all enjoy it. Bring some stitching to keep you busy on the ride. It will take over an hour to reach the Mauna Kea Hotel."

As they rose from the table, Edie stopped at Judy's side.

"Good job, standing up for yourself that way."

Judy merely nodded, but she seemed happy for the support.

"It may be time for you to think about a divorce," Edie continued.

Maggie was dismayed. What was Edie thinking, butting into something so personal? But before she could pull Edie out of the room, Judy was nodding her agreement.

"I realize now how miserable I've been, here in the back of beyond. In Scottsdale, I never would have gone out for drinks with someone like Sam. I appreciate having all of you for moral support."

"Well, what do you know," Maggie murmured to Victoria.

Lydia hugged her friend and led her out of the room.

CHAPTER 20

Quilt tour, day four. Friday.

As Lurline had predicted, it was a long but wonderful day. They left Hilo immediately after breakfast for the other side of the island, armed with cameras, sketchbooks and shopping lists. They began at the Mauna Kea Beach Hotel where two floors displayed the Hawaiian quilts specially commissioned for the hotel's art collection.

"These are just beautiful," Victoria said, taking photos of each one.

"I'm in love," Theresa exclaimed. She, too, had her camera out. "I just hope these photos turn out. The glass in front of the quilts is reflecting a lot of the building, and I hope that doesn't ruin them."

Maggie examined the little digital picture on her own camera. "It's fine. You can still see the quilt pattern even with all the reflection."

As they walked along to the next quilt,

Clare sidled up to Maggie and clutched her arm. "Have you noticed how odd Iris is acting?"

"Iris?" Maggie looked around, hoping to see what Clare meant. She'd noticed that Judy and Lydia both seemed to be dragging a bit. She suspected hangovers, though Judy had been almost manic, depressed one moment, giddy the next. Even after that confrontation with her husband, her current mood seemed extreme. But then Maggie had always thought Judy high-strung. Maggie felt sorry for Lydia, though she was being incredibly supportive of her friend.

"She's there at the back," Clare said, nodding toward Iris but keeping her voice as low as possible. "She's been following along, but she doesn't seem interested in the quilts."

"I think she's been here before," Victoria said. "Didn't she say something about this hotel when we first talked about setting up a tour?"

"Maybe." Clare seemed unconvinced.

"She may have a hangover," Louise said. "She had a couple of mojitos last night."

"I had a good time last night, all things considered," Anna remarked. "I've never been to a bar with a group of women friends before, and it sounds terribly naughty." She

238

smiled. "But I enjoyed myself. Despite our reason for going," she added.

Maggie could see the guilt cloud her face, as though she should not have had fun there because they had meant to investigate a murder during their visit. But then a smile crept across her features. A guilty little smile?

"That piña colada smoothie was delicious!"

"Don't beat yourself up about having a good time," Maggie said, putting her arm around Anna as they stopped before the next quilt. "None of us really knew Sam, so we don't have to give up our vacation just because he died. We didn't even like him, remember. It's okay to have a good time."

Maggie's advice seemed to work. They all tried not to let Sam's death get in the way of their long-anticipated trip. Instead, they concentrated on the quilts, the landscape, the flowers, fragrances and colors around them. Everything and anything could be the inspiration they needed for a fabulous quilt — isn't that the point Lurline had been trying to make?

They continued on to Waikoloa for shopping then stopped at Hapuna Beach for a picnic lunch specially prepared and packed by Manu. As Lurline had said, he'd packed "mainland food." They had potato salad and macaroni salad — two separate salads, not the local combination that had been in the bento box — coleslaw, fried chicken, thick slices of cheese and thinly sliced prosciutto to eat with crusty bread, grapes, apples and tangerines. The latter, Manu informed them proudly, were straight off the tree in the Blue Lily Inn's garden. For dessert, he'd made three kinds of cookies: white chocolate macadamia, oatmeal walnut cranberry, and a crisp refrigerator cookie rich with walnuts. He told them that the refrigerator cookie recipe came straight from his great-grandmother in Onomea. The drinks cooler contained a wide selection of soft drinks that included all the popular colas and the local fruit drinks as well.

Afterward, they stopped at Waimea and Honokaa for more shopping at quilt and fabric stores.

The women from Arizona had a wonderful time getting to see so much of the island. Rita pointed out the sights in her hometown of Waimea and introduced them to the workers in the local quilt shop. There was a lovely display of Rita's patterns there, and Clare took a photo of her standing beside the display rack, before purchasing several of the patterns to take home.

But best of all, Lurline and Makana seemed to relax for the first time since the luau. Makana even laughed as she told them about her first horseback riding experience, at a friend's ranch in Waimea. And Louise confided to Maggie that Makana seemed to have an appetite for a change. "Maybe it's getting away from the inn, or maybe just the outdoor air. I think the trip was good for her."

A happy but tired group returned to the inn near dinnertime.

"No worry," Manu assured them as he helped them off the bus with their bulging shopping bags. "I have a pork roast in the oven all day, and potatoes too. We'll have a good dinner, right on time."

The women entered the classroom, eager to show off their purchases and discuss patterns, fabrics and colors. Judy, who turned out to be quite an artist, showed off page after page from her sketchbook — beautiful drawings of plants and flowers, some colored in with pastels, as well as quick studies of the mountains and the beach. The expedition had been an excellent diversion and they all wanted the pleasant day to continue.

The talk of patterns and fabric did continue throughout Manu's delicious dinner, as they passed the platter of meat and bowls of vegetables. Until Makana's strangled groan turned everyone's attention toward the wide windows.

"Here we go again," she said. She'd been eating a fairly normal meal, Maggie noticed. But now she pushed her half-full plate away.

All heads turned toward the window that looked out over the driveway.

"You said Detective Sousa told you he knew where to find you," Edie remarked. "Looks like he's found you."

Sure enough, in the fading light of dusk they could just see Detective Sousa walking toward the house. Lurline rose and followed Manu to the door.

Makana remained in her seat, but her face had an almost green cast. Maggie was surprised she didn't run to the restroom. She wondered how long she'd be able to keep down her recent meal. Perhaps the girl did suffer from an eating disorder, but bulimia rather than anorexia. Keeping a worried eye on the young woman, Maggie turned toward the new arrival. Could he have news about an arrest?

Chapter 21

Quilt tour, day four. Friday evening.

Within moments, the detective was ushered to a chair, a slice of chocolate macadamia dream pie and a fresh cup of coffee placed on the table before him.

Maggie noted the excitement in Clare's eyes when the detective sat down beside her.

"What can we do for you this evening, Detective?" Lurline asked.

"Some new information has come to light," Detective Sousa said. "And I need to speak to all of you about it. Mainly the family, but since you were all there when Mr. Samson died, and some of you knew him before this tour," he looked pointedly at Judy, whose face turned a bright red, "I want everyone to hear it."

He had certainly gained the full attention of everyone at the table. There was a temporary lull in the sound of cutlery against china.

"It's like Monsieur Poirot gathering everyone in the drawing room," Clare breathed happily. "Are you going to solve the crime now, Detective Sousa?"

Maggie was glad to see Detective Sousa smile. "No, Ms. Patterson. I wish my 'little gray cells' worked as well and as quickly as Monsieur Poirot's. But unfortunately, I am still investigating."

Clare looked crushed. She loved those old movies where everyone gathered in the drawing room while the detective explained everything and named the killer. Still, Maggie was sure she would appreciate the "little gray cells" remark.

Having now lost his dramatic moment, Detective Sousa took a taste of the macadamia chocolate dream pie that Manu had placed before him. He sat completely still for a moment after tasting it, an expression of deep appreciation on his face. "Wonderful," he told Manu, who thanked him solemnly. "Absolutely delicious," he said again, before taking a sip of coffee. He urged the others to finish their dinners while he ate his dessert. It wasn't until everyone had finished with the main meal and had dessert before them that he stood to address them.

Smart of him to stand, Maggie thought.

He wasn't a big man. Standing not only gave him more authority, it offered a better overall view of the people seated at the table.

"You will all be interested to hear," he began, "that something unusual has come to light. As a matter of course, Mr. Samson's fingerprints were taken during the autopsy." He glanced around the table, and Maggie had the distinct impression that he was checking each person's response to this information.

"There was a little surprise when the results came back," he continued.

Maggie watched the family, but they didn't seem to have any idea where this was going. Clare, mesmerized by her closeness to the detective, watched him with her mouth slightly open, a forkful of pie forgotten several inches above her plate. The rest of the guests appeared to show mild interest, what Maggie considered an average response to Detective Sousa's mysterious hints.

"It seems that Mr. Samson was not really Mr. Samson."

Lurline looked puzzled. "What?"

Manu and Makana wore similar baffled expressions.

"What is that supposed to mean?" Edie asked.

"The so-called Mr. Samson was really Stephen Stimpson. There are warrants out for him on the mainland, for bigamy."

"Bigamy!" Lurline and Manu both exclaimed.

All the blood had drained from Lurline's face, leaving her looking pale and sickly.

Maggie, now more than ever interested in everyone else's reaction, noticed several of the women also whiten. Judy, Rita and Iris all lost color at this extraordinary news. But so did Anna, Lydia and Bernie.

"Yes. I have to tell you that it's unlikely your marriage was a valid one," Detective Sousa told Lurline. "Our information shows that Mr. Stimpson has married four different women in the past twenty years — not counting your own marriage to him. There is no record of his ever obtaining a divorce. He changed his name slightly with each marriage to confuse the issue. Not too much, usually just a letter or two. If someone caught him on it, he could claim a typo. After he'd used the name for a while, he managed to obtain all the proper ID in the new spelling. He started out as Stephen Stimpson, then became Stephan — with an 'a' — Stimson — no 'p,' then Steve Simson — dropping the 't' this time, then Sonny Stamson, and finally Steven 'Sam' Samson."

As Detective Sousa's stunned audience tried to digest this information, Manu stood, went over behind Lurline's chair and placed his hand on her shoulder. Maggie watched with interest as Lurline reached up and covered his hand with her own. The move appeared so natural, Maggie doubted Lurline was even aware that she did it.

"Mr. Stimpson was very clever in the way he moved from one rich woman to another, taking much of her money along with him each time."

"But I don't have any money," Lurline exclaimed. She seemed more confused than ever.

"You have the Blue Lily Inn. There's no way to know if he knew exactly what your situation here was; perhaps he thought it was a larger establishment. In any event, at the time you and he married, it seems he was being actively pursued by the last woman he'd married." He paused, shaking his head as though realizing how bizarre his story sounded. "It gets a little confusing, trying to keep the various names and all the wives straight."

As though realizing they needed a little time to digest all this new information, Detective Sousa paused.

"I suspect that he married you, Ms. Ilima,

to get away from the mainland. As I said, he was being actively pursued by his most recent wife. She was from an old Arizona family with important connections. She was determined to make him pay for making such a fool out of her. With her family and their political friends behind her, she had local law enforcement and the FBI on his trail. He fled to Nevada and happened to meet you. He probably thought he could hide out here — a small town on an island in the middle of the Pacific must have struck him as the ideal hideout. It apparently did work for all these years. The question now is whether or not one of those former wives managed to track him down here, or if a local love interest decided to get back at him. It's always possible that one of his former wives came here on vacation and recognized him. He wasn't exactly keeping a low profile once he got here. And it wouldn't be the first time a victim decided to take things into her own hands."

"Amazing," Clare murmured.

"I knew there was something strange about that man," Edie said.

Detective Sousa turned his attention to Edie. "Strange how?"

"Never could put my finger on it," Edie admitted. "I thought it was just that I didn't approve of his lifestyle. Must have been a gut reaction."

A few of her friends nodded their agreement with this statement. "Women's intuition," Clare muttered.

"No wonder he never wanted to go to the mainland." Lurline's voice was thoughtful. "I had offers to do workshops in Utah and in Colorado and he always talked me out of going. He knew I would have insisted he come along with me."

Detective Sousa paused while Manu cleared the dessert plates and refilled coffee cups. Everyone had finished their pie when he raised his second point.

"Some other interesting information has come to my attention." He paused, looking around the table once again.

"Ms. Fleming, I understand you have a permit to carry a concealed weapon in Arizona."

"Yes, I do." Iris's tone was defensive.

Aha, Maggie thought. Could Iris have brought her gun with her? Ever since Michael mentioned the possibility, Maggie had wondered. She'd refrained from telling everyone what Michael had told her about putting a gun in checked airline luggage, thinking it better to let the others feel safer in their incorrect conclusions. But unless

Iris had brought the gun with her, what difference could it make if she had a permit for Arizona? Or was it the mere idea that she would know how to handle a gun?

Iris defended her right to own and carry a gun. "It can be dangerous showing houses to relative strangers. I feel safer with a pistol in my purse."

"I can understand that," Detective Sousa said. "But why did you feel a need to bring it with you on vacation?"

There was a collective gasp around the table as everyone stared at Iris. Maggie could almost hear a dozen minds thinking: she's been carrying a gun this whole time?

Detective Sousa continued. "The TSA tells me that you filled out a form declaring a gun in your checked luggage."

"I did." Maggie thought Iris looked extremely uncomfortable admitting it too. And well she might, with a recent murder by gunshot at a time when she was not only present but quite near the victim. Maggie still couldn't believe that Iris felt the need to bring a gun on her vacation. What could she have been thinking?

"However . . ."

Maggie watched as Iris shifted in her chair, as though trying to get comfortable. Her eyes too shifted several times to the left.

Maggie suddenly recalled a program she'd watched on cable that claimed a person who looked to the left before answering a question was probably lying.

"Someone stole the gun from my luggage," Iris declared. "It wasn't there when I unpacked."

"You didn't report it." Detective Sousa's tone was dry. This was no polite inquiry. He already knew the stolen gun had not been reported to the airline or to the authorities.

"I thought it must have been taken by the handlers in Phoenix. It's where they x-ray the checked luggage, so they would all be able to see there was a gun there. And I've seen those shows where the hidden cameras have caught the baggage handlers going through people's luggage, like they're shopping at Wal-Mart. I planned to report it when I got back."

Maggie frowned. While there was a certain amount of logic to Iris's argument, it was not the most rational deduction Maggie had ever heard.

"I have another question for you, Ms. Fleming." Detective Sousa's eyes remained steady on Iris's face. "It seems you also knew one of Mr. Samson's former wives."

"I did?"

Iris looked surprised. Though not nearly

as surprised as Clare. The latter's mouth was once again hanging open. A dull murmur hovered over the room as the others whispered comments among themselves.

"Four years ago, you were involved in a serious car accident outside Tucson with one Lily Nowak Simson."

"That's right. I was in the hospital for months. Lily died." Her voice cracked slightly on the final words. "But she didn't use Simson. She dropped it after her husband left her. In fact, very few people at the agency knew she'd ever been Mrs. Simson."

"I understand you and Lily were very close. They called you the 'two flowers' at the real estate agency where you both worked, said you two did everything together."

"We were very close. We used to go to Rocky Point together, for weekends. We were coming back when our car was hit." Iris's face saddened. She looked ready to cry.

"Did you somehow learn that Sam was the bigamous husband of your friend and decide to kill him?"

"What?" Iris was startled. "That's the most preposterous thing I ever heard. How could I possibly know that?"

"That is a large leap of logic," Edie said.

Iris gaped at Edie, shocked to have the resident curmudgeon taking her side.

Detective Sousa shrugged. "This whole case is illogical. We have a dead man who was wanted on the mainland, and who apparently had a lot of local people in a position to dislike him. Yet the only people with real opportunity to kill him — all of you" — he gestured around the table — "don't have good motives. Except, of course, for you and your family, Ms. Ilima." His deep brown eyes zeroed in on the three family members, pausing briefly on each face. "After watching you here this evening, however, I do believe that none of you" — he nodded at Lurline, Manu and Makana — "were aware of his dubious background."

There was a moment of silence as they all considered his words.

"Are you going to tell us not to leave town?" Clare asked. Maggie knew she was dying to hear those words. It would made her involvement *real,* showcase her as a person of interest in the investigation.

Detective Sousa chuckled. "No. I know where to find you if I have more questions. Ms. Ilima has given me a copy of your schedule. I believe you have another six days to your tour."

With that, Detective Sousa rose from the

table, thanked Manu for the delicious treat and excellent coffee, and strode from the room.

No one spoke until they heard the door close firmly behind him. Then, there was an explosion of sound as everyone wanted to comment on this news and what it might mean.

As soon as she could get away, Maggie searched out a quiet corner so she could call Michael, Victoria trailing quietly behind her. "It's three hours later in Arizona," Victoria reminded her, her soft voice full of concern.

Maggie waved aside her friend's anxiety. "It's Friday night," she said as she touched her finger to Michael's name in her contact list. "And it's not that late." She pressed the phone to her ear.

"Michael. I didn't wake you, did I?" Then she winked at Victoria. "Where are you? It's quite noisy there." She grinned. "Are you at a club?"

"Ma. I can't really hear you. Let me call you back. Five minutes."

And he disconnected.

While she waited for him to call back, Maggie grinned at Victoria.

"I'm sure I heard a woman's voice. And loud music. He might be at one of those clubs in Scottsdale. I know he sometimes visits. I've heard him mention it to his brothers."

"Is he still seeing Lauren, from white-collar crimes?"

Maggie nodded. "He asked her to join us for Christmas dinner."

"That sounds serious."

"Her family is in Colorado and she didn't get home this year. I guess she had a lot going on at work and couldn't get away."

"They seem to make a good couple. Perhaps you'll have a wedding coming up soon."

Maggie gave a wistful sigh. Michael was her last unmarried son — and her youngest — and she would love to see him settled. She also enjoyed teasing him about his dates, or lack of them. So her first words when he called back — with a noticeable lack of background noise — were, "Was that a female voice I heard earlier? Are you out clubbing with Lauren?"

But Michael wasn't going there. He spoke as though she had not said anything at all.

"So, what's up that you're calling so late?" Then his voice rose enough in volume that Victoria clearly heard him. "Did someone else die?"

Michael muttered something Maggie

preferred not to hear. Just as well she couldn't quite make it out.

"No, of course not. Why would anyone else be killed?" She offered an exasperated look to Victoria. "I told you last time, this was something personal. Someone targeted Sam particularly, and I doubt there will be any other murders." She paused, then decided to add, "And it's not late here. We've just finished dinner."

"So why the call? Is anything wrong?"

"Why must something be wrong for me to call? Honestly." She added the last word under her breath, and Victoria patted her arm in sympathy.

When Michael didn't respond to what he recognized as a rhetorical question, she continued.

"Michael, Detective Sousa was here this evening. They've discovered that Sam was actually someone named Stephen Stimpson who is wanted on the mainland — for bigamy. He changed his name slightly each time he married so he went through several different names — Stimpson to Stimson without the 'p,' then Simson, Stamson and finally Samson. He used different forms and spellings of Stephen — Steve, Stephan. Nicknames like Sonny and Sam for Samson. It turns out Lurline's marriage was never valid."

"Hmmm." Michael took a moment to digest this. Maggie also imagined him making notes of the various names. "If she knew about that, it could be a good motive for murder."

"You don't think she would just be relieved that they were never married?" Maggie countered. "Save her the cost of a divorce?"

"Maybe." Michael considered that for a brief moment. "I don't know. It still strikes me as a possible motive. She could be mad at being taken in all these years. Does she have a temper?"

"Not that I've seen. But she admits to a passionate relationship with Sam and to a big fight on New Year's Eve. Their friends said they fought all the time. In public too."

"I know you don't want to hear it, Ma, but she sounds like a good suspect." He could hear her heavy sigh.

And I didn't even tell him about the missing gun or that New Year's Eve argument, Maggie thought.

"There's something else." Maggie paused, wondering if Michael was going to get upset about this new detail and demand once more that she return home. "It seems Iris Fleming was a good friend of one of Sam's ex-wives. They worked together at a Tucson real estate office and were involved in a bad accident, coming back from a weekend in Rocky Point. The ex-wife died — Lily Nowak Simson. Do you think you could find out about that accident?"

"When was it?"

"Four years ago, he said."

"Okay. I'll see what I can do. Don't get your hopes up. Tucson isn't even in the same county, so I don't know if I'll be able to get any information, especially on an old traffic accident."

"Michael . . ."

"Yes?"

"Mahalo." In Hilo, Maggie smiled. "That's 'thank you' in Hawaiian. We learned it from Lurline."

"Good night, Ma."

She couldn't hear it, of course, but Maggie was sure Michael smiled.

Chapter 22

Quilt tour, day four. Friday, after dinner.

Her call completed, Maggie and Victoria joined the others gathered in the large living room of the inn. The pleasant afternoon had turned into a rainy night and the open windows were soon closed. Sweaters were fetched from upstairs rooms to counter the damp chill. The two local women decided on excursions with their friends, Judy to take Lydia to a club Josh would never agree to visit, Rita and Bernie to visit relatives. Maggie hoped Judy and Lydia would remember to designate a driver. Lurline excused herself to see to some paperwork, and Iris pleaded a headache and escaped to her room.

The remaining women were the core group of the St. Rose Quilting Bee and they settled happily into the comfortable chairs and sofas grouped around the inn's main room. Running across the entire front of the house, the room had an old-fashioned feel, with crocheted doilies on the tables and dark, heavy pieces of furniture. Lurline had told them the style was called territorial, reminiscent of the early days of the twentieth century when Hawai'i was a territory of the United States. "A lot of this goes back to my grandparents' day here," she told them. Lurline's modern touch was the addition of numerous lamps, the type that offered illumination the most like natural light and that worked best for stitching.

Maggie and Victoria sat side by side on a love seat, Clare and Anna on an adjacent sofa, and Theresa, Anna and Edie on several overstuffed chairs close by. Each woman had her own lamp to illuminate her needlework.

"Wouldn't a fire be nice?" Anna asked as she took a pillow top from her bag. She had completed the appliqué on the *ulu* pattern they received on the first day and cut out a simple ti leaf as her first original project. Lurline had told them ti leaf plants were often planted near the entrance of a house, because they were considered lucky. So Anna decided that would be her second project.

Everyone agreed that a fire would feel good.

"It is a bit chilly with the rain, isn't it?" Victoria said. "I do enjoy a fire. It's one thing I miss in my condo."

Edie however, objected. "Have you noticed how old this house is? And it's all wood. A fire would be tremendously dangerous."

"Oh, for goodness sakes, Edie," Louise said. "Anna just meant she would enjoy sitting in front of a fire in a fireplace. And I agree, a little heat would be nice."

Edie sniffed.

"Let me close this window," Theresa said, rising to follow through on her suggestion and closing the last of the open windows.

"What do you make of that story about Iris?" Clare asked.

No one was surprised that Clare was back to her favorite topic.

"It's such a coincidence," Maggie said. "And in mystery books the detective always says they don't believe in coincidences. Michael has told me that he agrees with that, by the way. He says there are no coincidences."

"Were you just talking to him?" Clare said.

"Yes. I asked if he could find out about that accident. It's a tremendous coincidence, don't you think?"

"I wonder why Iris never told us about

it," Anna said.

"She said she wanted to make a fresh start, that's why she moved from Tucson," Victoria replied.

"That didn't keep her from telling us about her travel agency," Theresa commented.

"Or ranting about her ex-husband," Edie added.

"Though if you think about it, she never really provided any information about her ex," Maggie said.

"Or about the travel agency," Victoria pointed out. "She always just said she had one, and she lost it because of her sleaze of an ex-husband. She never gave any specifics."

"I'd noticed the telltale scars from plastic surgery," Louise told them. "I could tell she'd had an excellent surgeon, but if you know where to look the signs are there. I always thought she was just vain, and probably older than she admitted. But if she was in the hospital for months, it must have been done because of injuries from a very serious injury accident."

"Imagine her being friends with Sam's ex-wife." Clare shook her head, still surprised about this new information.

"Not an ex-wife, Clare. Not if he never

bothered with divorces," Edie said.

"So were they all wives of a sort?" Anna asked.

"It's like that TV program, *Big Love*. Or *Sister Wives*." Clare nodded sagely.

"Oh, it's not like that at all." Edie dismissed Clare with a heavy click of her tongue. "Those are polygamous unions, which are a whole different thing. There's usually some heavy religious basis for the participants."

"Oh." Clare hung her head, staring meekly at her stitching.

"That's not what Sam did at all, is it?" Victoria said. "He was just a con man." She shook her head, sad to have to give him such a label.

"Well, none of the marriages after the first one were legal, were they?" Theresa said. "So I don't know if you could call any of those women wives *or* ex-wives."

"Remember when we first talked about Sam and how little Lurline and Makana knew about him? You said he might have come here to hide out, Clare," Maggie said. "Hiding in plain sight, you said."

"And Judy suggested he was running from an old girlfriend or an ex-wife," Victoria added.

"And it turns out you were both right,"

Maggie finished.

Clare looked smugly satisfied at this compliment, and she stitched placidly for a few minutes. Her original piece was also a pillow top. She had done a cattleya orchid and had found a lovely purple fabric for the snowflake-style design. She'd paired that with a yellow-gold background for a very striking piece.

After a few minutes, however, she couldn't resist returning to the topic of Iris.

"Detective Sousa said it was a real bad accident. What if they got them mixed up?" Clare said slowly. She lay her stitching in her lap, ignoring it as her voice grew more excited at the thought. "Remember those teenage girls, returning to the valley after a trip to Disneyland? They identified them incorrectly and pronounced the wrong person dead. They didn't find out until the second girl woke up from her coma. And her friend's parents had been sitting there with her for two days."

"I remember that," Anna said. "Terrible thing."

"Maybe Iris is really the other woman, the one who was married to Sam." Clare's voice grew more excited with each word. "And Iris was the woman who died in the accident."

"That would actually make sense," Victoria said. "At least as far as explaining what happened with her travel agency. From what Detective Sousa said, Sam would marry a woman with money, then take as much as he could and decamp."

"Don't be silly." Edie made it plain that she didn't like Clare's conjecture. "That kind of mix-up sounds like the plot of a second-rate movie."

"But there was that mistake with the young women coming home from Disneyland. I remember it very well," Anna said. "I felt so sorry for the two sets of parents. Still, if there was a mix-up, wouldn't Iris have corrected them when she woke up?" She was obviously confused by Clare's theory. "That's what happened in the real case."

"The thing is, there are a lot of psychological issues involved with a really serious accident." Louise knotted off her thread and reached into her bag for the spool. "She may have been too injured in the accident to say anything for some time. And temporary amnesia is a common aftereffect of trauma."

"Well, that would make it all simple, wouldn't it?" Theresa mused. "If Iris was really one of Sam's wives, then she's probably the one who killed him. Could almost be justifiable homicide, wouldn't you think?"

But most of the others felt this theory far-fetched and didn't hesitate to say so.

"But what about the gun?" Anna asked. "Iris may have tried to bring one, but she said it was stolen."

"Oh, you're so naive," Edie said, shaking her head. In her hands she was creating a beautiful appliqué of a king protea. She wasn't using the snowflake technique, but had created her flower with a careful selection of green, pink and lavender fabrics. "That story stank like day-old fish."

"So you don't believe her gun was stolen?"

"Of course not."

"I thought that story sounded false too," Maggie admitted. "It was just too pat."

"That's true," Victoria said. "What I don't understand is why she would bother. If she didn't kill him, it makes more sense to produce the gun and say, 'Here it is. It was not the murder weapon.' "

"Good point," Maggie said.

"But if she thinks she's a suspect . . . not everyone thinks rationally when confronted with murder," Louise said.

"Has she acted any differently since the murder?" Maggie asked. She directed the question toward Edie, who was rooming with Iris. "One of the things Detective Sousa mentioned in our first interview was that people often behave differently when they have committed a murder and are trying to cover it up."

Edie considered. "Hmm. I've always thought Iris was a little odd."

"Odd how?" Clare asked.

"I'm not really sure. It's just that I've always felt like she was hiding something. I suppose she's just more private than some other people, but that's the impression I've gotten. And now, it turns out she *has* been hiding something all these years," Edie reminded them. "Something big."

"That you thought was rubbish," Maggie reminded her.

"I don't mean the ID thing," Edie said. "We don't know if that happened."

"But it could have," Clare insisted.

Edie shrugged. "I meant she's never told us about that accident in her past. And it sounded like a very serious accident, where she must have had a lot of surgery afterward. And she's never talked about this Lily, who was supposed to be such a great friend of hers."

There were some nods of agreement. It was odd that she'd never mentioned such a thing, as they often talked about health issues. All of the Bee members were over the age of fifty — some well past — so there were often serious health problems to investigate and discuss.

"Well, I can understand not wanting to talk about Lily," Victoria said. "That would be a painful episode in her life, and she might not want to discuss it with casual acquaintances like those of us in the Quilting Bee."

But Edie wasn't finished.

"She's been odd here too, when we're in our room," Edie continued. "Kind of secretive, maybe. Like she didn't want me to see her underwear or something. I thought it strange. We're all women. We all wear the same kind of underwear. Unless she brought along thongs or something. A woman her age and shape *should* be embarrassed about that." Edie shook her head, indicating her disgust at such notions.

"Was she any different the night of the luau?" Maggie persisted. "Or the day after?"

"She did seem nervous when all the police arrived on Thursday," Louise said.

"Oh, come on now, everyone was nervous then," Edie said. "None of us is used to this kind of thing. Even you, Clare. You might find it all terribly exciting, but you have to admit you must get nervous."

Clare nodded, a little embarrassed to learn she was so transparent.

Edie laid her sewing in her lap for a moment while she cast back in her mind. "Iris was definitely nervous about the police, but I don't think she was much different than anyone else. Judy was much worse."

"Judy is rather high-strung," Louise commented.

"As we've learned, Judy has issues of her own," Maggie said.

"You know, now that I think about it, Iris was acting rather oddly on the boat that night after the luau." Edie's expression was thoughtful. "I walked up to her at one point, when she was all alone at the other side of the rail — the side away from the view. I wondered if she felt all right. She had seemed fond of Sam, and I didn't want her to be brooding alone. I startled her, badly. She jumped about a foot and fumbled her purse, dropping things all over the deck. But she recovered well enough. Told me she thought she heard her phone ringing, then she couldn't find it in her purse. She has been carrying that great big bag around. I know those huge purses are fashionable, but it's like taking a small suitcase everywhere. It's no wonder she couldn't find her phone."

"It would be easy enough to hide a gun in

that huge bag of hers, wouldn't it?" Louise said.

"Did you know Iris had a concealed weapon permit?" Theresa asked.

"Oh, yes," Edie admitted. "I saw a gun in her purse one morning at the Quilting Bee and I asked her about it. She said it was because it was dangerous sitting alone for an open house. And since I know there have been some incidents in Scottsdale in the past, I thought that sounded like a darned good reason."

"Yeah, but bringing it with her on vacation? That doesn't make sense," Louise said.

"Maybe she just feels safer when she has it with her," Anna suggested.

"She does always say that a woman alone can't be too careful," Clare said.

"Did you ever notice that gun in your room, Edie? If it wasn't stolen in Phoenix, that is." Maggie looked over at Edie.

"No. I think I would remember seeing a gun in my bedroom. And you would have heard me talking to her about it too. I wouldn't have wanted to sleep in the same room as a firearm, especially a loaded one."

"She carries a loaded gun around in her purse?" Anna sounded shocked.

"Of course." Edie's tone was dismissive. "What good is a gun if it isn't loaded?"

"Does anyone think Iris could have shot Sam?" Clare asked.

Edie gave this careful consideration. It wasn't a simple yes-or-no question. "There's a hard side to Iris. I think she could maybe get to that point, but not in a cold, dispassionate way. There would have to be a deep connection, and even if Sam was her ex-husband — which I still don't think is so — I don't know if there was that kind of real depth. After all, we haven't known Iris for too long. She's only been coming to the Bee for a year, and she doesn't come every day."

"What do we really know about her?" Maggie asked the room at large.

"Pretty much only what we've just said here tonight," Victoria said. "While she talks a great deal during quilting sessions, she really doesn't say much about herself."

"That's exactly what I told Michael," Maggie said, happy to hear her friend felt the same way. She was feeling pretty good about her wall hanging too. The *obake* anthurium looked good. It wasn't as striking as Edie's king protea of course, but she was aiming for a traditional Hawaiian look.

"Your anthurium design looks very good," Victoria said.

Edie agreed. "I have to try one of those snowflake designs too. But I'm enjoying this

271

traditional appliqué. Aren't the proteas the most interesting flower?"

She looked proudly at her stitching before folding it carefully. "I'm going to call it an early night. We have the trip around downtown Hilo tomorrow and I want to be rested."

It didn't take long for the others to follow. No one knew how much walking would be involved in exploring downtown Hilo, so the general consensus was to get as much rest as possible.

Maggie sat up stitching for a while after getting ready for bed. Putting aside her *obake* appliqué, she quilted her *ulu* pillow top while she tried to get all the people, events and possibilities sorted out in her mind. But although she managed to finish quilting all around her appliqué design, she wasn't able to come to any conclusions about what had actually happened at the luau. There were still some vital missing pieces to the puzzle, of that she was certain.

CHAPTER 23

Quilt tour, day five. Saturday. Historic downtown Hilo.

On Saturday morning, Manu dropped the tour group off at the farmers' market in "historic downtown Hilo." The women were free to explore the downtown area until the bus returned for them at two o'clock.

Maggie, Victoria and Edie walked quickly through the stalls at the farmers' market. Tables overflowed with selections of fruits and vegetables of all kinds. There were people selling breads and different kinds of jam. There were cold drinks and frozen treats. There were pots and pails and vases of plants and cut flowers, some already prepared to take to the graveyard and set atop a grave.

"This is quite the sight," Victoria said. "But I must admit a quick pass is enough for me."

"Me too," Maggie agreed. "The flowers

are gorgeous, though, aren't they?"

"They are," Edie said. "But this isn't where I want to spend my money. Now if I lived here in town, I'd love to shop for some of this fresh produce. Did you see the beautiful avocadoes and bananas? Some of these other booths, though" — she threw her arm wide, encompassing the area across the street from the main produce booths — "remind me of the swap meet they used to have at the dog track in Phoenix."

Neither Maggie nor Victoria commented on that last, but they too did not want to spend too much time browsing here, even though the items for sale were very interesting. They had conferred among themselves as to the identity of several exotic fruit items, completely baffled by a spiny red fruit on offer at many of the tables. "Rambutan," a seller informed them. It was apparently not an uncommon question from people so obviously not local. "It like lychee," the seller added helpfully, though none of them knew what that was, either.

"Let's go on to that fabric store Lurline told us about," Maggie suggested.

"Now that I can get excited about," Edie said.

The three women trotted quickly through the rows of tables heavily laden with fresh produce to what Lurline had called Front Street, though Maggie noticed that the street signs read Kamehameha Avenue. The town's main street, it had a long row of stores lining one side of the street, many with tall false fronts reminiscent of a movie set. The stores stretched out from the area where the farmers' market was located and into the near distance. The opposite side of the street contained no buildings at all, just parking lots, a park with an old-fashioned bandstand, and a bus depot. The women knew that beyond those was an amazing arc of black sand, and then the blue Pacific.

When they first saw the bay from the bus, Anna had been amazed all over again at the long stretch of black sand. "It reminds you of the lava running into the sea, doesn't it?" she'd said. "It certainly makes you aware that this whole area came from black lava."

"It reminds you that we aren't all that far from an erupting volcano," Edie had retorted.

Once they had scouted out the "Front Street" area and determined how easy it would be to find their way around, the three women grinned like kids playing hooky and hurried up the sidewalk. The other tour members were still strolling about the farmers' market, which included much more than the fresh fruits and vegetables Maggie and the others had explored. On the opposite side of the street, there was another wide stretch of tents holding clothing, furniture, jewelry, and numerous other items. Still, the siren call of fabric beckoned, and they strolled down the street. Lurline had said the fabric store was a couple of blocks away.

"It was quite forward thinking of them to only build on one side of the street like this," Victoria said. "I assume they wanted to have the lovely view, and that's not the kind of thing men usually considered in the late nineteenth or early twentieth century."

"They didn't," Edie said. "Hilo did have stores and buildings on both sides of the street at one time. But there was a big tsunami back in nineteen forty-six — on April first, as a matter of fact — and it destroyed most of the buildings on the ocean side. After that they decided not to rebuild on that side of the street."

Maggie and Victoria both stared at Edie, startled at this guidebook-like knowledge.

Edie, looking slightly sheepish, shrugged. "I like to research an area before I visit. I want to learn as much as I can so that I can appreciate what the area has to offer. Hilo is a very interesting town and has had its ups and downs recently. Another tsunami in nineteen sixty caused tremendous destruction. Quite a few people died. That whole area where the farmers' market is located was cleared of buildings by the tsunami that year and never rebuilt."

All three of them looked back the way they'd come.

"Fascinating," said Victoria. As a former history teacher, she enjoyed hearing this kind of information.

"There's a tsunami museum in an old bank building between the fabric store and the bookstore," Edie told them. "I wouldn't mind seeing it."

"I'd enjoy that myself," Victoria said. "Let's stop in when we reach it."

It didn't take long to reach the fabric store described on their tour schedule. Maggie and Victoria were delighted to see a group of teenage girls taking a class at the back of the store. As women of "a certain age," they loved seeing young people becoming interested in their favorite hobby.

All three women were even happier to see the fine selection of fabric and patterns.

"Look at these Hawaiian prints," Victoria said, pulling out a bolt of fabric featuring petroglyphs, then a second with various colorful tropical flowers.

"I love these patterns that combine appliqué and sashiko embroidery." Maggie gestured to a rack of patterns on display beside a wall quilt. The quilt background was a specially dyed blue-green that mimicked the colors of the ocean. A purple orchid lei floated on "waves" worked in traditional patterns of sashiko, a Japanese style of embroidery using patterns created with rows of running stitches.

A tiny, middle-aged Japanese woman approached, a friendly smile on her face. "Isn't that lovely? Do you know the superstition about throwing your lei out when you sail away from the islands?"

Victoria replied, "I believe that passengers on the cruise ships throw out their leis as they leave, and if the lei floats back toward the island, it means you will return to visit again."

"Yes, that's it." The woman — her nametag said "Thelma" — smiled. "These patterns with the sashiko embroidery are created by a local quilt artist. We sell the patterns, but we also have some kits available with the specially dyed fabrics. Most people want to get the same effect as far as the water and the flower petals."

"I love it," Maggie said. "I'm definitely

getting the kit. The shade of blue in the background will be worth the price of the kit, I'm sure."

Thelma retrieved one of the kits from the shelf and handed it to Maggie. "Are you visiting from the mainland?"

"We're here on a quilt tour," Maggie said.

"A quilt tour?" Thelma seemed bemused by the term.

"We're at the Blue Lily Bed and Breakfast," Maggie said. "We've seen some wonderful Hawaiian quilts and a lot of the local sights. Plus we've had lessons in making and designing Hawaiian quilts. Perhaps you know Lurline?"

"Of course." Thelma's eyes clouded momentarily. "Terrible thing what happened to Sam."

"Yes. We were all there when it happened, you know."

"No." Her expressive face showed each reaction as it moved from shock to sympathy.

"Oh, yes," Edie said. "They took us to the luau at the resort so we could enjoy the local food and entertainment. It was a wonderful program."

"But how awful for you, to have Sam murdered there. My daughter works at the luaus. All the servers, they're real upset in

279

case they have to stop having the luaus because of what happened to Sam. It's good money they make working those."

"Oh, she won't need to worry," Edie assured her. "People are ghouls. They will probably want to attend more than ever, now that there's that kind of excitement attached to it. And as long as they know it wasn't the food that killed him."

"Oh, you think so?" Thelma seemed relieved to hear this view of events. "Maybe I call my daughter later — let her know what you think." She nodded firmly, as though reminding herself to do this later. Then she turned to Maggie.

"How is Lurline?" she asked.

Maggie was glad to see that Thelma was more interested in her friend than in gossiping about what had happened to Sam. But Maggie had to wonder if she could steer her toward some local gossip about the couple. Something that could provide a little insight into the people involved and help them locate a viable suspect. She exchanged a look with Victoria, who seemed to know exactly what Maggie was thinking. Unfortunately, Edie also knew and blundered in with her question first — her rather inappropriate question, Maggie thought.

"Were they terribly in love?" Edie asked.

"We were only at the inn for a day and a half when it happened, and it was hard to get a reading on the two of them."

Maggie sighed as Thelma suddenly became very busy measuring out fabric for Victoria.

"It's awfully hard on Lurline, Sam's death," Maggie said. "You know of course that the spouse is always the prime suspect when someone is murdered."

"They suspect Lurline?" Thelma seemed truly surprised. But surely she must have realized . . .

Maggie gave herself a mental head shake. Not everyone was as interested in mysteries as she and her quilting friends. Perhaps such information wasn't as widely known as she assumed.

"The police do seem focused on Lurline," Edie said. "They searched the bed-and-breakfast, you know. All the guest rooms too. They didn't tell us beforehand, but we saw all the police vehicles as we were leaving on Thursday, and I could tell someone had rifled through my drawers."

"I heard about that," Thelma admitted.

Maggie and Victoria exchanged another look. Someone had mentioned that Hilo was a small town despite it being the second largest city in the state. It appeared to be true.

"So you don't think Lurline would kill Sam?" Edie asked.

Victoria gasped at the audacity of the question. But Thelma replied as though it wasn't terribly rude. Perhaps tourists often asked rude questions, Maggie thought. She'd have to ask Lurline sometime.

"Oh, no. Lurline would never kill somebody. She's a gentle soul, even though she and Sam fought a lot. She's a passionate person, and passionate people feel things deeply. Intensely. There was a lot of passion between Lurline and Sam. You couldn't always see it, but sometimes, yeah, they got real romantic." She laughed. "I remember seeing them making out one time, during a Christmas party. It was a few years ago. They were acting like a couple of teenagers. A lot of us were jealous. Pretty special, yeah, to feel like that at their age."

"Love and hate are two sides of the same emotion," Victoria observed. "It's not surprising that two passionate people would show those extremes. Funny to think of Sam that way though. He seemed a little cold to me."

"Yeah." Thelma's eyes lost the amusement that had filled them at her memory of Lurline and Sam at the party. "Sometimes she did sound like she hated him."

"We heard this morning that Makana confessed to killing Sam." Maggie watched carefully to see what Thelma thought of this new development.

But Thelma didn't seem surprised to hear about the confession. Maggie suspected the small town grapevine again.

"Yeah, my cousin cleans at the police station. She was there when Makana came in, all emotional and said it was her did it."

Maggie almost smiled to hear her suspicion confirmed.

"Now her. She has a temper, that one." Thelma shook her head in disapproval.

"Really? Makana?" Victoria couldn't hide her surprise. "She hasn't shown any sign of that in front of us. She seems very upset about her family being under suspicion. And very concerned for Lurline."

"Makana has always been a drama queen. But she's smart too. She maybe confessed to throw the police off."

Maggie found this comment fascinating. She, Victoria and Edie all exchanged looks. No doubt they too were thinking that none of them had considered that angle. Maggie would have liked to continue the conversation with Thelma, but in the next few minutes the rest of the tour group filtered into the store. The long, narrow space became extremely crowded. No doubt Thelma was happy about that, but it wasn't the most comfortable way to shop as far as Maggie was concerned.

As soon as she saw Maggie and Victoria, Clare rushed over, an open bag in her hand. "Look at this," she told them, pulling out a lovely Japanese print fabric. "A little store back there had kimono fabric. *Real* kimono fabric, the kind that's only twenty-eight inches wide. Gorgeous stuff. I had to get some. I would have liked to get more, but it's so expensive."

Victoria reached into the bag to feel the cotton fabric. It was a small bundle, no more than a yard and a half. "Nice," she said, as the soft material slid between her fingers. "It will be lovely to quilt on."

"And you'll never believe it! The owner knew Sam!" Clare exclaimed.

"I'm beginning to think everyone in this town knows everyone else," Victoria remarked.

Thelma heard her and laughed. "Seems like, sometimes, but not quite. Some people say that everyone is related too," she added with a chuckle. "You see the tall young woman cutting fabric? With the red highlights in her hair?"

They all peered over toward the cutting

table, then nodded. Maggie had wondered about those red streaks in Makana's beautiful hair. She'd thought it a shame she'd bleached her lovely dark hair that way, but it must be a local fashion among the younger women.

"That's Lurline's niece." Thelma lowered her voice. "Some people say Sam was trying to make time with her. She's pretty, yeah?"

"Is she married?" Edie asked.

Thelma clicked her tongue. "Nah. These young people don't get married nowadays. I have two grandchildren, and my son still not married." She heaved a heavy sigh.

Victoria commiserated with her over her son's lack of commitment as they walked over to the register. Maggie paid for her quilt pattern and fabric kit; Edie and Victoria followed with their fabric and pattern selections. The voluble Thelma continued to speak.

"Alana's not married." She nodded toward the young woman so there would be no question to whom she referred. "But she lives with her boyfriend and his mother, out Keaau way. He's a scary guy, too — big Samoan. Lots of hair. Lots of tats. Rides around in one of those trucks with the giant tires."

The women exchanged a knowing glance.

This sounded like a viable suspect. Their hopeful look lasted less than a minute.

"We would have remembered someone like that approaching our table at the luau," Edie said. "He sounds quite noticeable."

"Oh, yeah, he is," Thelma said with a grin. "He was probably there, though. He dances — *da kine* Samoan fire dance."

They all remembered the fire dance. Not only was the dance impressive, so was the man performing. He was tall, wide and muscular, with long hair and many native tattoos — which did sound like Thelma's description of Alana's boyfriend. They would definitely have remembered if he had approached their table at any point during the evening.

"The person who shot Sam had to get up close and personal," Edie said.

"That's right. None of us knew he'd been shot. He just didn't get up from the table when it was time to go. No one saw any blood. Not even the EMT who came with the ambulance and checked him," Maggie said.

Thelma's eyes widened. "Wow. You think you would know if someone was shot right in front of you. Weird kine stuff, yeah?"

As they prepared to leave, Clare called out to them. "Wait up. I'm almost done."

She hurried to pay for her shopping so she could join them as they left for the bookstore. "I can't wait to see if they have any mysteries with local settings," she said.

"We may stop at a tsunami museum Edie read about," Victoria told her, explaining about Edie's online foray into local history.

But when they reached the former bank building that housed the museum, Clare decided against going inside. She went along to the bookstore alone, anxious to check out their selection of mysteries. Maggie suspected that she hoped to find one where the victim was thrown into a volcano.

By the time the others joined Clare at the bookstore, she had an armful of books already selected, only a few of them mysteries.

"They have wonderful books here," she told them, her enthusiasm spilling over. "I have some books with Hawaiian quilt pillow patterns, and some on local legends. And this really nice one with local flowers." She held up a thin book with a lovely orchid on the cover. "I asked the woman at the desk for some help, and you'll never guess what her name is!"

Maggie looked over at the desk, where a pretty brown-skinned woman with rather unlikely blonde hair was working the register. Maggie could see that she wore a nametag but, from ten feet away, could not read it.

It didn't matter. Clare didn't wait for her to ask — or to guess.

"Her name is Kate Ilima. She's Manu's sister-in-law; she's married to his younger brother."

Maggie had to laugh. "Unbelievable," she said, shaking her head. It really was a small town. And, as Thelma had just suggested, everyone seemed to be related to everyone else.

"We should ask her about Manu," Edie said. "See if he has a temper."

"But he's such a sweetheart," Clare said.

"This wasn't a crime of passion," Victoria said. "Someone planned it and planned it carefully. It wasn't a case of the murderer losing his or her temper and lashing out. Whoever did it had to plan to get a gun, hide it, then get close enough to discharge it during the noisiest part of the program. It was a cold and calculated plan."

Victoria's words had a sobering effect. For a moment they all stood together, thinking over her observation.

Then Maggie spoke. "Victoria is right. This crime was very carefully planned. But that doesn't mean we can't find out about Manu. Just for our own information. We don't know the people here the way we knew all those involved in the crimes we looked into in Scottsdale. Manu is a sweetheart when he's around us, but he's probably on his best behavior then too. After all, we're paying guests in his bed-and-breakfast, and he's being the gracious host. It's quite possible that he isn't the teddy bear he seems. Characteristics like a bad temper are often inherited traits, and Thelma said that Makana has a bad one. Still, I don't know how the information will help us. It will just be another piece of the puzzle for now."

For a moment Clare looked puzzled herself. "Thelma?" she inquired.

"The little Japanese woman at the fabric store," Edie said. "Didn't you notice her nametag?"

They waited to approach Ms. Ilima until they had all chosen their books. The store had a wonderful selection of books on all topics Hawaiian, including quilting and crafts. There was a huge selection of Hawaiian-themed picture books, which drew the grandmothers among them. Also shelves of local cookbooks, music and mythology.

All the other members of their tour group had joined them at the bookstore by then. Theresa and Judy almost got into a fight over the last copy of a lovely quilting book, until Maggie suggested Judy ask them to order a copy of the book for her since she lived in town.

Finally, it was time for Maggie to pay for her selections. She glanced casually at the woman's nametag, as though just noticing it. "Ilima," she said. "Are you related to Manu and Makana?"

Ms. Ilima wasn't surprised at the question. "You must be the group from Arizona at the bed-and-breakfast. Manu was really looking forward to your visit. This is usually a real down time for them." She shook her head. "Terrible about Sam. How is Manu holding up?"

"Good. He's a great cook. We're all delighted with the food."

"His brother is a good cook too — my husband. Their mother taught them good, yeah?"

"Manu is such a sweetheart. How did he manage not to lose his temper around Sam? It's so obvious that he's still in love with Lurline, and he had to see Sam flirting with all their guests."

"And any other woman he met," Kate

mumbled. She shook her head. "That Sam was a charmer, but I'm real glad *I* didn't marry him." She finished scanning Maggie's card and handed it back to her. "Manu is very laid back. He never gets mad. He really is sweet like he seems. My husband too. That family is all laid back kine people. Not like mine," she added with a laugh. "We lose our temper fast and loud, but we forgive fast too."

"We heard Makana has a temper," Edie commented.

"Oh, not too bad. Gets that from Lurline. Lurline can really let go." She handed over Maggie's package. "I heard about her confession. And then Lurline and Manu went confess too. One bunch *lolos.*"

It appeared to be unanimous now — everyone considered the confessions the acts of crazy people.

Chapter 24

Quilt tour, day five. Saturday, noon.

For their day trip into "historic downtown Hilo," the tour schedule designated "lunch on your own." So Maggie, Victoria, Anna, Clare, Louise, Edie and Theresa chose a cozy Chinese restaurant that served food family style. They had to pull several of the tiny tables together in order to squeeze all of the Quilting Bee around it, but with the help of the friendly staff, they soon had the tables adjusted and their order in.

"Where do you suppose the others have gotten to?" Anna asked.

"Bernie and Rita had planned to visit relatives today," Clare said. "And I heard Judy say something about a Japanese restaurant she's been dying to try. I'm sure she took Lydia and Iris there."

"I get the impression that Josh is a real homebody when he's not at work," Maggie said, her tone dry.

"And Judy is anxious to get out and about," Victoria said. "No doubt about that. It's nice that she's getting to visit these places now with Lydia and Iris."

"She may realize that all these spots she's been so anxious to visit aren't what she thought," Maggie said.

Louise nodded. "She's been bored, and dreaming that going here and there is going to change everything. I hope she's not too disappointed when she discovers that it won't."

"Perhaps having been to the clubs and restaurants, though, she'll be more content to stay at home and begin to quilt," Maggie suggested.

"Or work on her art," Victoria suggested. "Her drawings are really lovely, don't you think? I hope she'll be able to translate some of them into fabric."

"I wonder how she and Josh got along when they lived in Scottsdale," Anna wondered.

"Judy had friends there, like Lydia," Louise said. "She could do things with the girls, so she wouldn't have felt so isolated. And they have a son in Phoenix, don't they, Clare?"

"Yes," Clare agreed. "She told me he's finishing his degree at ASU next year. I think she really misses him."

Louise nodded. "It's a different atmosphere here. She doesn't fit in with the locals, and it doesn't look like she's managed to find a group of other mainland women to socialize with."

"She seems to be enjoying herself with Lydia and Iris," Victoria said. "I hope she won't be more lost than ever when we leave."

Louise nodded. "That could be a real problem. But we saw her assert herself with Josh, so we'll have to hope she continues to do so. Mainly, she has to stop feeling sorry for herself and find some activity she likes to keep her busy while Josh is at work."

The conversation ended as the waitress arrived with their food. They spent some time passing bowls and making their choices, but once everyone was served, they were ready to discuss their morning.

"Can you believe how everyone here seems to know everyone else?" Anna seemed amazed by the number of people they had met who knew Lurline and her family.

"Well, many of the people we've met have something to do with sewing or fabric," Maggie said, "so it's not surprising they might know one another."

"Can you believe how they're all related?"

Theresa said. She found that much more of a surprise than the fact that so many of the locals were acquainted.

"It's a small town," Maggie said. "Remember, everyone has been telling us that, and this morning really proved it."

"So, let's compare notes," Clare said eagerly. "Maybe one of the people we talked to will provide the clue we need."

Maggie appeared skeptical, but did not discourage Clare. However, she felt they needed a lot more than "a" clue, if they hoped to solve this murder.

"Why don't you start, Clare," Victoria said. "You went into the store that sold the Japanese kimono fabric. We missed that one."

"Well . . ." Clare finished chewing a piece of broccoli, swallowing quickly. "While I tried to decide which fabric to get, I told the woman about our tour and where we were staying. She was the owner of the store," she added for no particular reason before forking another bite into her mouth.

Edie almost rolled her eyes at this non sequitur and the ensuing wait while Clare chewed and swallowed. A sharp look from Maggie kept Edie from deploring the waste of time. After all, Maggie thought, they were on vacation. There was no hurry. The bus wasn't picking them up until mid-afternoon.

As soon as she finished swallowing, Clare began to speak. "Right away, she said it was a real shame about Sam. She liked him, called him a fun guy. And" — she paused, trying to create a dramatic moment for what she thought was her big news — "she said he did the club scene here. Without Lurline."

Her big news, however, dropped like a lead balloon. No one was surprised.

"There's a club scene here?" Theresa asked, that being the one issue in Clare's news that struck her as unexpected. "It's so much like a country town, I wouldn't have guessed that there's a club scene."

"Remember, Judy took Lydia out to a club last night," Victoria reminded her.

"I forgot," Theresa mumbled.

"They might have something on a small scale," Edie remarked. "I doubt if they have clubs that could rival those in Scottsdale. It would be a completely different kind of thing here." Scottsdale was well known for its trendy clubs, which attracted celebrities from the sports and entertainment worlds.

Clare returned to her story. "The store owner wasn't a local woman. At least not originally. I asked if she was from the mainland, and she was — from Oakland,

California. She said she's lived in Hilo for eight years now."

"That's certainly interesting, but not exactly a surprise," Maggie said. "We already knew that Sam liked to drink, and we know he played around. It makes sense that he would try to find other people with similar tastes. And it makes sense he'd be drawn to other people from the mainland. They probably had more in common." She pursed her lips thoughtfully as she poked at a piece of chicken with her chopsticks. "I don't think it helps much as far as leading us to his killer. We didn't see any strangers come up to the table during the program that night."

"Do you think we would have noticed with that loud show going on?" Theresa asked. "I've been thinking about that these past few days. It was all so colorful and eye catching. I doubt I looked away from the stage the entire time."

"There were twelve of us there. I think at least one person might have noticed," Maggie said. "Edie, for example, is very observant."

Edie sat up a bit taller, proud of the descriptive.

"Okay." Clare seemed disappointed, but willing to accept the group's verdict on her new information. "So did you learn anything interesting before I arrived at the fabric shop?"

"Thelma, the woman in the fabric shop," Maggie added, when she saw a question on the faces of several of her friends, "told us that Lurline is a very passionate woman who feels things deeply."

"No surprise there either," Edie said.

"She called her a gentle soul and doubts she could kill the man she loved. And she was sure she loved Sam," Victoria added.

"On the other hand, she called Makana a drama queen with a bad temper," Maggie said. "And she did have one very interesting opinion. She said Makana is very smart, and while the confessions were a dumb move, she thought Makana might have confessed to throw suspicion off herself."

A murmur rose quickly around the table as everyone considered this new idea.

"That's actually a great idea," Clare said.

Edie's droll voice cut in before she could elaborate. "Somehow I knew you would say that."

Maggie laughed. "It's a fascinating idea, and Makana certainly didn't like the man. Several times I saw her go out of her way to avoid him."

Victoria and Louise agreed, having observed the same thing.

"Lurline told us Makana had been trying to avoid Sam, remember?" Clare said.

"Still, it's nothing definitive," Maggie said.

With a heavy sigh, Clare had to agree.

"Lurline's niece works in the fabric store," Victoria said. "She was the young woman with the red streaks in her hair who was cutting fabric."

"For a moment there, I thought we might have something," Maggie said. "Thelma seemed to suggest her boyfriend might be the culprit."

"Really?" Clare was instantly interested.

"It didn't pan out," Maggie said.

Victoria nodded. "Thelma said Sam had tried to make a move on Lurline's niece, but she has a large Samoan boyfriend. He was the fire dancer we saw in the program the other night."

"Oh, he was wonderful," Anna said. "And a very large man."

"Yes, very large," Louise said, "and with lots of tribal tattoos. We would have noticed him if he'd approached the table, no matter how riveting the action on the stage. He was just too big to miss."

"That's what we decided," Victoria agreed.

"Thelma thought Makana had a terrible temper, but Kate at the bookstore, who's married to Manu's brother, said she's mild-mannered." Clare mulled this over. "And she was positive Manu hadn't an evil bone in his body."

"That's great," Theresa said. "He's such a sweetheart."

"That's exactly what she said. She said his brother, her husband, is the same way. And he cooks too." Clare, whose husband did not cook at all, found this especially appealing.

"Good. It would be a tragedy to have our fabulous cook arrested before we have to leave," Theresa said, to some laughter from the others.

"So, talking to these local people about Sam, Lurline and Manu hasn't helped much," Maggie said. "They draw pretty much the same conclusions we do. Except for Thelma thinking Makana had a volatile temper. Should we consider her as a prime suspect?"

"Oh, no," Anna said. "She's such a child, really."

"Ah, but she isn't, Anna." Louise asked Edie to pass the tea pot before she continued. "She's a young woman. Remember, she's been away at college for the past four years. Lurline mentioned that on the first day, and how glad she is to have her back.

She's had at least one serious boyfriend. I think she's not nearly as naive as we may think."

"What are you hinting at?" Maggie asked.

Louise sighed. "Nothing specific. I just don't think she's a child, as you suggest, Anna. She's a woman, and Sam definitely knew it."

"I have a feeling there's something you're reluctant to say." Maggie pursed her lips as she considered the points Louise had made.

Louise frowned. "I hate to say something outright that might reflect badly on a person when I have no proof, is all."

This tantalizing pronouncement got them all chattering, asking Louise to elaborate. But she refused to do so until she'd put more thought into it.

"It's just a suspicion," she insisted, "and I'll tell you all as soon as I reason it out. I need to do more observing to come to a conclusion about it."

Maggie pushed away her plate, finished with her meal, and looked around the table. "I hate to say this. But after what the local people have said — and remember they have all known Lurline, Manu and Makana a lot longer than we have — none of the three seem like viable suspects."

No one looked particularly happy at this

conclusion.

"But someone killed Sam," Clare said. Her voice almost pleaded with them to offer some creditable solution.

"That's why I think we have to examine our own group more thoroughly," Maggie said. She didn't look happy about the suggestion. Neither did anyone else.

"What do you mean?" Anna asked.

"As Clare said, someone killed Sam. The number of suspects has always been limited by the number of people at our table. Or who approached our table. If we decide his family seems unlikely to have done it, we're left with our own group."

No one said anything for a while. Everyone was thinking.

"You don't think someone here . . ." Anna looked around the table, her eyes wide.

"No, I don't." Maggie's voice was firm and sure. "But we aren't the only ones on the tour."

Anna's eyes widened as she considered who was not at the luncheon table.

"Well, I don't think Bernie could harm anyone," Victoria said.

Theresa agreed. "She's just been enjoying herself with her cousin and learning to quilt. I really like her. I hope she considers coming to the Quilting Bee sometimes once we get back."

Clare agreed that she liked Bernie too, and wouldn't mind seeing more of her. "Besides, Bernie doesn't have a mean bone in her body," she added.

Anna agreed. "She's a very kind soul."

"Okay," Maggie said. "That takes care of Bernie. How about Lydia?"

"I doubt it," Victoria said. "She did some flirting with Sam, even Bernie did a little. But with Lydia, I think it was mostly to keep up with Judy — some school-girlish fun. I don't think she'd plan such an elaborate scheme to eliminate him."

"That goes back to the whole coldhearted, planned killing rather than an emotional, spur-of-the-moment one," Edie said.

"And I think you're right. There's really no motive for either Bernie or Lydia to have killed him," Victoria said.

"What about Iris?" Maggie continued.

"Iris is a more difficult problem," Victoria said thoughtfully.

Louise frowned. "She did seem quite taken with Sam."

"Maybe we should leave Iris till the end," Maggie suggested.

Everyone agreed.

"And wc can probably eliminate Rita right off," Louise said.

Since there were no objections to this, Louise continued.

"Now, Judy . . ." Louise paused for a moment, giving them all a chance to consider Judy as a suspect. "The fact that she had a one-night stand with Sam does bring her right up front as a suspect. She felt pretty guilty about that affair, too, which could indicate she might possibly want to take further action."

"Also, she tried not to let on that she knew Sam before the quilt tour," Victoria added, "even lying to the police."

"So she murdered him so her husband wouldn't find out?" Clare asked, turning this over in her mind. "It seems weak as a motive."

"A bit of overkill, wouldn't you say?" Maggie suggested.

"It does seem a ridiculous reason to kill someone, doesn't it?" Theresa said.

"No more ridiculous than the idea that Iris is really Lily, Sam's ex-wife," Edie said. "And we all suspect that could be possible."

"Judy has been really upset since Sam's death, more so than I would expect for someone she barely knew," Louise said.

"And one of the things Detective Sousa questioned that first day was how everyone behaved, both before and after the luau.

Judy's behavior *has* been different since the luau," Maggie said.

"I guess if she shot Sam, she would be extremely upset, thinking she might be caught." Edie mulled this over, her expression thoughtful.

"She might just be concerned because everyone is talking about her," Clare suggested. "Lydia told me that she's truly sorry about her indiscretion and hurt that everyone is judging her."

"Indiscretion!" Edie snorted. "I guess since she went to confession, the sin has been downgraded to a mere indiscretion." She sounded disgusted.

Clare looked over at Edie, her eyes clouding in embarrassment at what she had to say next. "Lydia also said that since Judy doesn't know all of us, things that might seem minor to us bother her. Lydia mentioned that she's especially hurt by your attitude, Edie. She thinks your brisk manner is disrespectful."

"Hmpf," Edie said. "People have to earn respect. And you don't do that by sleeping with another woman's husband. She never said that Sam lied about his marital status, so she was well aware there was a wife at home."

Clare flushed a rosy pink, but kept her

gaze focused on Edie. "Well, now you know."

Maggie took over before more could be said. "Okay, let's just agree that Judy might need further discussion." She checked that no one objected. No one did. "What about Iris?"

"Iris is difficult," Victoria said thoughtfully.

Louise frowned. "She did seem quite taken with Sam. I have to admit I was surprised at that. She never struck me as the flirtatious type. She always seemed quite happy as a career woman, someone who didn't need a man to complete her life."

"Well, that was because she'd been so hurt by that ex-husband of hers," Clare said.

"Iris may have flirted with Sam," Maggie said, "but I don't think it's his death that has her upset now. She seems more worked up by the intrusion of the police and their investigation than the fact that Sam is dead."

Everyone considered this, and several of the others agreed.

"She was fairly distraught about the search at the inn, wasn't she?" Victoria mused.

"What about the accident and all that?" Clare asked. "And her relationship with one of Sam's ex-wives?"

"That's why Iris is a thornier problem," Edie explained. "But — I almost forgot. I didn't want to say anything at breakfast, with Iris right there, you know. But some time ago, I Googled Iris Fleming and travel agency, and there were no online references."

Maggie remembered being told about this back in Scottsdale, but Edie explained briefly for those who were unaware of her earlier attempt at detection.

"Anyway, after hearing about Iris and Lily Nowak yesterday, I Googled again. I did it after Iris went to bed, just picked up my netbook and went into the bathroom and closed the door. This time I typed in Lily Nowak and travel agency, and I did find references. There was an agency called Places to Go, run by a Lily Nowak and also a Lily Simson. I also found an article from the Tucson paper about the accident. There was a photo of the scene, and it was terrible." She stopped to take a steadying breath. It was obvious she didn't care to say more about the accident photo. "So I think Clare's original idea about the two women having their identities switched is a definite possibility."

"Were there any photos of Lily?" Anna asked.

"Excellent question," Louise said, "but not particularly relevant. As bad as everyone has said that accident was, and with all her facial injuries, even if Iris was really Lily, I doubt her current appearance would be the same as before the accident."

"There were some photos," Edie said. "And while there's a general resemblance to Iris, you couldn't look at them and say that woman is the Iris we know today."

Clare's eyes lit with excitement. "Oh, I knew it! I'll bet she changed her identity."

"But why?" Anna asked.

"So she could track down her awful ex-husband and get rid of him?" Clare suggested.

"How could she have known Sam was here?" Victoria asked more practically. "Detective Sousa said Sam might have come here to hide from mainland law enforcement, and he did seem to avoid detection. There were warrants out on the mainland, I believe he said. But Sam managed to disappear for all these years. Seven years since they met in Vegas, right? So how did Iris find him?"

"Don't forget he also changed his name," Louise said.

"But not too much. Detective Sousa said he just changed a letter here or there each time so that it could appear to be a typo." Victoria admitted that she found this quite brilliant.

"Con men are smart," Edie said, her voice dry. "It's how they survive. That's why it's so difficult for us to fight ID theft too. They keep coming up with new and better ways to scam us."

"Maybe she hired a private detective," Theresa said.

"She could have figured it out while she was planning our tour," Anna suggested. "Perhaps she talked to him on the phone and recognized his voice."

"That's an excellent deduction." Victoria's compliment had Anna's cheeks turning a bright pink. "Voices don't change much over the years, so she might have recognized him through his voice, even if it was just over the phone."

"Still . . ." Theresa was puzzled. "If there was a mix-up after her accident, why wouldn't she correct it once she was able? I can understand an incorrect ID immediately after a traumatic accident, but I don't see why the person who survives wouldn't correct the problem."

Maggie paused, her teacup halfway to her lips. "I'm not saying Iris is this ex-wife . . . but think about it. It would be a chance to start life over, to leave behind a very painful period of your life. I could see that it would be tempting, especially if neither of you had any family. She might have felt she was honoring her friend's memory."

"Or she could have been evading a stalker," Clare said. "Or running from creditors or something."

Maggie pulled out her cell phone. "Let me call Michael and see if he was able to get any information about that accident. I called him yesterday after we heard from Detective Sousa. I asked if he could find out anything about the accident and if a switch was a possibility."

Michael answered immediately and they exchanged a few words of greeting. But Maggie moved quickly toward her reason for the call.

"Michael, were you able to get any information about that accident involving Iris Fleming and Lily Nowak Simson?"

"I was."

Maggie remained silent, giving him time to gather his thoughts. His voice was unusually solemn.

"It was a bad accident, Ma."

"I assumed so. Louise says she'd always noticed traces of plastic surgery on Iris, especially around the face. She never asked about it, of course, because it could have just been cosmetic surgery."

"Lily and Iris were driving back from a weekend trip to Rocky Point." The Mexican resort on the Baja coast was a popular vacation spot for Arizonans, and they all knew people who traveled there often. "Outside Tucson, they were hit by a truck. The driver was speeding and highly intoxicated, and died instantly."

"There were only the two vehicles involved?" Maggie asked.

"Yes. The two women had to be cut from the car with the jaws of life. They were in bad shape, Ma. And by the time they got them out, their faces were bruised and swollen, making identity difficult. From the basic information provided on their drivers' licenses, it sounds like their height, weight, hair color, eye color — all those things were very close."

"I assumed that would be the case if there was any chance of a mix-up. How did they identify them?"

"It doesn't say in the report I saw, but I assume the emergency responders found purses or something like that beside them. That's the usual method in an accident."

"Not a very scientific approach."

Maggie felt sure Michael was shrugging at

his end. "There isn't much else they can do. Most people don't have fingerprints on file, so that doesn't usually help. And who would they have used for a DNA match — which would have taken a long time anyway. Neither woman had any family. They listed each other as the person to contact in case of emergency."

"Oh, dear," Maggie murmured.

"Yeah." Michael sighed. "It's a sad case. They airlifted them to hospitals in Phoenix, both unconscious. Lily was in a coma for a week and died without regaining consciousness. Iris had several surgeries and did not regain consciousness until after her friend died. And, Ma, she had a broken jaw. She couldn't talk."

He heard his mother's sharp intake of breath.

"I thought you might appreciate that little fact. Not only that, her right arm was broken. Is Iris right-handed?"

"Yes, she is."

"So, if a mistake was made, even if she wanted to correct it, she might not have been able to. At least not for several weeks."

"And by then," Maggie interrupted, "she may have decided that taking on a new identity was a good thing. It might have seemed that she was handed a chance to start a new life."

"I hate to admit it, but it's a possibility."

"But I still don't see how she could have planned such an elaborate scheme to murder her ex-husband. How did she even know where he was? And to plan a crime from three thousand miles away . . ."

She thought about it for a moment, then mentioned Anna's theory.

"Anna thinks Iris might have figured it out while planning our tour. That maybe she recognized Sam's voice while making the arrangements."

"Anything is possible, I suppose, and voices are hard to disguise. I do agree with you about one thing, though. I totally think Iris could be Lily. But as for her tracking down Sam and then killing him — that seems unlikely. Possible, but unlikely."

Maggie sighed. "It does sound far-fetched, doesn't it? Everything about Sam's death sounds far-fetched. And, yet, he's dead."

Hearing only one side of the conversation made the others eager to hear what they had missed. There was much speculation then, but they all agreed that the odds had gone up considerably in favor of Iris really being Lily, another spurned former wife of Sam's.

"I think we should call Detective Sousa and tell him Clare's idea about Iris and Lily switching identities," Anna suggested.

"I still think it sounds more like a movie plot than real life," Edie said. She shook her head, amazed that she found herself thinking the idea had any merit at all. "And I was the one who found out about the travel agency and Lily Nowak."

"I don't know." Victoria's voice was thoughtful. "I don't think we have all the pieces to the puzzle yet, and the whole story of Iris and Lily and the latter's connection to Sam is too coincidental."

Still, Clare loved the idea of sharing her theories with Detective Sousa. "Maybe we could meet him while we're here in town," she said. "Do you know where the police station is?" She seemed eager to follow through on that. Maggie imagined how thrilled she would be to visit a detective in his own office.

But no one knew where the police station might be. And they all agreed it wasn't really the kind of question a tourist asked of a waitress, friendly though she might be. Since none of the local women were there with them — thank goodness, with the way the conversation had gone — they turned to plan B.

Maggie pulled out her phone and called Detective Sousa. Luck was with them. He not only answered his phone, he suggested meeting them and even recommended a convenient place to accomplish this.

Within fifteen minutes, they were settled in an old art-deco building that they learned had once housed a popular department store. The building had been restored and currently housed several small, independent businesses. Detective Sousa had told them how to find the building and proposed meeting at a small snack bar inside.

He found the Quilting Bee gathered at the snack-bar tables, giggling together over shaved-ice treats. They had apparently all ordered different flavors and were happily sampling one another's.

"Well, I'm glad to see that you haven't been traumatized by Mr. Samson's death." He looked around at the smiling faces. "I like seeing visitors enjoying themselves here."

Maggie was charmed.

"So, ladies. What did you want to tell me that couldn't be said over the phone?"

His expectant look made some of the women squirm. Maggie knew they were wondering if calling him was really a good idea. With him standing before them, ready to listen, the idea seemed sillier than it had when they spoke among themselves.

As often happened, they looked to Maggie to speak for the group.

"We've been talking," Maggie began.

"Uh-oh." The detective grinned.

There were a few chuckles from the women.

"I called my son to see if he could find out about that accident Iris was in. You see, Edie and Clare have a theory about that."

As Maggie had already observed in previous encounters, Detective Sousa was a wonderful listener. He looked from one to another as they told him their theories and Edie explained her online research. He kept a bland expression in place, not saying a word until they had finished.

When he'd heard all their theories and speculation about Iris, he thanked them for calling him and for sharing. "I'm glad to hear you aren't trying to solve this on your own. Remember, we're dealing with a cold-blooded killer here, and I don't want you confronting anyone, even if you think it's an old friend."

Solemn nods traveled around the group.

"As for Ms. Fleming's identity, I have been looking into it. I, too, thought it a great coincidence that her best friend had been married to Mr. Samson. Too great. There are rarely coincidences in a murder case. However, while theories are good, I need proof. And I'm still working on that."

"We can get her fingerprints for you," Clare offered, so eager to help she almost slid off the small seat of the café chair.

Detective Sousa smiled. "Thank you, but that won't help unless I can find a copy of Lily Nowak's prints on file somewhere."

Clare's mouth turned down at the corners, and she looked so dejected Maggie wanted to laugh.

Clare caught her look and gave her a weak smile. "I know, I know." She sighed, disappointed that she wasn't living the amateur-sleuth life of her dreams. "This is real life, not TV."

Everyone laughed, even Detective Sousa.

"Again, I thank you for calling me. Don't hesitate to let me know if you have any other theories. I heard how helpful you were to Detective Warner in the past, so I'm interested in any insights you might have. Call me anytime."

Maggie shot a look at Louise, who gave a brief but definite shake of her head. Maggie suspected she knew where Louise's thoughts about Makana were heading, and she agreed about not saying anything until they were

317

more certain. Louise's new idea was too unformed to vocalize — especially to the police.

CHAPTER 25

Quilt tour, day five. Saturday evening.

"We arranged for you to attend mass this evening at Our Lady Star of the Sea Catholic Church. It's a beautiful little church with a mostly Hawaiian congregation. They greet visitors with lei, and sing hymns in Hawaiian. You'll like it." Lurline smiled at them, obviously delighted with what else she had to say. "I've also arranged a little surprise for you after mass. I think you'll be pleased."

They all did enjoy mass at the pretty little church. It was small and intimate, the people friendly. There were small but lovely stained-glass windows and beautiful island murals on the peaked area beneath the ceiling. Best of all, at the altar, the church had several Hawaiian quilt pieces the women admired.

"Perhaps you recognize the *ulu* pattern," Lurline told them quietly as they waited for mass to begin. "Remember, the *ulu* is the breadfruit, which was the bread of life for the early Hawaiians. So you can see why it would be significant as a piece of artwork for the church."

The mass was even more enjoyable than the atmosphere of the little church. Lovely and often familiar hymns were sung in Hawaiian, the words displayed on the wall for all to follow. Maggie was grateful to Lurline for the quick lesson in Hawaiian pronunciation she had provided earlier in the week. It allowed her to follow along well enough to participate.

When it was time to "greet those around you" the entire church began to move around in such a way that everyone got to hug or, for the more conservative, shake hands with everyone else. Maggie had never seen anything like it and immediately loved the friendliness of the congregation. She could see that it came naturally too. As she took back her seat for the communion, Maggie couldn't help thinking of the early sea voyagers, explorers and whalers, who called in at the islands and experienced this community in its purest form. It was a shame that the Anglo world proceeded to betray these kind people by taking over their kingdom. But now she could better understand how they were able to do so.

After mass, Lurline led the group to the building behind the church. There they found a large covered lanai and a spacious social hall. It was here that the local quilters in the congregation had set up a welcome for the mainland quilters. The tour group was flabbergasted when they saw the quilts stacked up on a table at one side of the room and the long tables groaning with food on the other.

Lurline introduced everyone then excused herself to go back to the inn and "take care of some personal business."

"I guess she have lots to do with losing her husband, yeah?" Winona said, watching her leave the room. Winona Akaka was a tall, brown-skinned woman of considerable bulk. Yet she moved briskly and with grace as she showed them to the front row of the seating area. "We thought we start by showing some of our work. We have lots of quilters here, so we proud to show off. After, we have dinner, yeah?"

The Arizona women happily agreed. It looked to be a wonderful evening. Quilt after quilt was unfurled, stories told of the makers, of the inspiration for the pattern, and of how some had been copied by friends and family of the creators.

"Now, we mostly share our patterns," one of the older women said. "Not like in the old days when they were more secretive and it was real shame to steal another woman's design."

"Yeah, they would make up chants and sing them to shame the stealer," someone said, laughter in her voice.

It took an hour for them to view all the wonderful show-and-tell items, and then the guests were invited to open up the buffet line. Sitting at picnic tables out on the lanai, they indulged in the wide variety of potluck dishes and enjoyed visiting with the local parishioners.

It was inevitable that they should discover that some of these new friends knew Lurline and her family. After all, the inn was just a few blocks from the church.

"We're enjoying Lurline's classes very much," Maggie commented.

"She's a good teacher," Winona said.

"And the food at the inn is wonderful," Theresa said.

"Yeah, it was a good idea Lurline and Manu had, starting the Blue Lily Inn. We couldn't believe it when Lurline got a divorce, but we were really shocked when she came back here with Sam," Winona said.

"Yeah. We all like Manu and hoped she would get over his little fling and forget the divorce," her friend Natalie commented.

"It wasn't Manu's fault anyway," Ruth said.

"You don't know that . . . ," Natalie interrupted.

"Oh, pooh," Winona said, backing up Ruth. "He's always been crazy about Lurline, even back in high school. And that Camellia, she was always trying to catch his eye, pull him away from Lurline."

Ruth nodded. "Camellia was always fast. I should know. She's my granddaughter. *Ai yai yai,* the trouble that girl gave her mother!" She clicked her tongue in disapproval. "She's still over on Maui — better for her mother she's not so close. She likes to party and there's lots of *haoles* over there to buy her drinks. She's still good-looking, even though she middle-aged. Takes after her grandma, yeah?" She chuckled merrily and her friends kidded her about her modesty.

Maggie was enjoying the interplay among the women. "Did you all go to school together?"

There were several nods.

"We all graduated from Hilo High," Natalie explained. "Except Ruth there — she

323

went to St. Joseph."

Maggie didn't say it, but it was apparent that Ruth was much older than the other women too. But then they did admit to being in school with her granddaughter.

"I was in the same class as Lurline and Manu," Winona offered.

"I was a year behind. With Camellia," Natalie said.

"We heard Sam really charmed Lurline right after her divorce," Maggie said.

"We couldn't believe it," Winona said again. "She seemed too sensible to fall for someone like Sam. But you know what they say about love. It's blind."

"And it makes you crazy too," Natalie added with a laugh.

Winona nodded sadly. "Sam got her on the rebound. We all thought Lurline would have her fling in Vegas, come back to the bed-and-breakfast, and realize she'd made a bad mistake. And Manu would be there waiting for her."

"But that Sam." Natalie picked up the story. "As soon as they got back here, he whisked her off to Fiji for one honeymoon. She was so excited. There's no real quilting tradition in Fiji, but they famous for the beautiful bark cloth they make there. She couldn't wait to see some of that, learn as much as she could about the native art. She made some wall hangings using some of the motifs they use on their *tapa*. They were real nice and won some ribbons at the county fair."

"I don't believe we've seen those," Victoria said. "I'd like to."

There was some discussion about using the old patterns to create modern quilts, and then the conversation wound back around to Lurline.

"Lurline seems a very passionate woman," Maggie said. "Women like that feel everything very strongly. Love, hate . . ."

"Oh, yeah. That Lurline can have a temper!"

Her friends laughed.

"Remember that time in high school when Camellia tried to grab Manu away from her at a dance? Hoo, boy, we thought they were going have one catfight." Winona chuckled.

"Who do you think killed Sam?" Edie finally asked.

Maggie's brows rose. Leave it to Edie to just blurt that out.

The laughter stopped. The local women exchanged looks. Then Winona shrugged. "Could be anybody. Lots of husbands and boyfriends hated him."

"Lots of women didn't like him much

either," Natalie said.

Edie gave them her most serious look. "You know the police are thinking Lurline, Manu or Makana did it."

Once again the women glanced at one another. Maggie, however, was unable to determine if they thought one of the three people mentioned might be a killer.

"We don't think Lurline did it," Maggie stated. Might as well make her position clear, that she wanted to support their friend. "If Sam had been shot or stabbed in a moment of passion . . . then I would say Lurline probably did it. But this was a coldly plotted crime. Someone had to go to a lot of trouble to plan exactly how to shoot Sam without everyone nearby knowing what happened. I don't think that's Lurline's style."

Lurline's friends seemed relieved.

Natalie nodded. "You know her pretty well, even though it's only been a few days."

"The same for Manu," Winona said. "Maybe he would lash out in a moment of passion, though I never saw him act like that." She heaved a big sigh. "I always used to hope he and Lurline would break up so he would notice me — back in high school, you know. Teenage crush. Never happened, of course. Even after the divorce, Manu never noticed anyone else."

Ruth agreed. "Manu wouldn't go to such lengths. He's not a real planner, except when it comes to meals."

"If Sam was poisoned, I might suspect Manu," Winona said with a chuckle. "That seems more like something Manu might try. I always wondered why he didn't. He's always been right there, cooking for them and their guests. Crazy, yeah?"

"We couldn't believe it when he refused to give up his share of the inn. Can you imagine having to live with your ex right there all the time!" This came from a younger woman. She had the same red streaks sported by Makana and Alana, but her hair was short and spiky. Maggie remembered that she had shown them a wonderful wall hanging of the goddess Pele reflected in the flames of the volcano.

"Manu fixed up that place out back for himself," Winona told them. "It used to be a big storage shed. Lurline's grandfather was quite the gardener and had built this large shed where he could store supplies and start seeds and all *da kine* stuff. There was a chicken coop on one end too, where they had laying hens. We used to collect the eggs for her grandmother." She smiled in happy nostalgia at the memories.

"I remember playing there with Lurline when we were kids. Her grandparents lived there then. It made a great playhouse," Natalie added. "It had water and everything. Made it easy to turn it into an apartment, I guess."

"Enough about Sam." Winona looked at Maggie. "We don't want to let him spoil our evening. Tell us about your projects. I hear you've already done some original designs. Who's making the king protea I heard about?"

Edie proudly told them about her project while everyone continued to visit the food tables. They talked quilting and, eventually, food. Maggie raved over the homemade sweet bread, while Edie asked for tips on making the excellent sushi. Everyone exclaimed over the teriyaki sauces; there were several varieties, used for both chicken and beef. It seemed that everyone had their own special recipe, and their own secret ingredient — not that they weren't more than willing to share. The locals laughed, however, at the careful way the Arizona women sampled or outright avoided some of the local specialties containing raw fish, seaweed, or shellfish.

As the conversation continued, musical instruments began to appear — a couple of guitars, numerous ukuleles. One person would begin to strum, the others would join in. Voices began to sing. Here and there someone would get up to dance a graceful hula. It was time for *kani ka pila* — Hawai'i's version of jamming. The quilt tour women sat back and just enjoyed it all.

When Manu appeared with the yellow bus, Maggie was shocked to see that it was past midnight. She did feel pleasantly mellow and tired. The music and company had been most enjoyable, and she'd had way too much to eat. Several of their new friends copied down e-mail addresses, asking them to share photos of their new projects. And more than one woman promised to drop recipes off at the inn in the next few days.

CHAPTER 26

Quilt tour, day six. Sunday morning.

After enjoying the local entertainment at the church until late on Saturday night, most of the tour group women slept in on Sunday morning. Perhaps anticipating this situation, Manu had set up a continental-style breakfast that worked well. The women ate as they wandered in, then moved on into the classroom to work on their projects.

The three Ilimas let everyone know they planned to visit the funeral home that morning. Lurline had to make arrangements for Sam's funeral — once the body was released by the police. Sunday, which had been put on the schedule as a free day, seemed like the best option.

"I think you're due for a day of rest anyway," Lurline told them, as she explained why she would be gone. "You've had several busy days, and I'm sure you would all like a chance to work on the pieces you have started. I can't wait to see some of your original designs put into fabric. What you've already accomplished is amazing. This is the most talented class I've ever had."

"I'll bet you say that to all your classes," Theresa said with a grin.

Everyone laughed, but pride in the compliment, and in their work, shone in the happy faces.

"I'll be here if you need any assistance," Rita assured them.

Edie was surprised to learn that Manu would be going along with Lurline. She could understand Makana accompanying her mother while she planned for her husband's funeral. But her ex-husband?

She confronted Manu when he walked by her with a platter of banana macadamia coconut muffins. "Do you really think you should go with Lurline and Makana?"

Manu was unfazed by her blunt disapproval. "Makana and I just go along to support Lurline. We both love her. Me, I'm mainly chauffeur. I'm taking my ukulele and I can sit in the car and play while they take care of business."

Edie seemed somewhat appeased by this explanation. At least, she said no more about it.

While some of the women finished breakfast, and others began work in the classroom, Maggie and Victoria gathered up their projects and moved outside to the front porch. Why sew in the classroom when there was a big, old-fashioned porch available? The long, wide space was filled with rattan rockers and Adirondack-style chairs, perfect for sitting and stitching. Also, Maggie thought the natural light an improvement over the fluorescents in the classroom.

Others from the Quilting Bee soon joined them, coming out one by one as they finished eating then gathered together their sewing supplies.

They sewed in companionable silence for a while. The morning was bright and clear, the sky a beautiful azure with a few puffy white clouds. The sun was bright and had made a good start to warming the day, beginning with the porch where they sat. Light trade winds blew the clusters of blue lilies that lined the porch and walkway, making them wave in their own form of hula.

"I love this porch," Anna said with a long sigh. "It reminds me of the farmhouse where I grew up. Of course, we didn't have agapanthus. We had tulips and daffodils to line the walkway in the spring, and petunias in the summer. We had azaleas along the front of the porch."

"That sounds very nice. Just like this. It's a lovely spot for stitching," Victoria said. She took in a deep breath, releasing it slowly. "It doesn't smell quite as good as that ginger lei Sam gave Lurline at the beach, but there is a definite hint of tropical flowers."

"Did you know that the ginger plant is an invasive pest?" Edie announced. "It takes over the forests and clogs drainage ditches."

"That's a shame, because the flowers are beautiful," Louise said. "That had to be the prettiest lei I've ever seen. And the scent! Just wonderful!"

"I think that light floral scent here is mainly from the plumeria trees," Theresa said, looking over toward two large specimens on the lawn. A straggly-looking tree, the leaves and flowers only appeared in clusters at the ends of the long branches. "Don't you love the plumerias?" she continued. "I decided to do a plumeria pattern for my wall hanging. It seemed like a good one to start with. What do you think?"

She held up the pattern she had created, depicting the long oval leaves separating groupings of three blossoms. It wasn't very original, Maggie thought, then promptly scolded herself for such a negative response. Theresa's piece might reflect some of the pillow patterns they had seen, but it was a fine start and she was excited by it. She had also added a scalloped border that Maggie admired. Lurline had explained that many Hawaiian quilts had scalloped borders reminiscent of the waves in the sea that surrounded the islands.

"I thought this hand-dyed fabric with the pink and yellow in it was just perfect." Theresa ran her hand gently over the appliqué she had already stitched.

Everyone agreed with her fabric choice. They had seen many of the trees, and yellow and pink seemed to be the commonest colors for the blossoms. Theresa had chosen a lovely gray-green for her background, and Edie complimented her on her choice, leaving a surprised Theresa smiling with pleasure.

Maggie smiled at Theresa's enthusiasm. "I can see what will be keeping you busy from now on."

"I *love* these Hawaiian quilts," Theresa admitted. "I plan to concentrate on making them from now on, rather than the pieced ones. But don't worry, I won't desert the Quilting Bee," she assured them. "I really enjoy quilting together with all of you."

"Maybe we could do something Hawaiian for the raffle," Victoria said. "Not a whole big quilt," she added quickly, as she saw the astonishment of the others that she would even suggest such an enormous project. "Lurline has a very nice rose pillow pattern."

"Oh, yes," Clare broke in. "She told me the rose is the official flower of the island of Maui. Did you know all the islands have their own colors and flowers?"

"Yes," Edie said shortly before turning to Victoria. "What did you have in mind?"

"I thought if we each did one of the pillow-size blocks, we could put together a nice top with the appliqué rose blocks and something else. Some pieced blocks, or some large print fabric squares. You're good at that kind of thing, Edie."

For a while, they discussed the potential for such a project, with Edie throwing out ideas that they all agreed sounded terrific.

"Think of what that might mean at the auction," Louise said. "We need some really good quilts this year, as Father wants to refurbish the restrooms and it's going to be an expensive proposition."

There was a pause in the conversation, as everyone concentrated on stitching and on enjoying their exotic surroundings. A mourning dove cooed, the plaintive call reminding them once again of the sadness surrounding their new friends at the inn and their errand that morning.

In any case, Clare soon prodded them back toward her main topic of interest.

"So, now that we're all gathered together here . . ."

Clare giggled. Actually *giggled,* Maggie thought in disgust. Whoever would have suspected a woman her age could giggle that way?

"What?" Edie snapped. "Are you planning on a wedding?"

Clare, momentarily caught unawares, took a moment to catch Edie's reference. But she recovered quickly. "No, silly. Not a wedding. It's like in an Agatha Christie book when everyone gathers together in the library to solve the crime."

"No, it's not," Edie admonished. "In Agatha Christie, the detective in charge brings all the suspects together. Like the other night when you suggested the same thing to Detective Sousa. This is a completely different thing."

"Oh." Clare looked disappointed. "I guess you're right."

"But we are gathered together here," Victoria said, stitching carefully at her potted moth orchid. She, too, had added a scalloped border to her wall hanging. "We can discuss any theories you have, Clare."

Maggie knew Victoria didn't want to disappoint Clare in what she seemed to think might be their big moment of crime solving.

Clare, however, deflated even further. "I don't have any theories."

Edie clicked her tongue, but didn't even look up. She was finishing up the bright pink petals around the outside of her king protea and kept her eyes on her work.

Within minutes, Clare perked back up. "Unless . . . maybe it's like *Murder on the Orient Express.* You know, like maybe all the women Sam has been hurting all these years got together and killed him. Or all his ex-wives."

"Except he wasn't shot twelve times," Edie said.

"Oh," said Clare, deflated once again.

"Also," Maggie reminded her, "a number of people approaching Sam at the table would have been rather noticeable, don't you think?"

"Maybe they hired a hit man," Clare suggested, hope shining in her eyes. She had recently discovered a series with a hit man as a main character and had been surprised to find him sympathetic.

"Only if it was a movie," Edie said dryly.

Maggie reminded them of the main information gleaned through all of their previous discussions. "Everyone is sure Lurline and Manu could not kill anyone. Nothing we learned yesterday from old friends of Lurline and Manu lead me to change my mind about this. I still think we have to look within our group."

With what Clare later called impeccable timing, Iris took that moment to arrive on the porch, her *ulu* pillow top in hand. As she settled herself in an Adirondack chair painted a cheerful yellow, she asked, "Look within our group for what?"

Everyone on the porch glanced toward Iris. Anna hung her head, embarrassed to be caught speculating on a murder suspect who had just walked into the middle of their discussion all unaware. She looked like a near-sighted woman who had lost her glasses as she peered at her appliqué.

"We were just saying that from everything we've learned about Lurline, Makana and Manu, I don't think any of them capable of murdering Sam. If it had been a crime of passion, then, yes, Lurline would be at the top of my list. But this was coldly plotted and carried out." Maggie moved restlessly in her chair before meeting Iris's eyes. "I was just saying I think we need to examine the tour group."

Iris ignored the fabric in her lap and stared at Maggie. "Look among our group for the murderer?"

Maggie and several others nodded.

"I'm not saying it was someone from our group, but we have to consider it."

Iris continued to stare, hot anger glowing in her eyes. Maggie was surprised she didn't yell "traitor" and storm back into the inn.

After a moment of silence, Iris finally reached into her bag, gathering the supplies she needed to start sewing. She still looked upset, though she was considerably calmer. Maggie didn't blame her for being angry. She'd worked long and hard to set up a nice trip for them. It wasn't her fault things had gone wrong — unless she herself killed Sam.

Maggie took a deep breath and finally asked the question they had been wondering about for the past two days. "Iris, what really happened to your gun?"

Iris stopped searching for her green thread and looked up, indignant. "I told you, it was stolen from my suitcase."

"No one believes that ridiculous story about the baggage handlers in Phoenix taking it," Edie said. "I'm surprised Detective Sousa didn't call you on it."

Iris sat up, inhaling until her chest looked

twice its usual size. She appeared ready to lose her temper in a big way.

Then she slowly deflated. Her breath swooshed out, and she slumped in her chair. She fidgeted with the fabric in her hands, with the cord that held her scissors — looking anywhere but at the other women. Her face slowly turned a deep red.

Just as Maggie began to worry that she was having an attack of some kind, she finally opened her mouth to speak.

On the other side of the porch, Edie pulled out her phone and dialed Detective Sousa's number. She did it so quickly, Maggie wondered if she had him on speed dial. After identifying herself, she said quickly, "If you can get over to the inn right away, you might hear something important."

Edie returned the phone to her bag to find Iris staring at her. Iris's mouth hung slack and there was a look of betrayal in her eyes. It was quickly replaced with a tearful glare of reproach. "I thought we were friends, Edie."

"We are," Edie said in her matter-of-fact way. "Or perhaps I should say 'we were.' You didn't tell me you were bringing a gun along. I didn't even know you were allowed to put a gun in your checked luggage. As your roommate, I feel I should have known that. In fact, after Detective Sousa told us about you filling out the papers to bring a gun in your luggage, I searched our room."

"*What?*" Iris really looked offended now. Maggie recalled her indignation about the search warrant. Iris was apparently someone who felt strongly about her personal things remaining private.

Edie nodded. "While you were in the shower I searched all the drawers, and in the closet. I didn't find anything. But it's made me very curious about what you were doing on the excursion boat that night. When I startled you, remember?"

"I would like to hear about that."

Detective Sousa's quiet voice startled the women. They were all so intent on the interaction between Edie and Iris, none of them had seen or heard Detective Sousa's car arrive. He now stood at the foot of the steps leading up to the porch. The women still in the classroom saw him, though, and they trailed out of the house to see what his presence might mean.

While Iris stared blankly at Detective Sousa, her mouth not quite closed and her face the color of white bread, Edie explained what had happened that night after the luau.

"We were all at the rail of the boat, watching the streams of lava coming down that slope toward the ocean, and I realized that Iris wasn't with us. I was concerned, because she had been friendlier toward Sam than some of us. I thought she might be upset so I went to find her. She was in a shadowy area of the deck, in a place where she couldn't have seen the lava flow."

Detective Sousa nodded. "In other words, where she could not see the event you all were there to view."

"Yes. When I called her name, she jumped about a foot. She dropped her purse and fumbled around with it, saying I startled her. Then she said she'd moved there to answer her phone, but it stopped ringing before she could get it out of her bag."

"I see." Detective Sousa leaned his shoulder against the railing, one foot on the first step and one on the second. He appeared quite relaxed, but Maggie felt sure he was very busy exercising his "little gray cells."

"Would you like to tell us what you were really doing when you were interrupted, Ms. Fleming? I doubt your cell phone was working out there on the ocean. It's pretty desolate out there, the coast decimated by recent eruptions. Were you disposing of a gun perhaps? A gun you used to kill Mr. Samson?"

If possible, Iris grew even paler. A tear

trailed down her left cheek. Another quickly followed on the right.

"No. Of course not." She drew in a deep breath. "I did not kill Sam."

"So what were you doing?" Edie asked.

Iris drew in a raspy breath and swiped at her tears.

"I did bring the gun on the trip because I was considering . . ." She stopped, drew in another breath and started over. "I think you all suspected what happened after the car accident — that Lily and Iris were mistakenly identified."

For this final admittance, her voice dropped so low everyone leaned forward, hoping to hear better.

"It's true. When I finally awoke after the accident, I was shocked to discover that everyone thought I was Iris. But admitting the truth wasn't easy. I couldn't speak, you see. My jaw was broken and wired shut. And my right arm was also broken, so it was very difficult to write. I had to lie there and listen as everyone called me Iris. And while they didn't tell me she had died, I knew she must have. Otherwise, why would they think I was her? But the more I heard it . . . the longer I thought about it . . ." She heaved a deep sigh. "The more I thought about it, the more I liked the idea of starting over as someone else."

"But how could you change your whole identity like that?" Clare's question wasn't accusatory. She was fascinated and curious.

"We knew each other very well, so I was able to slide into her identity easily enough. And I moved as soon as I was able, so I could really start all over again. It didn't hurt anyone," she added defensively. "Neither of us had any family left. That's one of the reasons we became such great friends. Two childless divorcees, with no family to speak of. We started spending holidays together, then weekends. Evenings at the theater or at a ballgame."

"So why did you bring the gun?" Anna asked.

"I had so much time to think while I was in the hospital, then in a care home. That's all you can do when you're in that kind of situation, just lie there and think. You're trapped in a body that won't work properly, and there's so much pain. But your mind just whirls. It never stops. All I could think about was how Sam had ruined my life. He was Steve then, of course. But he romanced me, made me love him, then eventually ran off with as much money as he could take. It ruined my life and my business."

She stopped, wiping again at new tears.

Clare handed her a small package of tissues that she took from her sewing bag. Iris nodded her thanks, pulling out a tissue and dabbing at her cheeks.

"I decided that if I ever had enough money, I would trace him and seek revenge. It was part luck, part accident, but I managed to track him down here. I found him just before the subject of the Hawaiian quilt tour came up, and then I couldn't believe my luck. It was all so perfect. I registered my gun with the TSA so that I'd have it with me." Her face set. "I wasn't sure I would be able to shoot the bastard, but I wanted the opportunity to try. I really would have liked to push him into one of those steam vents at the volcano — but that was too public. And the opportunity never arose anyway. It was what he deserved, though." As her anger grew, her voice steadied.

Detective Sousa remained silent but fully alert.

"And did you?" Clare asked, sitting on the edge of her seat by now, her stitching lying forgotten on her knees. "Shoot him?" she clarified.

"No. It turned out I wasn't able to do it. Oh, I thought about it. I tried to get to know him again, and I found I couldn't hate him as much as I had while I was lying in a hospital bed feeling sorry for myself. He turned out to be an aging playboy more worthy of my pity than anything."

"Didn't he recognize you?" Anna asked.

"Oh, no." Iris dismissed this with a quick wave of her hand. "I had to have a lot of plastic surgery after the accident. And since I didn't have any family, the doctors only had a driver's-license photo to work with. And it wasn't even my photo. Iris and I had a passing resemblance, but that was all. So, no. No one who knew me before the accident would recognize me now."

Maggie and Victoria shared a quick look. Both found that statement unutterably sad.

"So what were you doing on the boat when I found you?" Edie asked. "If you hadn't just shot Sam, why did you give the impression you might be dumping a gun into the ocean?"

Once again Iris sighed. "Actually, seeing Sam dead scared me. I didn't know he'd been murdered of course, but it still terrified me. After all, I had been thinking about killing him myself. And just like at home, I had my gun in my purse. So that night on the boat I was considering tossing out my gun — until you walked up and startled me." She shuddered. "I'm used to having a gun in my bag. I like having it there. It makes me feel safe. But here I'd been considering shooting a man, and he suddenly turns up dead. It scared the life out of me."

"Poor choice of words," Edie mumbled.

"When you found me, I was thinking that I should throw the gun away, but I was hesitant. It's an expensive item and I'm used to shooting with it. I'm comfortable with it. I hated to throw it overboard like so much garbage. So I was debating with myself. And then you walked up and scared me half to death. I felt lucky the gun didn't fall out of my purse right then along with all the other things that spilled out."

"So where is the gun now?" Clare asked. Her fabric slipped off her knee and she grasped at it, catching it just before it reached the boards comprising the porch floor.

Iris looked at Detective Sousa, still afraid of where all this truthfulness might lead.

"Go on, Ms. Fleming. Whatever your answer, you realize you will have to come with me to the station for questioning. You'll also have to make another statement."

Iris released a breath with a rasp of a sob. "I know." She breathed in and out for a minute before continuing. "I really panicked when the police turned up here and everyone said you were searching the inn. I still had the gun in my purse, just like always. But suddenly Sam's death was suspicious, and we didn't know how he died. So I decided I'd better get rid of the gun right away. I lagged behind on the trail when we were at Rainbow Falls — when we walked up that trail leading to the river before the falls. I stayed back a little and then stopped to adjust my shoe. And that's when I took the gun from my purse and just shoved it deep into the undergrowth." She released her breath on a long sigh of relief. "It's probably still there. You can get it and see that it's not the murder weapon."

"Didn't it occur to you that if you had just given it to me, we could have proven that days ago?" Detective Sousa's words seemed to indicate exasperation, but his tone was patient.

"I guess." Iris sounded exhausted. The confession had taken a lot out of her. And she faced further interrogation in town. "It's hard to think straight when you're terrified that you may be accused of murder."

"I'd like you to come with me now, Ms. Fleming," Detective Sousa said.

Maggie was impressed by his courteous manner. He should be angry with her, but he was being polite instead.

They watched the two of them leave together, one sad, dejected older woman and one young detective. Still, it was a far cry from the famous "perp walk" they'd all seen so often on television.

Lurline, Manu and Makana returned in time for lunch but too late to witness the scene with Iris and Detective Sousa.

Always well organized when it came to their meals, Manu hurried inside to lay out his usual excellent repast. Maggie noted that he had planned a cold collation, probably with the thought that everything could be done ahead of time. Undoubtedly, he'd made lunch at the same time he prepared their breakfast. The main dish was a seafood salad served with bread newly made earlier that morning and bowls of fresh fruit salad, all topped off with another of his delicious pies for dessert. Today's was something he called *Haupia* Pie, a lovely coconut-cream delicacy on a graham-cracker crust.

As they all took their places around the table, Lurline glanced around the room, her gaze settling on the empty chair. "Where is Iris?"

Several people spoke at once, trying to explain. Bewildered, Lurline and Makana stared from one to another of their guests.

Finally, Maggie's voice rose above them all. "One at a time, please."

Lurline threw a grateful look her way.

"Edie, why don't you explain," Maggie said. "You had a major role in what happened."

Clare looked disappointed that she wasn't the one called on to elaborate. But Edie sat up a little straighter and began the story.

"We were stitching out on the front porch," she began. "Talking about this and that. And, as keeps happening" — she glanced pointedly at Clare — "we got back to talking about Sam and how he died. Maggie just came right out and asked Iris what had happened to her gun. None of us believed that story about baggage handlers in Phoenix stealing it out of her luggage."

Lurline's eyebrows rose. Her salad lay neglected before her. "What did she say?"

"She finally admitted that her story was a fabrication. And I called Detective Sousa. Because I also remembered how odd she acted on the boat after the luau that night."

In a few succinct sentences, she recounted the story once more.

"She was the woman who used to be married to Sam?" Lurline seemed shocked, even though the possibility had seemed obvious to the women from the Quilting Bee. "And she wanted to kill him."

Lurline mumbled the last sentence, but Maggie had no trouble hearing it. She thought that everyone had.

Makana looked from her mother to Edie, trying to take it all in. "So was she trying to dispose of the gun?"

"That is what I wondered," Edie said. "But apparently not. She says she just panicked and decided it might be best to get rid of it. However, I came upon her before she was able to do anything. But it was seeing all the police here on Thursday morning that really scared her. She said she was so upset about that, while we were at Rainbow Falls she slipped the gun into some thick shrubbery."

"So, Iris is off with Detective Sousa, to make another statement and to show him where she dumped the gun," Clare finished.

"At Rainbow Falls?" Makana's eyes widened, as though she couldn't believe the strange tale.

"That's what she said." Clare eagerly picked up the story. "Iris said she dropped back as we walked up the trail, then she just leaned down and pretended to fix her shoe. That's when she shoved the gun into some bushes or shrubs. On the way up to the area that takes you to the riverbanks behind the falls."

That afternoon, the tour group was treated to a quilt class with Rita, where she showed them how she created her unique wall hangings with their beautiful embroidery embellishments.

"I'm heavily influenced by the Tahitian tradition of *tifaifai*," she explained, as she displayed the beautiful quilts and wall hangings she had brought to share. "The Tahitian quilts are not quilted with batting, as the Hawaiian and the mainland quilts are, but they are embroidered."

The afternoon was spent trying out embroidery stitches and techniques, and a good time was had by all. Lydia was in her element.

Just before dinner, the Quilting Bee again managed to escape to the porch for some private stitching time. Iris had returned, but pleaded a headache and escaped to her room. Though disappointed that she wouldn't be telling them about her day with the police, they could understand her reluctance to visit.

"She probably does have a headache, poor thing," Victoria commented.

"So, now that Iris has been eliminated as

a suspect, only Judy is left," Clare said with a sigh.

Maggie looked thoughtful. "Judy is still a suspect, I suppose. She and Sam had some kind of relationship. It's obvious she's unhappy in her marriage, and feels isolated here in Hilo."

"Could be island fever," Louise suggested.

"Don't forget the three people in the family. The police did always feel it was one of them." Maggie's sigh was echoed by several other Bee members. "We keep eliminating them, then coming back to them."

"Out of those three, I think we should concentrate on Makana," Edie declared.

"Makana! But why?" Anna asked, shocked. "She's just a girl."

"Oh, no," Edie said. "She's already graduated from college. She's over twenty-one."

Louise looked thoughtful, and Maggie nodded sadly.

Louise exchanged meaningful looks with both Maggie and Edie. "I guess you both noticed what I imagined I noticed earlier — what I was afraid to comment on yesterday in case I was wrong." She sighed heavily.

"You're thinking that Sam may have gone farther than just complimenting her on her looks," Maggie said.

"Oh, no." Anna moaned softly.

Both Edie and Louise nodded slowly.

"It wouldn't surprise me to learn she's pregnant," Louise said. "That was what I was debating yesterday. I guess I mostly hated to think it might have happened. But she has all the early signs — thick, luxuriant hair, a glow to her skin even though she's often pale. And her appetite is strangely up and down — the way some women get early on because they feel nauseous. She seems to have cravings, too; the other afternoon I saw her scooping up pie and ice cream with those greasy island potato chips."

"Eww . . . I'm glad to say I missed that," Theresa said.

"Her mother said she broke up with her boyfriend just before she graduated, remember? Do we know if that was in June or December?" Victoria asked.

"She graduated in December," Clare said, but then turned to Louise with a doubtful look on her face. "She's told me she has trouble sleeping, though, when I asked if she was feeling all right a few times. No matter what you think about a 'glow,' her color isn't very good, and she always seems to have terrible circles under her eyes. Don't newly pregnant women usually sleep a lot?"

"She may have just said that, you know," Louise suggested. "About having trouble sleeping. Or it may be true. I'm sure she doesn't want to let everyone know about the pregnancy, especially if there's a possibility Sam had been abusing her."

But Clare held to her differing opinion. "I still think she's trying to work through choosing a proper diet and portion-control issues after losing all that weight."

"Well," Louise said, "I guess that *could* explain the binges and the erratic appetite."

They thought that over.

"Clare's right," Victoria decided. "It could be that."

"Diet and weight issues would reinforce a low self-esteem, and I do believe she suffers from low self-esteem." Maggie looked over to Louise who nodded. "That kind of problem could easily lead into a bad relationship."

"Or," said Louise, "she could have low self-esteem issues *because* of being abused by her stepfather."

"True. There's no easy answer here."

They were no closer to a resolution when Manu called them to dinner.

CHAPTER 27

Quilt tour, day seven. Monday morning.

"Only two more days here," Bernie said as they sat down to another of Manu's wonderful breakfast spreads. "I'm not counting our travel day, because it's hard to do anything that day except pack. Then it'll be back to cereal in the morning for me. Boy, am I going to miss your cooking, Manu."

While all Manu's meals were outstanding, true to the nature of a bed-and-breakfast, his morning spreads were amazing. He always had several kinds of juices and breads, fruit, scrambled eggs, both hot and cold cereal, either pancakes or waffles, and bacon or ham. One morning he'd offered fried Spam, telling them it was a special request from Makana. Just as she had at the beach, he explained that it was a local favorite. Still, only a few of the women indulged. Recipes making use of local products like macadamia nuts, coconut, papaya, pineapple and mango, however, were greeted with great enthusiasm and so kept reappearing.

With a quick wave and an appreciative *"mahalo,"* Manu hurried back to the kitchen.

While the women debated their favorite breakfast dishes, Maggie noticed that Iris was much more subdued than usual. Her afternoon with the police seemed to have had a profound effect on her. Everyone wanted to hear what happened the previous day, but she was reluctant to talk about it.

Finally, she gave a deep sigh. "Detective Sousa drove me over to Rainbow Falls so I could show them where I'd pushed the gun into the ground cover."

"Did they find it?" Clare asked eagerly.

"Oh, yes." Iris appeared strained, her voice dull. It was very unlike her and caused some glances of worried concern from her associates. "It was right there. I found the spot without any trouble and pointed it out. One of the uniformed officers just pushed some undergrowth aside and poked around a bit and came out with it. Detective Sousa told him to take it right over to the lab and find someone who could check it against the bullet taken from Sam's body."

Lurline winced.

"Oh, it sounds just like a TV show," Clare said.

Iris shot a nasty look her way. "It wasn't though, Clare. This is my life we're talking about here. I knew I didn't shoot Sam. I knew my gun wasn't used. But it was still the most unsettling thing that's ever happened to me. Even the hell Steve — or Sam — put me through years ago, or that awful accident and recovery period, didn't compare to this. I kept imaging cell doors slamming, like they do in the movies — that awful clanging noise that echoes down the corridor."

Her voice cracked and Maggie thought she might cry. But Iris managed to control her voice — and her emotions — pulling herself together enough to drink some of her coffee.

"I'm sorry." Clare's apology was sincere and graciously accepted with a nod from Iris. "It's just that I get so excited hearing these real-life stories. I can't help myself," she added, with a meek bow of her head.

Maggie offered Clare what she hoped was a supportive look.

"Did you go back to the police station after finding the gun?" she asked Iris.

"Yes." Iris poked at the waffle on her plate, but didn't seem to be eating. "I sat in an empty room for a long time — an interrogation room, I guess. At that point, I was just glad it wasn't a cell," she added. She turned toward Clare. "I'm sure you would have found that quite exciting, Clare, but I was so close to a panic attack, I spent all my time just trying to control myself so that I didn't have one."

"Oh, Iris, I'm so sorry." Clare felt so bad she had tears shimmering in her eyes. "It must have been terrible for you."

Iris nodded. "They gave me some water, and I prayed. It helped."

Anna, seated beside her, patted her arm. "Praying always helps, doesn't it?"

"It did. Once Detective Sousa came back, he assured me that the gun wasn't the one used in the murder. That's when I began to feel like I might get through it okay."

Maggie noticed that both Lurline and Makana winced at the word murder. It had to be difficult for them, coping with a family member killed, and having a group of strangers so eager to talk about it at every meal.

"He still kept me for over an hour, asking questions over and over." She sighed. "I don't know why they always ask the same questions so many times."

"They're seeing if your answers will remain the same," Edie said, matter-of-factly. "That's how they can trip up real criminals."

"So, we may never know who killed Sam," Bernie said with a sigh.

"Oh, I think we will." Maggie's tone was so confident she received startled looks from more than one person.

Clare and Victoria nodded.

"We discussed it last night, and we think we know what happened," Louise said.

Makana started. Lurline looked either fearful or angry; it was hard to determine which. Manu, just entering the room again, with a newly refilled plate of macadamia nut pancakes, appeared mildly interested.

"You know who killed Sam?" he asked.

"No kidding," Bernie said. "In that case, you're a lot smarter than I am."

"So who did it?" Rita asked.

"Where were you having this discussion?" Lydia inquired. "Where were *we*?"

"It was while we were stitching together just before dinner last night, and again just before bed," Maggie replied. Her calm demeanor indicated such discussions were nothing new for them. Which they were not. They had used their time over their stitching to solve several other murder cases back in Arizona. "We called Detective Sousa and asked him to check on a few things for us.

He should be here soon."

Iris gave up on her meal, pushing her plate aside and heaving a giant sigh. "I was hoping I wouldn't have to see him again."

Makana, who had been nibbling at a slice of banana bread, put it down and raced to the bathroom.

Lurline rose, looking after her, obviously conflicted. To follow her child, or stay and find out what the women suspected? In the end, she sat down heavily and finished her coffee, keeping an anxious lookout for Makana's return.

Detective Sousa arrived just as the group moved from the dining room to the classroom. He glanced around the room, then asked Lurline to get Manu and Makana. Makana had still not returned from her trip to the bathroom. When she did come in, holding on to her father's arm, she appeared fragile and slightly green.

Detective Sousa greeted Makana kindly and asked if she was ill.

"No. I'm fine." Her voice could barely be heard, and her eyes were dull. Maggie thought she seemed afraid.

"I'm glad to hear that," Detective Sousa said. His tone was kind, but it didn't seem to offer any comfort to Makana.

"Please take a seat." He gestured Makana

and Manu toward two available chairs near the front of the room. Once they were seated, he addressed the room at large.

"I received a very interesting phone call last night," he began. "Your students, Ms. Ilima, have some theories about Sam's murder which they were kind enough to share with me."

Once again, Lurline winced at the word "murder." Maggie knew Detective Sousa saw it, though he didn't give any indication of it. His gaze moved past her, running along the line of women from the Quilting Bee.

"And I must commend them on passing on their suspicions rather than trying to confront a suspect on their own."

"Oh." Makana's soft gasp drew some quick glances, but everyone was anxious to hear what more Detective Sousa would have to say.

"On the advice of Ms. Lombard" — he nodded toward Louise — "I reviewed our interviews with you, Makana. I also spoke to your friends and teachers. And most important, I reinterviewed your recent former boyfriend. You see, the Arizona women here suggested that you show some signs that you might be pregnant."

Makana gasped. Not the soft surprise of a

moment earlier, but a full blown gulp of shock. She suddenly appeared so shaky, Louise rushed over to stand beside her, grasping her wrist and checking her respiration against her watch. Lurline also rose and hurried to Makana's side but merely stood there fretting.

Detective Sousa waited until Makana had settled back down and the other women resumed their seats before he continued.

"The women here said they were told that your longtime boyfriend broke off your relationship and that it was very upsetting to you. But I discovered that he is still very much in love with you, Makana. In fact, he said *you* broke up with him. He said you were a psychological mess this past semester and worse after the Thanksgiving break." Detective Sousa's sharp gaze locked on Makana's pale face. "Now something occurring over Thanksgiving break would account for what the women here said indicate signs of very early pregnancy. So tell me, Makana. What happened over the Thanksgiving holidays?"

Makana suddenly had the appearance of cornered prey. Her mouth opened and closed. "Tha . . . Thanks . . . Thanksgiving?"

"Makana, dear, you told us how Sam used to come on to you." Louise used her most

soothing caregiver voice, but Makana stead-
fastly refused to look at her, keeping her
eyes focused on the fabric of her skirt. "But
you show several classic signs of sexual
abuse. Your self-esteem seems to be extremely low for such a lovely young woman
as yourself. You still don't seem to realize
just how attractive you are. Clare told me of
your recent weight loss, but I'm not sure
even that accounts for your rather odd eating habits. But abuse might. Also, pregnancy. And you have terrible circles under
your eyes. Newly pregnant women often
sleep for long hours, but you don't look as
though you sleep at all. And that's another
effect of sexual abuse — sleep disorders and
depression both."

Detective Sousa was smart enough to al-
low the women to question her.

"Sam did more than just flirt with you,
didn't he?" Victoria asked in her most
gentle, caring voice.

"What?" Lurline leaped to her feet, outrage
plain in every line of her face and her
posture. "Are you implying that my
Sam . . ." Lurline became so choked with
anger that she couldn't finish the sentence.

Detective Sousa shifted slightly so that he
stood a little closer to an anxious Lurline.

"Why don't you let Makana tell us," he

suggested.

With so many pairs of eyes watching her, Makana broke down and cried. Tears spilled down her cheeks as she slowly began to speak.

"It was only one time," she said, swiping at the tears that continued to stream down her face. "He only did it one time."

Louise came forward with a handful of tissues and pushed them into the younger woman's hands.

"It was the Saturday after Thanksgiving," Makana said, once she had controlled her tears. "You and Sam went to a party," she said, turning toward her mother. "You both came home drunk. You were arguing. I could hear both of you shouting from my room. Then there was some banging around and I heard a door slam. Next thing I knew, Sam was knocking on my door. I was already in my nightgown, just sitting in bed studying. He came in and tried to start something with me, telling me how great I looked. He went on and on, and he was getting raunchy. It was embarrassing. I told him I was studying and he had to leave. And he did."

Beside her, her mother tightened her hand on her shoulder. The mother bear protecting her cub, Maggie couldn't help thinking.

But too late.

Makana wiped her eyes again, blew her nose and hiccupped. Rita opened a bottle of water and thrust it into Makana's hand, and she sipped gratefully.

"But later . . . he came back later. It was dark. I was asleep. Or half asleep. I awoke. I must have realized someone got into the bed with me. And he was . . . was touching me . . ."

She stopped again, and Lurline's hand — the one not on her daughter's shoulder — curled into a fist. Maggie imagined her wishing she could push that fist into Sam's solar plexus. Or perhaps another, more tender area of his anatomy.

"Did you cry out?" Louise asked, her voice gentle.

"I tried to, but I couldn't. He put his hand over my mouth. I could hardly breathe. And then, and then . . ." She took a deep breath. "He, he did it. And when it was over, he said if I told anyone, he would see to it that Lurline never sewed again. He . . . he whispered it. 'She might be blinded. Or she might break all her fingers.' He whispered it, in this menacing voice. He scared me to death."

Lurline put her arm around Makana. "I never knew."

Manu also hugged his daughter. "I would have killed him . . ."

He stopped, as though realizing the import of his hasty words.

But Detective Sousa raised his eyebrows. "And did you? Kill him?"

Manu looked startled. "No, of course not." Manu's gentle face screwed up with fear of how those gut-reaction words might be interpreted. "Just *da kine* figure of speech, yeah?"

Sousa nodded. "I thought so. How about you, Ms. Ilima? Would you have killed Sam if you knew he attacked Makana?"

Lurline ignored Detective Sousa, turning to her daughter. "Why didn't you tell me?"

"I was afraid. Afraid of what you would think of me. Afraid I did something to make him think I was offering an invitation. Afraid of what Sam might do if I told anyone. That voice, making the threats. I thought he might kill you. Or . . . or hurt you worse than dying even. Or me . . ." Her soft crying turned into wracking sobs.

"It was the drink," Lurline explained. "Sam just wasn't the same when he drank."

Maggie almost gasped in shock. How could Lurline possibly excuse such disgusting behavior with that feeble excuse?

"You too," Manu stated quietly.

Lurline shot an angry look his way. "Me? Me, what?"

"You drink too much too, Lurline. I love you, but when you drink you're not the same. You get mad about everything. You pick fights. You need to stop drinking, Lurline."

All the women in the room were watching. Like attendees at a tennis match, their heads moved from side to side as their attention swerved from one family member to another. Detective Sousa continued to observe quietly, on the alert for any indication of a confession.

"He's right, Mom." Makana spoke up to support her father's opinion. "When you drink, you get different too. Both of you did. I could hear the two of you fighting whenever you'd been out partying. That's why I was so glad to get away, to Honolulu, for school. To get away from all that."

"So it was my fault?" Lurline sounded shocked, her voice subdued with pain. "You think it was my fault that Sam attacked you?"

"What, you think it was mine?" Makana suddenly sounded more adult than her mother. Her voice was somber and quiet, resigned to what she apparently saw as her parent's poor opinion of her.

"No matter what you think, dear, it was not your fault." Louise's voice, firm and definite, carried across the table to her.

"Never your fault," Detective Sousa assured her. "If you had called us, Sam would have been arrested. Even though you are over twenty-one, his behavior toward you was completely unacceptable. And if we'd arrested him, we would have discovered the bigamy warrant. Sam would have been out of your hair for good. Not that you could have known that, of course," he added.

"But you decided to rectify things, didn't you, Lurline," Maggie said quietly. "If I'm not mistaken, *you* took Sam's gun sometime after New Year's Eve. You told us about that fight you had that night so that we'd all think he got rid of the gun then. You hinted that he was afraid he might start waving it around again one night and maybe shoot someone so he took the gun and left it with some friend. But you planned carefully and did it yourself, didn't you? So he could never harm your child again."

Lurline stared at her, her mouth agape. So did some of the other tour members.

"Would you like to say something, Ms. Ilima?" Detective Sousa asked. "Answer these charges?"

Lurline's body suddenly turned limp, and

she collapsed into a chair. She did not cry. Her face hardened into an expression of terrible agony.

"I found out. Sam never could keep his mouth shut about anything. And even though I was horrified, even though I was shocked . . . he wasn't even a little remorseful. Not even a little!" Her voice turned raspy with bitterness. "I threatened to divorce him right away, but he threatened back. He claimed he could keep us in court for years to come, challenging every little division of property."

"Oh, my." The classroom had become so quiet, Clare's softly voiced exclamation was easily heard throughout the room. "Do you think he could have done that?"

"Possibly," Detective Sousa said. "Some people know how to work the system. Sam, however, was merely threatening. He couldn't risk going to court, where his true identity would be sure to come out. Also, your marriage was never valid because he was already married at the time. He would never have risked going to court. So he had to intimidate you to prevent you ever filing the papers."

Now Lurline did begin to cry. "So I did all this for *nothing*. Nothing! I could have gotten rid of him fine if I just went ahead and filed for divorce."

"I'm not saying it was a sure thing, but probably. I *am* sure he would not have taken the chance. Not with several warrants out against him on the mainland." Detective Sousa's voice was kind. "There's no way for us to know what he would have done, Ms. Ilima. He might have harmed you or Makana. Or he could have just disappeared, as he did with his previous marriages."

Louise walked up to Lurline and put her hand on her shoulder. "You need to get a good lawyer, Lurline. There were extenuating circumstances here, and I'm sure a good lawyer will be able to make some kind of deal for you."

"Maybe even convince a jury to let you go," Edie said. "Sam wasn't much of a person, and you were just trying to protect your daughter. Even if you did choose the wrong method."

Detective Sousa's response was quick and firm. "We cannot condone vigilante tactics, Ms. Dulinski."

"There was no guarantee Sam wouldn't follow through with his threats against Lurline and Makana," Maggie said. "And he could easily have attacked Makana again. Most abusers do not stop after only one time."

There was no comfort coming from Detective Sousa, however. He read Lurline her Miranda rights, handcuffed her, and led her from the room. Manu, still in shock, followed them, asking about sending a lawyer. Makana buried her face in her hands and sobbed.

There were no congratulatory toasts for solving this crime. The women watched sadly as Lurline was led away. They couldn't even find it in them to be angry that she had chosen their tour to gain her freedom from Sam. Instead, they rallied around Makana, offering her all the support they could. They knew she would need a lot of love to sustain her through her pregnancy. Maggie was glad to know there was a large group of family and friends ready to come to her aid. Throughout the day, cousins and aunties dropped by to see how she was doing. Many of them brought gifts of food and flowers.

"It feels like a funeral around here," Edie remarked. There hadn't been nearly the same outpouring after Sam's death. Maggie felt it was an indication of the esteem Lurline had earned from her friends.

Now that they had divined her secret, Makana felt free to speak of the upcoming birth. While the women stitched on their various projects, she talked about having the baby and asked questions about pregnancy and childbirth. They were happy to learn that she did not believe in abortion and planned to keep her baby — even if it was Sam's.

"I pray every night that it's not. I want it to be Loki's, but wishing won't make it so, yeah?"

"Didn't you use protection?" Edie asked.

"Oh, Edie," Louise said. "You know as well as I do that the only birth-control method that is one-hundred-percent effective is abstinence."

Makana blushed, her cheeks turning a bright pink that rivaled the color in the outer petals of Edie's protea. It gave her a healthier overall look and made her look very pretty.

When Makana moved to the other side of the room to help Lydia with her reverse appliqué, Clare whispered, "Thank goodness Sam wasn't her biological father."

That evening everyone sat in the comfortable living room once again, sewing contentedly. The puzzle was solved, there was nothing more to worry over. They were free to speak of nothing but the new quilting patterns they were learning about, or the beautiful sights they had seen on their tour. And another full day of quilting unmarred by an unsolved murder mystery.

But of course, Clare was still focused on their big adventure.

"I can't wait to tell everyone about our tour," Clare said.

"What will Gerald think?" Maggie asked. She was pretty sure she knew, but wondered if Clare was going to be realistic about it. She was.

"Oh, he's going to be terribly upset with me." She looked over toward Judy, still stitching carefully on her *ulu* pillow top. "If Gerald had been here in town, he probably would have rushed right over to pick me up, just like your Josh did."

Judy seemed relieved to hear it wasn't only her husband who would act so foolish. "Well, it wasn't fun being a suspect in a murder case, even if it was just you all that suspected me."

"We suspected everyone," Clare told her. "Just like the police did, I'm sure. It wasn't anything personal."

Clare seemed surprised when everyone laughed.

Manu chose that moment to enter the room, asking if anyone wanted a late snack. He was rather amazed to be answered with

374

a resounding yes coming from multiple voices. Stitching was laid aside, spools of thread and scissors carefully put away.

"We could really use one of your fabulous desserts, Manu," Maggie said.

Everyone else agreed.

"And some of that great Kona coffee?" Edie suggested.

"I'm going to remember the food from this trip for a long time," Theresa said.

"Amen," echoed around the room.

CHAPTER 28

One week later. Scottsdale, Arizona. Sunday brunch at the Browne family ranch.

"So, how was your Hawaiian vacation, Ma?" Hal asked. "We heard there was a lot of excitement."

"Well, except for the murder, we had a wonderful time."

Sputtering laughter erupted from Maggie's sons and their wives.

"While I can't condone murder, of course," Edie said, "Sam was not a nice man and no real loss to this world."

"A bigamist, a womanizer. And he raped his own stepdaughter." Louise shook her head. "Not a nice man is putting it a little too politely. He was scum."

"I still can't believe it was Lurline." Clare sighed. "She was such a nice person. And a fabulous quilter."

"She was the lioness, protecting her cub," Louise said.

"If she gets a sympathetic jury, she might not have to spend too long in prison," Hal's wife Sara said. "There were certainly extenuating circumstances."

"Extenuating circumstances!" Michael was annoyed at the women's spin. "May I remind you, she planned it carefully. Cold-bloodedly. *And,* she tried to make it look like someone from Ma's tour group was responsible. How can you have any sympathy for her? This was vigilante justice, plain and simple."

Maggie shrugged. "She was a mother, protecting her child. And Sam had no moral fiber."

"What's going to happen to that poor girl?" Merrie, one of Maggie's other daughters-in-law asked.

"She and her father will continue to run the bed-and-breakfast together," Maggie replied.

"And you know how these things go," Michael said. "They'll probably get a lot of business from people curious about the murder."

"Really, Michael." Maggie shot him a "be good" motherly look. "Lurline had a very good quilt program going, and Makana knows all about it. She'll be able to pick herself up and take care of all the groups they already have scheduled. And probably manage to book more on her own. Also the extended family was very supportive once the true story came out, so they'll be there for her too."

"Is she pregnant? By Sam?" Sara asked.

"Oh, she's pregnant all right. Louise was right about that. But she doesn't know if the baby is her boyfriend's or from the rape," Maggie explained. "She doesn't believe in abortion, I'm glad to say. She'll have the baby. Manu will take good care of them for now."

"After what Detective Sousa said about her former boyfriend, I'm sure he'll try to reestablish that relationship." Clare smiled at what she hoped would be a happy ending for Makana. "Especially if the baby is his. He's already asked for a DNA test once the baby arrives."

"If Makana goes to counseling and can build up her self-esteem," Louise said, "she'll have a good chance at creating a good relationship for herself. It won't be easy for her, though."

"And she and Manu will have to deal with whatever happens with Lurline too," Maggie said. "Hopefully, her lawyer will get her some kind of plea deal and avoid a trial. I hope she can do that for her daughter's sake. After all, she claimed to have killed Sam for that reason."

"The prisons are in Honolulu," Victoria added, "and they even send some of the prisoners to contract prisons on the mainland. So if she goes to prison, Lurline will be far from her family. It won't be easy for them to visit, and I think that's going to be hard on all of them."

"Poor Manu." Clare sighed. "He loves Lurline so much. He was really upset about the whole thing."

"Manu didn't know what was happening?" Michael's voice indicated that he didn't believe it for a second.

"He says not, and I believe him," Maggie said. "Remember, he didn't live in the house with Lurline and Makana. So while he was there all the time, he wasn't in the midst of things. He kept to his own apartment when there were no guests, unless Lurline and Sam asked him to cook for them. And in the period we're talking about, there were no guests, plus it was the holidays. Lots of stresses, then, and they probably kept to themselves. They were having a lean period, which is why Iris was able to arrange such good prices for us."

"And it was the holidays too, remember," Louise reiterated, "which had to be a difficult time for that odd family."

"All those people who know Lurline well — they all said she couldn't have done it. Not unless it was in a fit of passion. During an argument, for example. No one considered how she might act if he'd attacked her daughter. That was a slow, simmering rage that had time to grow. They didn't have any tour groups between Thanksgiving and Christmas. We were the first. It gave her lots of time to plan something. It was just unfortunate that our group was the first to arrive after she developed her plan."

"She was a good actress, too," Victoria said. "Oscar quality, I think. At first, she pretended she didn't know anything about Sam and Makana. She was outraged, and quite believable, wasn't she?"

The other women agreed.

"She did act completely shocked, like she was hearing it for the first time," Clare said.

"So, where's Iris? Or is she going to go back to Lily?" Hal asked.

"Iris, or Lily, left for a vacation in Rocky Point," Clare told them. "Bringing up the whole thing about her accident and her best friend made her want to get away. She said she wanted to go to Rocky Point and revisit some of their favorite places, as a kind of tribute."

"I wouldn't be surprised if she decides to get a condo there, maybe even settle down there for good," Victoria said.

"Is she going to keep the name Iris Fleming?"

"Yes," Clare replied. "She said neither of them had any family, so the mistake in identification didn't hurt anyone."

Louise explained further. "She also said that for years she nursed her hurt against Sam — or Steve, as she knew him — and planned what she would do to him if she could find him. She said that kept her going while she endured all that pain during surgeries while she was recovering from the accident. She planned how she would track him down and make him pay. She probably needed something like that to focus on, to get her through painful surgeries and therapy."

"She admitted to hiring a private detective," Maggie said, "who, by the way, located Sam in Hilo, Michael. The authorities couldn't find him during all that time, but a private detective managed it in less than a year."

Michael shook his head. "We're all short-handed and underfunded."

"Not a top priority felony, either," Hal said. "They might have put more resources into it if he'd *killed* all those ex-wives."

"When we confronted her about the name/accident thing, I really thought she might have killed him," Clare said. "For revenge, you know. Mystery stories always like the revenge angle."

"But, as we keep telling you," Maggie said, "this is real life, not a mystery story."

Everyone laughed. It felt good to be home, Maggie thought. Much as she had enjoyed the vacation at the Blue Lily Inn, much as she liked the briny sea air and the beautiful gardens filled with tropical flowers, and much as she enjoyed learning all about Hawaiian quilting — to her, there was nothing like the Arizona desert.

"A toast," Hal called out, raising his glass of orange juice. "To the St. Rose Quilting Bee. Welcome home."

A host of other glasses rose into the warm dry air. The desert sun sparked sharp pinpoints of light off the golden rims of the glasses, shooting sparks into the air like frenzied but harmless sparklers. Hawks, or perhaps vultures, soared overhead. In the distance, a lone coyote called out.

At the Browne family ranch, many voices also rose and crystal clicked against crystal.

"Hear, hear."

A NOTE FROM THE AUTHOR

I want to take a bit more of your time to make a few things clear. Hilo is my hometown, and I love it there. Although it is the second largest city in the state of Hawai'i, it retains an old-fashioned, small-town feel that I attempted to convey through the eyes of my group of urbanized mainland women.

St. Rose Goes Hawaiian is a work of fiction. While there may be stores and hotels in the town of Hilo which appear similar to those in my story, I want to assure you that all the downtown stores, the resort hotel where the luau is held and the Blue Lily Inn were constructed from my very fertile imagination. The trick, of course, is to make people familiar with the location wonder — could it be . . . ?

While I try to be as accurate as possible, in the case of this particular story I used artistic license in the matter of the local gun laws. A flight attendant on a recent flight did assure me that it is possible to pack a gun in your luggage with the proper paperwork. However, Hawai'i has some of the strictest gun laws in the nation; I sincerely doubt Lily would have been allowed to take her gun with her on her vacation. But I needed that particular plot point, so decided to go with my fictional version. It is also unlikely that the agapanthus lilies so often mentioned would be in bloom in Hilo in January. However, I couldn't resist the image of the beautiful blue lilies swaying in the tradewinds.

I want to acknowledge those people who helped me with particular information that helped with the writing of this book. Special thanks to Doctor Doug Lyle, to paramedic Joe Collins, and to Captain Randy Medeiros of the Hilo Police Department. And a big *mahalo* to my brother-in-law Tom Naylor, who visited many of the local sights with me so that I could refresh my memories.

RECIPES

I thought I'd share some family recipes that helped inspire a few of Manu's creations.

ALOHA QUICK-BREAD

This quick bread is a family favorite. It is what I had in mind when Manu makes "Banana macadamia coconut muffins" one morning. My father used to supply me with macadamia nuts for all my baking needs from several trees in his yard. Unfortunately, I have to buy them these days.

Cream:
1 cup margarine
2 cups sugar

Add:
4 eggs
1 cup mashed ripe bananas

Gradually add:

4 cups sifted flour

2 teaspoons baking powder

1 teaspoon baking soda

3/4 teaspoon salt

When this mixture is well blended, add:

1 (20-ounce) can crushed pineapple, un-
  drained

1 cup shredded coconut

1 cup unsalted macadamia nuts, chopped

Mix just enough to combine. Dough will be
lumpy.

Preheat oven to 350 degrees F.

Grease and flour mini-loaf pans. Bake for
40–45 minutes. Top will be lightly browned.
Remove from pan to cool.

Makes 8 to 10 mini-loaves, depending on
how much you fill them.

BANANA NUT BREAD

This is the recipe we used at my house
whenever we had overripe bananas. Overripe bananas are common, too, when you
have banana trees in the backyard. The
entire bunch of bananas ripens at the same
time. Those little things you buy in grocery

stores are not bunches, they are "hands." You can probably get at least a dozen hands off one bunch, although they do vary in size.

Cream:
1 stick of margarine (1/2 cup)
1 cup sugar

Add:
2 eggs
Beat until smooth.
Repeat for:
1 cup mashed bananas

Add:
2 cups flour
1 teaspoon baking soda
1/2 teaspoon salt
blending only enough to moisten flour.

Fold in:
1/2 cup chopped nuts — use macadamia, walnuts or pecans, as available.

Pour into greased bread pan.

Bake at 350 for one hour.

Makes one 9 × 5 inch loaf.

PORTUGUESE RED BEAN SOUP

Every Portuguese family has their own recipe for Portuguese Red Bean soup. This is the one used in my mother's Silva family. Mom sometimes added elbow macaroni, which her father liked, but I prefer it without. It's been my favorite meal since childhood.

Take:

1 small package (1 pound) dry red kidney beans

Sort, wash, then cover beans with water. (The beans may be soaked overnight. I usually just cook them on a low heat for 2 hours. Because of the hard water in my part of AZ, I use bottled water for cooking beans.)

Add to pot with beans:

1 ham hock

1 linguiça (Portuguese sausage) — mild or hot, according to taste.

Cook on low heat about 2 hours, or until beans have softened. Then add remaining ingredients:

1 clove garlic

1 teaspoon cinnamon

1–2 teaspoons salt
1 medium onion, diced (or 2 tablespoons of
    minced dried onion)
2 medium potatoes, diced
1 small can tomato sauce

Cook another 30–40 minutes, or until potatoes have softened.

Serve over rice.

We always serve this with a side of thinly sliced cucumbers in a vinegar dressing.

For dressing: Mix 1 cup white vinegar with 1 teaspoon shoyu (Japanese style soy sauce). Salt and pepper to taste (about 1/2 teaspoon of salt and 1/4 teaspoon of pepper).

ICE-BOX COOKIES

Mom made these cookies quite often; they were my favorite after-school snack. It is one of the cookies Manu makes for the group's picnic lunch.

Cream:
1 cup white sugar
1 cup brown sugar
1 cup margarine

Add:
3 eggs

Gradually add sifted dry ingredients:
3 1/2 cups flour
2 teaspoons cinnamon
1 teaspoon baking powder
1 level teaspoon baking soda

When thoroughly mixed, add:
1 cup chopped walnuts

Form dough into rolls and put into refrigerator for a few hours. These may also be put into the freezer and brought out to bake as needed. Slice into 1/4″ rounds and bake on greased pans at 350 degrees F. until lightly browned.

Makes about 10 dozen cookies.

TERIYAKI SAUCE

My mother also had a recipe for teriyaki sauce marinade. We usually used it to marinate thin slices of steak, but it can be used for chicken or pork as well.

1/2 cup shoyu (Japanese style soy sauce)
1 small clove garlic, crushed
1 small piece of fresh ginger, crushed
1 teaspoon MSG*
1/2 teaspoon salt

* MSG under various brand names was a popular

1/4 teaspoon pepper
2 tablespoons brown sugar

Mix all ingredients to make marinade for steak, pork or chicken.

VINHA D'ALHOS (PORTUGUESE MARINADE FOR FISH OR PORK)

Another of my mother's recipes is for Vinha D'alhos, a Portuguese marinade. Mom cooked by instinct, so many of her recipes were a bit vague. We had to press her for amounts when we requested the recipes. This is my absolute favorite for ahi steak, cooked well done (baked or fried).

Sprinkle salt and pepper on fish or meat. Add 1 clove garlic, chopped fine, and 2 chili peppers, also chopped. Cover with 1/2 cup white vinegar and 3/4 cup water. Soak overnight.

---

condiment in Hawai'i during my growing up years. Today, I just eliminate it when I cook these old recipes — I haven't noticed any difference without it.

ABOUT THE AUTHOR

Annette Mahon is a retired librarian, an avid reader and quilter. She loves to include quilts in her stories. A native of Hilo, Hawai'i, she currently resides in Arizona with her husband and a spoiled Australian Shepherd.

Annette loves hearing from readers. Visit her Web site at www .annettemahon.com or her Facebook page at www.facebook.com/author.annettemahon. E-mail her at annette@annette mahon.com.

The employees of Thorndike Press hope you have enjoyed this Large Print book. All our Thorndike, Wheeler, and Kennebec Large Print titles are designed for easy reading, and all our books are made to last. Other Thorndike Press Large Print books are available at your library, through selected bookstores, or directly from us.

For information about titles, please call:
  (800) 223-1244

or visit our Web site at:
  http://gale.cengage.com/thorndike

To share your comments, please write:
  Publisher
  Thorndike Press
  10 Water St., Suite 310
  Waterville, ME 04901